ABOUT THE AUTHOR

Adrian Wright is the acclaimed author of several biographies including the life of L P Hartley *Foreign Country*, the life of John Lehmann *A Pagan Adventure*, the life of William Alwyn *The Innumerable Dance*, and a collection of theatre pieces *No Laughing Matter*. His three books on British musical theatre, *A Tanner's Worth of Tune, West End Broadway* and *Must Close Saturday*, are standard works on the genre. His novel *Maroon* was published in 2010. The first of his 'Francis and Gordon Jones' series, *The Voice of Doom*, appeared in 2016. He lives in Norfolk.

ALSO BY ADRIAN WRIGHT

Fiction
Maroon
The Voice of Doom

Non-Fiction
No Laughing Matter
Foreign Country
A Pagan Adventure
The Innumerable Dance
A Tanner's Worth of Tune
West End Broadway
Must Close Saturday

WHAT READERS SAY ABOUT THE FRANCIS AND GORDON JONES STORIES

'These are gloriously sunny tales. And, as is often the case with comic writing, the serious moments grab the reader all the more for the comedy that surrounds them.'
The Bookhound

'These stories are delightfully charming on the surface, but what invokes involuntary giggles and snorts of laughter is the cheeky and sly way that Wright pushes the envelope into a loving pastiche of the genre.'
Patricia Michael, actress

'A delightful read from one of the great authors of our time … Seriously funny, charming and very witty'
David Eastaugh, Future Radio

'This book makes for delightful reading. The writing is witty and erudite, the characters sharply focused and the stories charming'
Alexandra Poxon

'Only Francis and Gordon, like Holmes, Miss Marple and Poirot, can find their way through the webs of intrigue!'
James Bugden, social worker

'Every reader will have their favourite in this collection'
Roger Mellor, biographer

The Coming Day

The Francis and Gordon Jones Mysteries

Adrian Wright

Copyright © 2018 Adrian Wright

The moral right of the author has been asserted.

Apart from any fair dealing for the purposes of research or private study, or criticism or review, as permitted under the Copyright, Designs and Patents Act 1988, this publication may only be reproduced, stored or transmitted, in any form or by any means, with the prior permission in writing of the publishers, or in the case of reprographic reproduction in accordance with the terms of licences issued by the Copyright Licensing Agency. Enquiries concerning reproduction outside those terms should be sent to the publishers.

This is a work of fiction. Names, characters, businesses, places, events and incidents are either the products of the author's imagination or used in a fictitious manner. Any resemblance to actual persons, living or dead, or actual events is purely coincidental.

Matador
9 Priory Business Park,
Wistow Road, Kibworth Beauchamp,
Leicestershire. LE8 0RX
Tel: 0116 279 2299
Email: books@troubador.co.uk
Web: www.troubador.co.uk/matador
Twitter: @matadorbooks

ISBN 978 1789016 369

British Library Cataloguing in Publication Data.
A catalogue record for this book is available from the British Library.

Printed and bound in the UK by TJ International, Padstow, Cornwall
Typeset in 11pt Adobe Garamond Pro by Troubador Publishing Ltd, Leicester, UK

Matador is an imprint of Troubador Publishing Ltd

In memory
Frank Herbert Wright
1923–2018

Contents

The Coming Day	1
Continuous Performance	52
Seeing is Believing	93
The Kiss of Venus	132
Happy Bunny	184
Afterword	252

The Coming Day

*U**ncle* Billy knew the gloomy days.

They were easier to bear when his nephew Gordon was at home, but in the long hours of an unusually overcast May the boy was at St Basil's, doing whatever grammar school pupils did. Billy faced such days bravely, but since being made redundant at Northcrack Staithe Power Station, time hung heavy. His years in the Navy had instilled a passion for tidiness. Today he was turning out drawers of the Welsh dresser he had rescued from Gordon's parents' house, following their deaths in the motor accident that had left three-year-old Gordon an orphan. Billy had rescued Gordon, too, and never regretted it.

Socks and vests in ship-shape order, he was about to close the last drawer when he found the camera. The sight of it unsettled him; his stomach clenched. There was no point in keeping it, for he would never use it again, although it had been a good one in its day, sanctioned by the British government. Under the camera was a package done up with string. Photographs. For the briefest moment, he wanted to untie it, his chest seizing as if he were about to have a heart attack, but he knew he would leave it untouched. The images were in his head and would never go. Seeing them would only remind him of what he would never forget, and he remembered it all, that one day, everything but the weather.

The only thing Billy couldn't remember was the weather. He remembered everything else.

'*He* looks like that man from *Wuthering Heights*,' said Francis.

'Is that one of the new bungalows next to the railway line?' asked Gordon.

Francis gave his cousin an exasperated glare.

'Heathcliff! Wild and wind-tossed and a magnificent example of manhood. Emily Brontë's hero.'

'It doesn't do to flaunt your knowledge,' said Gordon. 'People might think you were showing off.'

'He's known as Rufus Wolfe. His real name is Rufus Darting. He's Lady Darting's nephew, and he's moved into the Lodge at Darting Hall.'

'And he looks like that *Wuthering Heights* chap?'

'Well, he looks like my *idea* of him,' said Francis. 'He's an actor.'

'Oh. You mean, like his uncle?'

'Hopefully not.' Francis remembered Lord Darting's performance as Cinderella in the village pantomime. 'Rufus Wolfe has been called the new Wolfit.'

'More wolves!' complained Gordon. 'And that would be a compliment, would it?'

'I'm not sure Rufus Wolfe would think so. He's one of the New Wave.'

'As distinct from a Marcel Wave?' It was one of Gordon's more irritating mornings.

'He got rave notices at the Old Vic for his Hamlet,' explained Francis, 'but he's turned his back on the established theatre. Now, he performs on railway platforms and Peabody housing estates. He's just done *Cymbeline* at Wormwood Scrubs.'

'Prisons? Isn't Lord Darting a magistrate? That means his nephew is acting in prisons full of people his uncle *sent* there. Ironic isn't the word. Still, anyone with Lady Darting as an aunt must be interesting.'

'Talk of the devil,' said Francis, jumping from his chair and moving to the window. The Darting Rolls Royce had glided soundlessly to a halt outside Red Cherry House. The chauffeur, Dimple, was opening the rear door from which the skeletal form of Lady Darting emerged, dressed as chief of the Branlingham Girl Guides. Her crow-like face gleamed with pleasure.

'Our boy detectives!' she called. 'Is La Stupenda at home? No doubt she has succumbed to the self-raising when she should be cultivating her coloratura.'

"La Stupenda" being the title her ladyship had given to Mrs Jones, Francis explained that his mother was busy in the kitchen.

'How fascinating,' cried Lady Darting. 'A *kitchen*! I believe we have one at the Hall. It was certainly there when I went into it in 1948 to enquire about the progress of a suet dumpling.'

On cue, Mrs Jones appeared at her rosiest, rubbing her pastry-mottled hands on a crisply laundered towel.

'Our own dear diva!' cooed Lady Darting. 'In good voice, I trust, for your opening aria at the church fête?'

'Morning, your ladyship. Fingers crossed. I had a good gargle first thing. It didn't sound too bad when I did the scales in the bath, but I've been up to my eyes with baking. Reverend says as he wants two hundred Sussex pond pudding tartlets with lemon drizzle by ten o'clock sharp.'

'And each to be stamped with the Darting family crest,' declared Lady Darting imperiously. 'I shall be distributing them to the miserably poor of the parish directly after the winner of the Guess the Weight of the Pig competition has been announced.'

'Very gracious, I'm sure,' said Mrs Jones. 'Let's hope they'll be a bit less miserable after. How grateful they'll be for your bounty.'

'Oh, very,' grunted Mr Jones from a corner. 'Old Mrs Watson needs new dentures, and Bob Badham's roof's sprung that many holes that he's planning to turn his place into a planetarium, but they'll be thrilled to get a Sussex pond pudding with lemon drizzle.'

'We must pull together to protect the fabric of St Barnabas at Knee,' pronounced Lady Darting as if she were launching a ship, of which she still lived in hope. 'A great sum must be raised, but we must keep our feet on the ground, our hand at the tiller, our hopes high and push the boat out. As aristocrats, we Dartings can offer something quite unique to the less fortunate …'

'Those ruddy tartlets again, I suppose!' mumbled Mr Jones.

'Fêtes are a Darting speciality,' insisted her ladyship. 'My husband absolutely adores them.'

'Will he be telling fortunes again this year?' asked Gordon.

'Most certainly. His lordship will once again appear as Gypsy Rosalinda. He is in Norwich today having his ears pierced.'

'Well,' said Mrs Jones, feeling at her bravest, 'I was staggered with what he told me last year. I thought it was physically impossible.'

'And was it?'

'I'm pleased to say it was,' replied Mrs Jones.

'Now, to the matter in hand' (and now Lady Darting assumed an official manner). 'Two of my girls will be assisting Francis and Gordon in the First Aid marquee, and our new general practitioner will be available should any more serious medical situation arise. We would not wish for the Lady Mayoress to faint as she did last year.'

'I should hope not,' sighed Mrs Jones. 'She made a right mess of my raspberry blancmange.'

'The gates open to the public at fourteen hundred hours. Reconnoitre Central Tent 13.30. Come, Dimple.'

Saluting, Lady Darting swept into the street, her official ribbons dancing in the sunlight.

In his bedroom at the vicarage of St Barnabas at Knee the Reverend Challis sent up a prayer of thanks. Kneeling as he did each day at sunrise, he clasped his hands and lifted his eyes in supplication.

'Thank you, God, for this new dawn. By what magic does it reappear, at start of day? We are grateful for your organisational abilities. We give thanks that you have arranged matters so cleverly, that without fail afternoon follows morning, followed in turn by evening and then night with which you cloak the earth in impenetrable mysteries, ever ready, should we have need, to lead us through the darkness with a torch that has no need of a battery. Just as well with the price of them nowadays. You know that there is much evil, too much of it in this wicked world, into which you will shine the torch, or possibly as best suits your needs, the lamp that shows the way. Direct its beam on to the people of Branlingham, O Lord, that Mrs Jones's pastry will rise if not formed of plain flour, that Mary from the Dairy will bring forth a child whose name shall be appropriately biblical, that my congregation will swell, especially at matins when the numbers recently have been absolutely shocking, that the solemnity of Harvest Festival will no longer be interrupted by the unfortunately ribald laughter initiated by the suggestive shapes of malformed vegetables, and that Francis and Gordon resolve the unsolvable. In the great scheme of things, we are as nothing here, a mote in the eye of the world, but we turn our faces to you O Lord, as I have turned my face to you since a young boy in that pair of rompers with little giraffes all over them that Nanny lengthened and made do with until I went on that holiday in Ambleside when it never stopped raining and there was that incident with a ladies' umbrella. Make us good, O Lord, and shine into the shadows that threaten us all, rich or poor, poet or peasant, Marks and Spencer or Marshall and Snelgrove. And please may the sun shine for the fête. I would be much obliged if it could come out around two o'clock, when the scouts will entertain us. I would hate them, O Lord, to get wet. Amen.'

How dismally the morning dawned, but by lunchtime the sun struggled through imposing clouds and dominated the sky. By a quarter to two, a tidy crowd was already gathered outside the vicarage, admission fee in hand. The gates opened five minutes early, and most of Branlingham and much of the surrounding district ran across the reverend's lawn to obtain the best seats in the main marquee.

The event was officially opened by Mrs Jones dressed as Britannia and singing "Land of Hope and Glory". The patriotic fervour was lightened by the Boy Scouts' vocal selection from *Call Me Madam,* with which the Reverend Challis was enchanted. After great applause, the audience dispersed to raid the many stalls, including jellied eels, a tombola, a shooting gallery, winkles and ice-cream (but not at the same time), and a Hog Roast, thoughtlessly placed next to Bertha, the pig whose weight would remain a mystery until the close of proceedings.

A section of the grounds had been marked off for the Girl Guides' display of physical jerks, for which Lady Darting changed into a khaki ensemble of generously-gusseted shorts and monogrammed blouse. Her husband, who had gone to Buntings department store to buy a fetching assortment of Romany garments, was encouraged by the queue outside Gypsy Rosalinda's tent, and was soon making extraordinary medical predictions to the local housewives.

In the First Aid HQ, all began calmly. Outside it, a substantially constructed woman in Red Cross uniform gave the impression that only the prospect of imminent death warranted anyone entering the premises.

'Let's hope no one needs the kiss of life,' Gordon whispered to Francis.

A crisply-dressed nurse greeted the boys. She was instructing two of the guides in bandage winding.

'Nurse Dalton, isn't it?' asked Francis.

'That's right. How nice to see you both. We shall have people pretending to be ill just for the privilege of meeting the boy detectives! Are you on the First Aid rota?'

'Not officially,' said Francis, 'but we can lend a hand if needed. Hopefully, you'll have a quiet afternoon.'

Two hours later, the only casualties had been a grazed knee, a nosebleed and a sarsaparilla that had gone down the wrong way, a disappointment to Gordon who had read in the *Eagle* how to apply a splint to a broken leg and what to do with a brain tumour. Business was so slack that the boys took turns touring the stalls and keeping Nurse Dalton (who insisted on them calling her Mary) company.

'Just as well it's quiet,' said Francis. 'You'd be hard put to deal with a lot of people, being on your own.'

'Oh, I'll manage,' said Mary Dalton. 'The new doctor said he'd be here by the time the fête started, but he hasn't arrived. He's not the best time-keeper in the world.'

'A new doctor? We hadn't heard. What's happened to Dr Anderson?'

'You may well ask! Dear Dr Anderson. So fussy and particular, but a wonderful physician. He sold the practice. Didn't you know? I thought boy detectives knew everything.'

'We don't have much to do with doctors.'

'So I should hope, fit lads like you. He's gone to live with his sister in Cambridge. He was most concerned about who would take over from him. The new man's settling in but it's not easy for him, what with Dr Anderson having been here almost fifty years. Of course, Dr Hendel is well qualified. The patients seem to take to him well enough, but people don't like change. What is that poor girl up at Hilltops to make of it? It could have a devastating effect on such patients.'

The flap of the tent waved to one side to reveal a tall, handsome young man in his early thirties, wearing a well-cut brown suit and homburg, and carrying a medical bag. His face had an open expression, his eyes full above a slightly curved nose. Prim wired spectacles distanced his gaze.

'Ah! Do I hear the name of my excellent predecessor? The kindly Dr Anderson … He lives on in legend!'

Francis and Gordon's immediate hope was that the new doctor hadn't heard what Mary Dalton had said. She blushed slightly, but introduced him to the boys.

'I am pleased to meet you both,' said Hendel. 'You are prominent personalities in local parts. I know of your reputation.'

Francis was a little miffed by the 'local', but smiled as the man took his hand.

'Well,' said Mary, 'now that you're here at last, doctor, perhaps I may take a stroll?'

'Certainly, nurse. My young friends and I will hold the fort. Such a very English affair, isn't this? The fête worse than death, isn't that the saying?'

'Not the same sort of fête,' laughed Mary, and left the tent accompanied by Gordon, who had taken an order for tea and cakes.

'And how do you like Branlingham, Dr Hendel?' asked Francis.

'I think the question is does Branlingham like me, but yes, I like it very much. I imagine this is what all England should be like. No sense of hurry or worry. And charm … What an important word that is to you English. Charm.'

'You are not an Englishman?' asked Francis (idiotically, because of course the man wasn't English, and Francis had made it sound like an accusation).

'What can I say? I hope I may become one. I think I will be accepted, difficult as it is to follow in the footsteps of the admirable Dr Anderson. A foreign accent is not always a good thing in your country. Without it I would perhaps pass for what I think you call "an ordinary Joe". Who knows, the accent may wear off in time.'

'I hope it won't. I think it's very attractive. German, isn't it?'

'I was born in Düsseldorf, but did my medical training in Hamburg. I came here after the war.'

'Have you always worked in Norfolk?' asked Francis.

'Not always, no. Here and there.'

Hendel removed his hat, mopped his forehead and opened his bag.

'What are you and your cousin working on at the moment?' he asked.

To Francis, the shift of emphasis seemed awkward, as if the man didn't want to discuss his past. He busied himself with consulting a notebook, while Francis sat watching the tent flap, hoping that a patient was about to appear. The silence was broken by Gordon returning with a tray of tea.

'Ah!' cried Hendel. 'This is Englishness at its best. The cup that cheers. Everything stops for tea in your country.'

Francis had already made up his mind that he liked Dr Anderson's successor.

As the boys and Hendel ate and drank, the afternoon grew hazy, lending a mystical glow to the maypole dancing by St Mildred's School for the Advancement of Deserving Girls. Marred as it was by sudden gusts of high wind and a severe knotting of the ribbons during "Merrie Robin's Rout", the effect was nevertheless stunning and was wildly applauded by many of the older Branlingham men. Even Police Constable Cudd, responding to a complaint about Gypsy Rosalinda's predictions, tapped his feet. It was as the goose-pimpled girls of St Mildred's were hurrying back to their changing tent that the day took a turn for the worse.

Mary Dalton, returned from her stroll around the garden, seemed impervious to the heat. Other women wore sleeveless dresses and summer frocks, but she hadn't removed her long sleeved cardigan with its strong woollen cuffs. She told Hendel that he might as well take advantage of the lack of business by taking a look around the stalls.

It was an hour later when a child arrived complaining of

biliousness. Mary diagnosed too many toffee apples, a couple of banana splits or a bag of monkey nuts. She was about to lecture the victim on the perils of greed – the real cause was three knickerbocker glories – when bedlam broke out. Suddenly, the tent was a mass of groaning people clutching their bodies as if they might lose them at any moment.

Hendel, whose trip around the stalls had already involved meeting several ailing visitors complaining of biliousness, returned to the tent looking hot and fuddled. In his arms, being violently ill, was a young man of cinematic handsomeness, his extravagantly wayward raven-black hair suggesting he had just crossed some forsaken Yorkshire moor.

All faces turned to him. The tent fell silent.

'Name?' asked Mary Dalton.

'I'm Rufus Wolfe,' croaked the cinematically good looking young man, 'and I've been poisoned.'

A few days later, Francis and Gordon were sitting with Rufus in the front room of Red Cherry House.

'Who would want to poison *me*?' he asked. 'I've nothing in *principle* against poisoning actors, but I mean to say. You boys helped me enormously.'

'All I did was hold the bucket,' said Gordon.

'Ah, but the way you held it … And as for your bedside manner, Francis … It's going to be both a blessing and a curse to you in later life.'

'But you *weren't* poisoned, were you?' said Francis. 'Not specifically. You were one of – how many were there? – at least fifty or so. It was like something out of the Old Testament.'

'It's a good job Nurse Dalton doesn't break under pressure. She had everything under control,' said Gordon.

'And Dr Hendel, of course,' added Rufus. 'As for Nurse Dalton, she must have been the inspiration for Betjeman's poem, the one about the nurse's chintzy chintzy cheeriness.'

'Please try to avoid literary allusions when Gordon's around,' suggested Francis. 'He always needs an explanation, and I don't suppose he's ever heard of Leamington Spa.'

'I think Gordon's got a grand mind. And please call me Rufus. I feel much better, anyway, although that upset at the fête knocked me up for a couple of days. I hope everyone else is over it too.'

'They seem to have made a full recovery,' said Francis.

'It was something in the water,' suggested Gordon.

'In the food, more like,' said Francis. 'You know they sent mum's Sussex pond pudding tartlets to the Public Analyst. When they checked what people had eaten, mum's tartlets were the common denominator.'

'It would be a brave Public Analyst who put the blame on your mum,' laughed Rufus. 'Those tartlets were divine. I'll gladly stand up in court and put the blame on the winkles.'

Mrs Jones, scarlet-faced and tear-stained, brought another plate of the libelled tartlets from the kitchen.

'Why, thank you, Mr Wolfe! I'm sure I never was so put out in all my life. Those nasty accusations from people who've never so much as lifted a rolling pin! Look here! I've done one with your family crest on specially for you.'

'Oh, no need, Mrs Jones. I don't hold with the family snobbery. I'd give away the Darting fortune and live in a caravan and have my name removed from Debrett's if I had my way. And you must all call me Rufus.'

'Well, I'm Doris,' said Mrs Jones, 'and I don't mind who knows it.'

'Doris! Doris! Why did they give the Muses those ridiculous names? Calliope! Terpsichore! They should all have been called Doris! I've heard some of the greatest singers in the world, watched as one Tosca after another threw herself off the parapet, sobbed as Lucia after Lucia became dangerously unhinged, but never have I heard such a voice as yours. Your "Land of Hope and Glory" ... It was an Ordnance Survey of this great country!'

'Thank you, I'm sure,' said Doris Jones, who was probably blushing beneath the permanent redness of her complexion. Flushed with excitement, she went back to the kitchen. She would ask Miss Simms at the Post Office to get her a copy of *Wuthering Heights*. It would make a change from her usual Mills and Boon, whose heroes paled into insignificance beside Rufus. Francis had told her that the hero of that book was very much like Rufus, and the idea made Mrs Jones put salt instead of sugar in the scones. Gordon had to get back to Bundler's Cottage because Uncle Billy would have tea ready. He collected his bicycle and rode off.

Something in Francis quickened to be left alone with Rufus. He supposed that Rufus was the first bohemian he had ever met, bohemians being short on the ground in Norfolk, not that he was at all sure what a bohemian was. He'd read about them in books, imagining that they lived in attics in Chelsea or Paris and broke every rule and went to wild parties and never washed properly and turned up in operas by Puccini. Sadly, Francis didn't think he stood much chance of ever becoming a bohemian.

'I must dash,' said Rufus. 'I'm doing a reading at Strangeways next week.'

'What sort of reading?' asked Francis.

'It's a one-man show I do about Verlaine and Rimbaud. Great French poets and huge chums. Tell you what, Francis. It's a bit of a cheek, but how do you fancy lending me a hand? Could you be on book for me tomorrow?'

'On book?'

'You hold the script and see if I've got the words in the right order.'

The Grove, an avenue of stout, red-bricked houses fronted by well-maintained gardens and gold-topped iron railings, had been built in Branlingham by a local builder towards the end of Victoria's reign. The builder had lived in the grandest of them for more than fifty years, but when the last of his family died, Hilltops was put up for sale. The estate agent, Dempster & Pageant, listened as prospective purchasers complained that Hilltops was too forbidding a place, the gardens shambolic, the rooms inconvenient, and the plumbing beyond hope. A staff of servants had supported the builder's family, but after the war domestic help was at a premium. Dempster and Pageant was reconciled to having the property on its books for ever, but in 1947 a caller at the office expressed interest, viewed it and signed the contract, all in the space of one afternoon.

Mr Parks impressed both Mr Pageant and Mr Dempster, and had not quibbled about the asking price. They knew nothing of him except that he wore good clothes (Mr Dempster thought him the sort of man who bought his pyjamas and handkerchiefs in Jermyn Street), and was cultivated and business-like. He was also foreign, which they did not mind.

Ten years later, Hilltops had shaken off none of its forbidding exterior, but had come to terms with its current inhabitants. A part-time handyman restored the gardens to something like their Victorian glory, and a woman came in twice weekly. There was a housekeeper, Mrs Davies, who lived at the top of the house, but whose domain extended throughout it. This morning she stood in the study facing her employer. Had some of the house's original Victorians been asked their opinion, they would have called her poker-faced.

'Miss Ann should be brought down,' she said. 'It's a fair day, Mr Parks.'

The man she addressed stood at French windows that opened onto a terrace. Although not tall, he had an upright bearing that made him seem less slight. He wore a well-cut suit and polished shoes. Despite his hair being freshly pomaded, his spotted bow tie, and a goatee beard that was clipped as close as well-tended privet every morning before breakfast, there was nothing of the dandy about him. His face never lost its seriousness, but the suggestion of pleasantness put others at ease. He was smiling now, a lilt that suited his voice, which Mrs Davies had told her sister was mellow, like a warm sugared drink before bedtime.

'How long have you been with us, Mrs Davies?'

'Long enough to be able to speak to you when it's needed. The wind has dropped. She won't take harm if she's wrapped up well. To be out in the open … to see the trees and catch a glimpse of spring …'

'Spring … yes, it comes round again. Everything comes round in England. I have wanted to speak to you, Mrs Davies.'

'Well, here I am, Mr Parks.'

'How long have you been with us? It must be several years.'

'Nine. I climbed up the hill nine years ago, sent from the agency. A rainy day in September.'

'Time flies. You have been indispensable, but you know that, of course.'

'Others would have managed as well.'

'Not so well, no. You might have had an easier position, with a proper family.'

'I don't know what you mean by that,' said Mrs Davies. 'This family is proper enough to be going on with, thank you very much.'

'A more proper family would have brought life to the old house.'

'There is that, I suppose.'

'As it is, we are very much alone here.'

'That's been your way,' said Mrs Davies. 'The house hasn't helped. It keeps people to itself, close by it. That's what these old places do. It hugs them and doesn't want to let them go. It has suited your purpose.'

'Ann must have quiet. Too much of life unsettles her. It is thanks to Dr Anderson that my daughter is still with us. His leaving has been a blow to us.'

The unexpected tightness in his voice suggested it would be unwise to question him, but Mrs Davies ploughed on.

'Of course. Dr Anderson was full of advice. But carefulness may not always be enough, and Dr Anderson has gone. He won't come again, and Ann must be looked after. I know you would do anything to make her happy and bring her good health.'

'That will not happen,' said Parks sternly. 'We should not delude ourselves in that.'

'That's as may be, but you will need to call the new doctor. Mary Dalton's been very obliging since Dr Anderson went, but she has her work cut out at the surgery and can't always be running up here to keep an eye on Ann. You need to get the new doctor in, and that's all there is to it. His name is Hendel. He's German.'

Parks' eyes flickered. A slant of sun blurred his vision for a second.

'We were so used to Dr Anderson.'

'You're as bad as the rest of the village, saying how Branlingham will never be the same now he's gone. If you ask me, Anderson was a bit of an old rogue.'

'Mrs Davies!'

'Oh, not in a serious way, but professionally he was on the make. Stands to reason, doesn't it? Private practice. You don't suppose he spent all that time every week up here out of the goodness of his heart, do you? Dr Anderson had a healthy list of wealthy patients, to whom a long visit was never a problem, and a nice bill to be presented at the end of each month. A country doctor in a village like this depends on such clients unless he fancies living like the church mouse.'

'We kept him in bread and cheese?'

'Brandy and cigars, more like.'

'That's untypically ungenerous of you, Mrs Davies. Anderson was a good man.'

'I'm sure he was, but that's the past. It's time you gave this new man a chance.'

'What did you say his name was?'

'Hendel. I've heard people in the village speak well of him. He came up trumps at the church fête, when all those people went down with gastroenteritis. I could call him if you like.'

Parks stared at the garden. After a moment, he said 'Very well', and turned back to give the instruction, but Mrs Davies was already in the hall lifting the telephone receiver.

*

Making hay of a bright morning, Gordon cycled alongside Francis to Darting Hall. He chopped logs in the back yard of the Gothic lodge where Francis and Rufus Wolfe sat in the gnome-like parlour. Rufus sprawled on the faded plush velvet of a flea-bitten sofa that Lady Darting had excommunicated from the Pink Room at the Hall. Across the room Francis squatted on the floor with a volume of Verlaine's verses and a typewritten script on his knee.

'Bastard!' said Rufus. 'It's a bastard text, but it's the best we have. The trouble with translations is you never know if they're what the writer meant to say.'

'Doesn't that make them dangerous to read?'

'Goethe, the Greek poets, Ibsen, Tolstoy; they come to us through the conduit of someone else's mind. All we can do is accept and make what we will of them. As a poetry lover, you know that, Francis.'

'Do I?'

'You're a grammar school boy. I mean, you *do* poetry, don't you? Keats and stuff? That lonely knight ailing at arms where the sedge has withered.'

'And a bit of Wordsworth. Walter de la Mare, and "The Highwayman" – Noyes, isn't it?'

'All good middle of the road stuff,' said Rufus without a hint of condescension.

'And I like Hilaire Belloc,' said Francis. In fact, saying it made Francis realise for the first time how very *much* he liked Hilaire Belloc.

Rufus jumped to his feet and did a little apache dance, clapped his hands and chanted '"Do you remember an inn, Miranda, do you remember an inn?" Put a collected Belloc in your knapsack, Francis, and you'll never walk alone.' With a final Pyrenean flourish, he stopped twirling and collapsed into the sofa again.

'What do you want to do in life, Francis?'

'Do? I don't know. At school they want us to go into insurance or banking. Doesn't matter what, so long as it's respectacle.'

'Heaven forbid! That's not you.'

'No, and it's not Gordon either.'

'Well, he might become a professional wood chopper.'

'Oh, I'm sure Gordon's life'll be much more thrilling than mine. I think mine will turn out deadly dull. But not Gordon's. He'll explore places no one knows, and do amazing things. You must never let on, but he's worth ten of me.'

'He won't be pigeon-holed, anyway. Neither will you.'

Francis didn't have time to agree. Gordon put his head through the window. His cheeks were alarmingly mottled, his ginger hair, crowned with wood shavings, seriously deranged.

'Wood's chopped,' he shouted. 'Shocking blisters. And there's been a bit of a do at the Bide-a-Wee Tea Rooms.'

Rufus and the boys hurried to the Bide-a-Wee. As ever, the front doorbell tinkled as they entered, but now the tap of bone china cup on bone china saucer, the timid ring of apostle spoons and tiny clatter of dessert forks gave way to the moaning of a battlefield. The door was wedged partly open by a customer who had collapsed behind it. One or two people still sat at tables, as if transfixed. A man in a raincoat who had started on a plate of chocolate éclairs was consoling others strewn untidily around the room. The Bide-a-Wee's proprietor Beryl Sanders was slumped across the kiosk at which her customers paid their bills. They groaned in harmony.

'What's happened here?' demanded Rufus.

A woman appeared from the back regions of the premises, her face a ghastly white. Beads of perspiration peppered her forehead, her eyes so unfocused that Rufus was sure she could not recognise him.

'Nurse Dalton!' he called. 'What on earth has happened here?'

'Oh God,' cried Mary Dalton. 'I feel so ill. Has anyone telephoned for an ambulance?'

'Yes,' said Beryl. 'I managed to get through before I succumbed.'

'We need Dr Hendel,' said Francis. 'This looks like a repeat of the church fête.'

'No point in telephoning the surgery,' said Mary. 'Dr Hendel himself was here only half an hour ago. He had to go into Norwich unexpectedly, an emergency call. I feel so useless. It's me who should be helping everyone, but …'

'Nonsense,' said Francis. 'You're in no state to do anything.'

'Water!' shouted Rufus. 'Dilute the problem. Gordon, fill up any containers you can and bring them in here.'

Gordon vanished into the kitchen, grabbing at jugs and buckets and teapots and anything that would carry water. The distant sound of an approaching ambulance filtered through, and before long the boys were helping the worst affected of the customers into the waiting vehicle. Struggling to stand, Mary insisted on playing her part, but refused to get into the ambulance herself.

'No,' she protested after the last of the patients had been despatched. 'It's quite right they should go, but I know it will pass off. Another couple of glasses of water and I'll be right as rain.'

To Gordon, she seemed far from well: her hair was disarranged, with her natural auburn showing at the roots. 'The hospital will have quite enough on its hands without me to worry about.'

'Take it easy,' said Rufus comfortingly.

'My day off, too! Dr Hendel and I came in for a quiet coffee and … oh dear … we were having such a nice chat. Just as well he was called away or he'd have gone down with it too.'

'Let's hope he hasn't succumbed to it as well,' said Gordon. 'Whatever "it" is.'

'*Two* outbreaks of food poisoning in the village in the last month … It's a bit out of the ordinary, isn't it?' wondered Francis. 'In the way of things it's inevitable that these upsets should occur now and again, and there's nothing to link the sickness at the fête with the Bide-a-Wee Tea Rooms.'

'Not that we know of. What did the hospital say?'

'Much the same as they said about the fête: it was general food poisoning. Everyone recovered within a day or two, with no lasting ill-effects.'

'I don't know about that,' laughed Gordon. 'Miss Simms swears she'll never set foot in the Bide-a-Wee again. It's left her very wary at the Post Office. She's even refusing to lick the stamps.'

'It's a coincidence that such a thing happened twice. If it wasn't, imagine the panic there would be. Beryl Sanders has had the food inspector in from the council, and he's pronounced everything fit for human consumption, but who knows? Perhaps the cream for the afternoon teas had gone off.'

'Serves Miss Simms right. She puts too big a dollop on her scones. Anyway, Dr Hendel was unaffected. Funny, really. He'd been at the Bide-a-Wee only a little before everyone fell sick, but had no ill effects at all, although he'd had one of Beryl's afternoon teas there with Nurse Dalton.'

'And they've never discovered the source of the problem at the fête,' said Francis, 'so we don't know if it was the winkles or the toffee apples or the Hog Roast.'

'Or Aunt Doris's baking,' suggested Gordon, holding up his hands in mock horror.

Dr Hendel made his first visit to Hilltops. Since he had been in Branlingham, he had been called to two other addresses in The Grove, and was surprised to see how markedly different Hilltops was from its neighbours. It reminded him vaguely of the home he had lived in with his parents in Germany, recalling the happiness he had enjoyed there. He stifled the thought and rang the doorbell.

Mrs Davies mentioned the weather, took his homburg and showed him into the drawing-room. He was admiring the view that fell away from the terrace when a man in a flannel shirt and corduroys came up from the lawn.

'Dr Hendel! Good of you to come. Excuse my costume. I have been helping Evans with the bonfire.'

'I miss a garden,' said Hendel, looking out. 'This is beautiful. I am in lodgings at present. My landlady is most particular about her box hedge and aspidistra. She prefers neatness to naturalness. I have caught your garden between chaos and geometrical precision.'

'That is how I wish it to stay. A garden without edges, where nature does as it pleases. I sometimes think Evans would prefer a box hedge and an aspidistra.'

'You are German?' asked Hendel.

'Yes,' said Parks, but his eyes suggested he didn't welcome the question. 'I think we are countrymen.'

The conversation faltered for a while as they looked at one another, then Parks settled his visitor in an armchair and sat across the room from him.

'Thank you for coming, Dr Hendel. Your predecessor has been visiting us for several years.'

'Dr Anderson had a special relationship with his private patients. That is commendable, of course, but I should make it clear that I do not plan to take on many private cases. The practice is already busy, and growing. Other than Nurse Dalton, I have no help at the surgery, no partner, so that all the work falls to me. If I am to do it to the best of my ability, I will not have as much time for private patients as did Dr Anderson.'

'That will disappoint some of us,' said Parks.

'A very few. There are only a handful of private cases.'

'I suspect Anderson spent most of his "private" time on us.'

'Us?' Hendel looked puzzled. 'Are you not alone? Nurse Dalton hinted at something, but I know nothing of your circumstances.'

'Circumstances?' echoed Parks. 'What a word that is, what a multitude of events it embraces. Ah! Here is Mrs Davies with the coffee.'

The housekeeper poured it into two cups and distributed them with quiet deliberation.

'It smells wonderful,' said Hendel.

'Dr Anderson preferred something stronger,' she said, winking as she leant over. Left alone, the men stirred the coffee. Parks set down his cup and saucer and settled in his chair.

'Circumstances … I will tell you a little of them. When the war started, I was a professor at one of the great German universities. My speciality was German history. It was not a subject that sat comfortably with what was happening at the time. Throughout my career, my head was full of theoretical idealism about the future of my country, based on the solidity of its past. No matter how much fine learning I had, I had not realised how frail civilisation is, how hope can be misleading. What had passed for wisdom was swept away by political fancies. The past was something only to be stamped on, altered out of all recognition, obliterated … If I had been a man without responsibilities, I might have rebelled against what was happening around me. Perhaps even then I would have lacked the courage. But I had a family … my wife Helga, a brilliant political journalist who fiercely campaigned for her countrymen's rights, and my young daughter. I had to keep them safe. There may be words to excuse what I did. I have not found them. You see, I subscribed to those terrible changes that corrupted the air we breathed. I traded our safety for my conscience. Every fibre of me resisted the dark empire being built, brick by brick, around us, but no argument showed a way out of the predicament. I made the pretence of agreeing with the tyrants who were undermining everything I had ever believed in.'

'I am a countryman,' said Hendel softly. 'You may say these things to me, and perhaps I may understand.'

'So it went on throughout the war. I abandoned every moral principle. Don't ask me for details. I would not give them even if I could remember. Fortunately, so much has been sponged from my mind. There are days, even now, when I almost convince myself that I did only what I had to do, that there was no choice. Sometimes I have almost forgiven myself.'

'Circumstances,' repeated Hendel. 'Which of us can say we would not have done the same?'

The coffee was untouched. Parks stood and walked to the fireplace. On the mantelpiece was a framed photograph of a man and woman. He took it up, gazed at it for a moment or two, and handed it to Hendel.

'Helga and I on our wedding day.'

He saw the change in Hendel's eyes.

'As the war progressed, I blamed myself for not having left Germany. I should have removed my family to a place of safety long before it began. My existence became a living hell. In those final months, I thought of taking my own life. Dreadful to confess it, so cowardly as it would have been, and leaving Helga and my daughter to face an uncertain future, but in the end I knew I could stand it no longer. I planned our escape. We would begin a new life in England.'

'That was brave. You risked everything.'

'Others risked more, and lost. The escape could only be managed by involving others that I thought I could trust. I learned that trust is a marketable commodity. We were betrayed. In her writings, Helga railed against the Nazis. I pleaded with her to take care. She was a person of greater integrity than the man who asked this of her, but it was too late. They took Helga away. My fifteen-year-old daughter and I left Germany without her.'

'It shames me,' said Hendel. 'It shames all of us.'

'You are young. You need burden none of the shame. Let us who were there take that burden from you. Ann was horribly affected by what happened; it changed her life forever. She had been such a bright child, inquisitive, outgoing. I thought that once in England she would improve. Perhaps I did not appreciate how traumatically she reacted to Helga's disappearance. How naïve to imagine that time would make her whole again. Since that day Ann has hardly spoken. She barely moves.'

'In all this time?'

'All those years. When I returned to the house that evening, she was inconsolable. Two men and a woman had come for Helga. When the purpose of their visit became clear, Ann remonstrated with them. I remember her words between her sobs. The woman smiled. She said "Good afternoon. You are back from school early. Is your mother at home?" and the men slipped past Ann, ran upstairs and found Helga in her bedroom. My wife had time only to snatch a winter coat and hat. She didn't even take her handbag. There would have been no point, for she knew where she was going. When Ann heard the cries upstairs, she fought with the woman who was still standing in the open doorway. She pleaded with her to go away and to take the men with her. For a while, it seemed as if the woman might relent. She knelt down and spoke to Ann face to face. She told Ann that her mother was going to a good place where she would be happy. And even as she was kneeling and looking so kindly into my daughter's eyes, she softly brushed aside some strands of Ann's hair with her wrist. Then the men came down the stairs with Helga in her winter coat and hat. She was never seen again.'

'Where did your wife die?'

'One of the camps. The records of deaths were so chaotic at that stage of the war. After all, it isn't as if they were considered important. We cannot be sure of the location.' Parks smiled wryly. 'There were many camps to choose from.'

'Your daughter …'

'Ann.'

'Ann … did her health deteriorate at once?'

'Yes. The collapse began that day. By the time I got home, she was stiff with fear. At first I could not understand what had happened. Of course I feared the worst. I knew that Helga was gone and that was all I needed to know. I could barely make sense of what Ann was saying, but between her sobs I understood. With the help of a trusted friend we escaped the next morning. We came by boat to England. In a way it was another desertion, another sign of the weakness in which I had already excelled.'

Hendel listened attentively, his face alert with sympathy, but now he looked at his wrist-watch, got to his feet and sighed.

'You asked me here for a consultation, Mr Parks. May I now see your daughter?'

At the top of a twisting staircase that went up from the recesses of the entrance hall, Ann Parks was sitting in a bath chair at an opened window through which a muted sun shone. Hendel thought the room might once have been a nursery where children spent their days before being taken down to spend the evening half hour with their mother, but now the tall, light-filled space gave no hint of careless happiness. Although not a child, the flaxen-haired girl seemed extraordinarily frail. Despite the warmth of the day, a tartan rug was spread across her lap. The persistent conversation of two blackbirds came from the garden. Looking from the window, Hendel thought 'If I had to look at one view every day of my life I could do worse than this', but looking to Ann he saw no sign of contentment in her face. Her features bore no expression; she might be thinking anything, or nothing.

'Ann, my dear,' said Parks, bending to her, 'I've brought Dr Hendel to see you.'

Looking across at him, Parks was surprised by how nervous the young doctor seemed. Anderson's bluff manner had easily cut through the sick-room atmosphere with its permanently medicinal atmosphere, not that Anderson had ever spent much time in it. If he were honest, Parks had never warmed to the old man, although it didn't do to let Mrs Davies know. Hendel walked up to the chair and put his hand on the girl's shoulder.

'Hello, Ann. I am Richard Hendel, and I am pleased to meet you.'

The sight of her unsteadied him. She was a pathetic thing. Her head drooped as he moved closer, but it slowly lifted. She gazed at him with such intensity that he didn't know what to do or say next. The unworldliness of it startled him, as if this were a face he had dreamed of in some old painting or long forgotten half-sleep, with lips that needed to say little or much, but stared out at the world in wonder.

Her father touched her cheek, saying that he would have tea brought in, and left them alone. Half an hour later, Mrs Davies showed the doctor out. As he got into his car he looked up at the window of the sick-room and (was it imagined? Did he only wish it had happened?) could have sworn that a thin hand lifted from the arm of a bath-chair.

After the misfortunes at the church fête and the Bide-a-Wee Tea Rooms, Branlinghamers treaded carefully. The WI regarded members' homemade Victoria sponges with suspicion, and the fishmonger did less business. Thinking that everything in the village was back to normal, Francis and Gordon made the most of the sunny days by cycling to the coastal town of Sheershore, relaxing in a sheltered hollow of the dunes and reading. Gordon was struggling with *Wuthering Heights*, conjuring up the image of Rufus at every mention of Heathcliff, as well as hurtling through a Biggles adventure in which Ginger was currently endangered. Francis was rereading *The ABC Murders*. They discarded their books for frequent dips in the sea.

The tartan rug was removed from Ann's room. Each morning Mrs Davies flung open the windows as Dr Hendel recommended. She was pleased to see Hendel at the door. He visited more regularly than his predecessor, spending time with his patient rather than in the study making short work of a whisky and soda.

One intensely hot day, he invited Francis to accompany him. Although he felt awkward trying to communicate with Ann, Francis enjoyed being shown round the garden by Mr Parks. Sometimes Hendel would not speak to Ann's father at all, but wave to him as he worked in the flowerbeds.

Hendel was untrained in psychology, but knew this case involved much more than a physical complaint. He reduced the medication prescribed by Dr Anderson. One of the pills was little more than a tranquilliser, and Hendel stopped it.

Rufus Wolfe's visit to Strangeways won him many new admirers. Two inmates who had almost finished digging an escape tunnel said they would forgo their freedom if only Rufus promised to return to the prison. Such passion might have turned the head of others, but Rufus remained unspoilt, full of self doubt and consumed by sudden spasms of passion for anything or anyone that he thought beautiful, male or female, animal, vegetable or mineral, and then descending into despair because all life was worthless, and then being uplifted by a mere snatch of the most commonplace music that reduced him to tears. He related his visit to Strangeways to Francis in detail, bringing it to life so vividly that Francis felt as if he had been there.

'But that's enough of me,' said Rufus. 'What shall we do now that Verlaine and Rimbaud have been put to bed, so to speak …? Tell me what you are detecting. I'm longing to know!'

'Nothing, I'm afraid. It's one of our fallow periods.'

'Surely not. What about the fête? Remember? The day they tried to poison me, and half of Branlingham for good measure! Me: a Hamlet from heaven according to the critics, but usually when I'm wondering whether to be or not to be I'm really thinking about how nice it will be to get home and walk through a snowstorm or cuddle up with a mug of Horlicks. And that outbreak at the Tea Rooms? I know you've had your suspicions, Francis. I can hear your restless detective mind whirring from here.'

Francis laughed. He had begun by being star-struck by Rufus, but now felt relaxed as never before.

'Everything's gone quiet … but something tells me things will begin to happen again.'

'There! Just as I suspected!'

'People think detectives need a magnifying glass to examine cigarette ash or footprints below a window, or the questioning of suspicious characters. But it's not necessarily so. I've been detecting from a distance.'

'My goodness! I felt sure something must be up! How does that work?'

'Village life has its dynamics that are always changing. You only have to have spent time with Miss Marple to know that. Sometimes it's as simple as people coming and going. The old country doctor retires from his practice, and a new doctor takes over. The effect on the village is bound to be considerable. The new man doesn't know that Mrs Grumble is a hypochondriac, or that Mr Bumble is addicted to Syrup of Figs with quite disastrous consequences, or that for years the old doctor has prescribed useless sugared pills to his patients just to keep them quiet. The new man hears that a local distillery is closing and doesn't realise it's because he's taken over from an old soak of a rascal who drank his private patient's cellars dry. By keeping an eye and ear alert, you can learn a lot of what is going on.'

'And what have you been learning, oh boy detective?'

'Well, remember that I was at the scene of the two poisonings. That gave me a start. But there's more ... Mrs Davies, the housekeeper at Hilltops, often meets mum in the butcher's shop. One afternoon mum gave me something to take up to Mrs Davies; it might have been one of her specially commissioned corsets, and of course I don't ask questions when female undergarments are involved.

'It was a very warm day. I got to Hilltops and Nurse Dalton was bending down to tuck Ann's rug under her feet when she rolled up the sleeves of her cardigan. What surprised me was the look on Ann's face.'

'Look? What sort of look?'

'Well, that's it. I don't know. It was just, you know, a *look*. And later in the afternoon, when I was leaving after Mrs Davies had given me some tea, I saw Dr Hendel with Ann in the sitting room. The afternoon had got even hotter, and he'd loosened his tie and taken off his jacket and was rolling up the sleeves of his shirt, and ... the look on Ann's face. You see ... *it was the same look*. Frankly, I don't know what to make of Dr Hendel.'

'You are a horse of dark complexion,' said Rufus, screwing up his eyes as if trying to get Francis into focus. 'So, what happens next?'

'We wait.'

They didn't have to wait long. The following Saturday, Seth Booth, a cow hand from Pardley's Farm, and Delia Rowes, the most glamorous boot operative in the Norwich shoe industry, were married by the Revd Challis at St Barnabas at Knee. His reverence was momentarily alarmed at the size of the bride's bouquet, but half an hour later he was seated in the Wedded Stoat at the top table of the wedding feast, beside the bridegroom's widowed mother, her already generously bosomed figure alarmingly enhanced by one of Mrs Jones's most cunning constructions. The garment was not only sublimely comfortable, but had given the woman such confidence that she was seriously considering what it would be like to be the wife of a vicar.

With the history of the village's medical upsets still fresh in everyone's mind, all possible care was taken with the preparation of refreshments. Only the most trusted of the community were allowed to give a hand. Lady Darting had kindly supplied vegetables from the garden at Darting Hall, although Uncle Billy (honorary chef for the day) said he'd never seen such shrivelled specimens, and that one of the mouldiest carrots bore a striking resemblance to her ladyship. Lord Darting added a spark of originality to the proceedings by serving at table dressed as a Lyons Nippy. Nurse Dalton was at her busiest, helping wherever the need, and threatening to box the ears of two of the Booth family's boys who had matching red ears and ran amok around and under the tables. Careering into her, they upset her capacious bag, sending its contents flying.

Rufus was in control of the soup, a recipe poached from the kitchens at Wormwood Scrubs. Mrs Jones' giant Bramley apple pie attracted as much attention as the three fire tongs, two sets of fish knives, and sets of home-knitted baby clothes in blue and pink that many imagined would all too soon be in use, that formed the centrepiece of the presents. It was, of course, Mrs Jones' wedding cake that proved the cynosure of every eye. On close inspection, the miniature bride and bridegroom perched at the pinnacle of the third tier bore an uncanny resemblance to Seth and Delia, whose shape suggested that even when placed on an iced cake she seemed to be interestingly corseted. Beryl Sanders had closed the Bide-a-Wee Tearoom for the afternoon, and donated that day's scones and fancies to the festivities.

The Revd Challis, anxious to avoid his eyes fixing on Mrs Booth's undulating chest, was delighted to see Francis and Gordon at the heart of the event, turning their hands to whatever was needed. So long as there were such splendid youth in Branlingham, he felt assured the little community that looked to him for spiritual comfort would flourish.

There was only one cause for concern. He had thought nothing of it at first, seeing Francis dipping into a box of chocolates that had appeared on the fringe of the tables at the furthest point of the room. After all, the boy must be hungry, never having stopped fetching and carrying from the moment the wedding party had sat down. There was, however, such a thing as excess. Francis could barely have swallowed one chocolate before he helped himself to another. The Revd Challis watched as a raspberry delicacy was speedily followed by a coffee delight. Those around Francis were flagging after the demands of the day; the boy's energy was not only undimmed but accelerated. It was a little later that Gordon noticed the change. What was the manic gleam that fired from Francis's eyes, as if some alien being had taken possession of him? It was only natural that the celebrating families, fuelled by milk stout and Babycham, should break out into rude jokes and untidy dancing, but history repeated itself as one by one the revellers complained of stomach pains. It seemed less natural that Francis, egged on by an hysterical crowd, was waving at them from the top of a lamppost.

'I think there is no need for you to call so often,' said Parks.

Some of the usual warmth had gone from his voice.

'This is your second visit this week, and we are no longer private patients.'

'I have not called as often as I might have wished,' said Hendel. 'I believe Dr Anderson was a much more frequent visitor.'

'Ah! Dr Anderson ... He kept a fatherly eye on Ann.'

'Mine is hardly that, Dr Anderson having been so much older. But it must be as you wish, Mr Parks. As a matter of fact, I was about to suggest that I spend less time here.'

'Then we agree. That may be a sensible way forward.'

'But I do not think I have wasted my time here, and I hope I have been of a little service to you.'

'You must not think me ungrateful, doctor.'

'And Ann?'

'My concern is that she has become ... unsettled. You must understand, her condition ... it is not always easy to know what she is thinking or feeling, but I sense a difference ... a restlessness. I don't know if it is good or bad.'

'The reason I was about to recommend that I spend less time in the house is because I think Ann should get away from it.'

Parks almost shuddered.

'What do you mean?'

'You oblige me to speak frankly, Mr Parks. I know that I lack the gravitas or experience of my predecessor, and I do not disrespect his memory or question what he did for your daughter's well-being. Perhaps you are right in thinking me a callow fellow, but over the weeks I have been coming to Hilltops my understanding has altered. From the beginning I saw that Ann could not have a more devoted father. She would not have survived so long without your diligence and care. But she is cocooned here. The world is kept at bay and she has no idea of what happens in it.'

'My one thought has been for Ann's welfare. Her fragility demands protection, and that is what I have provided. Do you suppose she would be as well as she is if Dr Anderson had not kept her safe?'

'He wrapped her in cotton wool. He closed the shutters and kept out the sun and rain. What sort of life has that left her?'

'Dr Hendel, if you were not so young and well-meaning, I might think you impertinent.'

'Keeping her locked away from what's frightening may see her through a few more years, but what for? What would be the point? You have already given her so much; why not open the door to everything? There are dragons around us all, but let her face them. Better that she has a chance to breathe fresh air than the medicated dust of the sick-room. There is a theory that we grow immune from danger by exposing ourselves to it.'

Parks waited a space, and breathed deeply.

'I am grateful for your opinion, doctor, but since Dr Anderson left I have become more concerned about Ann. Nurse Dalton has bridged the gap, and been most kind and attentive. She, too, has spoken to me of Ann's recent deterioration, the lack of colour in her face.'

'A reflection, perhaps, of the lack of colour in her *life*,' insisted Hendel.

'I do not think you callow, Dr Hendel. Reassure yourself of that.'

'And I do not need you to be grateful. I only ask that you consider what I suggest.'

'Which is?'

'Lend Ann to me for the occasional afternoon.'

Parks raised his eyebrows and half smiled.

'I can't imagine why I should agree to such a thing, but I too was once young and impertinent. Nevertheless, I can't see how that would help her.'

Hendel leaned forward, his hands spread-eagled on his knees, his face made more vivid by the shaft of light that cut across it, his spectacles accentuating the intensity of his gaze.

'I don't know either. But it might.'

'Well …'

'Tomorrow at two o'clock? Make sure she is well wrapped.'

The next day, Mrs Davies helped Ann into Hendel's Austin 7. The car returned to Hilltops two hours later. As they accompanied her back into the house, Mrs Davies could have sworn something like the ghost of a smile crossed the young woman's face, but it was gone in an instant.

Mary Dalton was standing at the door. Parks had asked her to call, as if by chance, because he wanted her opinion of how Ann seemed after the excursion. He need have no fear, Mary told him. Ann was in good hands with Dr Hendel, and surely her father could see the bright tint in the girl's cheeks? Of course, the new doctor's was a different approach to that taken by Dr Anderson, but Mary was all for it.

It was three weeks later that Hendel mentioned the possibility of a birthday party. Ann would be twenty-five. Mrs Davies wore away at her employer, casually suggesting he might open the house to visitors that day. There would be no problem about catering; she would see to it all. It would make a change, people flowing through the quiet rooms.

Parks was naturally dubious. There was no denying the slight improvement in Ann's condition, but he needed to protect her, and was nervous of what excitement and the unknown might do. Added to this was his guardianship of the house itself. He had kept it removed from the village; surely that was something the British might understand, defending his house as if it were a castle.

He had heard something of the troubled church fête, the sickness at the Bide-a-Wee Tea Rooms, and the chaotic wedding reception at the Wedded Stoat, but those were public occasions, and such things (still officially unexplained, although theories involving inadequate sanitation or food that had gone off in the warm weather abounded around the village) happened. Somehow, Hilltops seemed above and beyond such events. Parks' faith in Hendel, in Mrs Davies's good management, and his desire to see more changes in Ann did their work, and invitations were sent out.

The day of the birthday party was the hottest of the year. It was as if Hilltops breathed easily for the first time in its existence. Rufus persuaded Mr Parks to put up bunting, and something about Rufus's very presence, insisted on by Richard Hendel, gave the occasion an especially festive air. In the intervening weeks, Parks felt himself changed. He too knew what it meant to be cocooned. Rufus had been to the house once or twice, reading Ann poetry and singing songs of Arcady and reciting scraps of poetry and pulling funny faces until hers almost reacted to such nonsense. He meant to be her troubadour, and longed for a flicker of recognition in her eyes.

Mrs Davies had laid careful plans. Only when the morning came did she realise that she alone could not cope with all the preparation. She knew she could rely on Doris Jones to help with the food. Her Sussex pond tartlets had long been absolved of all blame, and by eleven o'clock three trays of them were queuing up for the oven at Red Cherry House. Mr Jones wouldn't be able to transport them to Hilltops because he was off to the football, but Mary Dalton happily offered to fetch the tartlets, and Mrs Jones, from Red Cherry House.

Dr Hendel had already secured an invitation for Francis and Gordon, and for Uncle Billy, who, Hendel knew, had been in Germany during the war. Uncle Billy and Mary Dalton arrived at Hilltops almost simultaneously, one car drawing in after the other. Mrs Jones spilled out of the nurse's Morris Minor and called to her brother.

'Billy! I don't think you know Nurse Dalton.'

'Why,' said Billy, getting out of his car, 'not sure that I do.'

'No,' laughed Doris Jones, 'you won't catch our Billy at the surgery. Never had a day's illness in his life, have you dear?'

'Probably not,' said Billy, but his voice was unclear, and in the general confusion he didn't know what was what. Mary Dalton smiled at him as she went out to her car to bring in more provisions. He stood still for a second, until his sister pressed a pile of trays into his hands, and directed him into the kitchen. Mrs Davies had always liked Billy and was pleased to see him, and the cakes. She said something she hoped might amuse him, but he seemed to be in a daydream.

'Sorry, missus,' he said. 'I was just wondering ... something or other ...'

Gordon was helping to ferry food when he overheard two women in conversation.

'It was at the Wedded Stoat, wasn't it?'

'Yes! The most exciting wedding I've ever been to! If it hadn't been for the fact that a qualified medical person happened to be passing we'd have been in even more of a pickle.'

Gordon's freckles almost blushed. Francis had been almost out of his mind that afternoon at the wedding reception. Others rolled their eyes, complaining of stomach pains, but Francis beamed with delight. Even when Gordon had persuaded him to climb down that lamppost, Francis had been unstoppable, a wildness in his eyes that seemed not to recognise anything around him. He'd only reached the ground when he ran off again, charging away up the Norwich road as if an army of demons was after him, returning home three hours later, having been spotted only ten minutes earlier jumping a five-bar gate eight miles away. Gordon had firmly taken hold of him, and wouldn't leave his side until, hours later, Francis came back to himself, unaware of the extraordinary behaviour he'd exhibited. Gordon's task was to ensure that nothing like it ever happened to his cousin again. He would stay close to him all through the party at Hilltops.

The assembled guests were in the drawing-room, awaiting the entrance of Ann Parks. Commissioned by Parks to make a dress for his daughter, Mrs Jones had sent off for the finest silk and tulle, and scoured the papers for patterns of the latest French models. This had been one of her greatest challenges. It was in her power to make something exquisite of this strange, silent creature, something that would show her to the world as she had never been shown. When the moment came, they were expecting Mr Parks to bring her down, but as he got to the foot of the stairs he turned back and looked into the room.

'Dr Hendel! I think *you* should fetch my daughter.'

Afterwards, Mrs Jones said it was like Cinderella arriving at the ball. She couldn't believe how beautiful the girl looked, although her eyes were so misted over she couldn't see anything plainly. The rustling dress fell exquisitely about her in folds of fairy-light net, deepest pink, russet and white. The guests stood transfixed as Hendel carried her slowly down the stairs. It was as if in that moment something had changed and could never go back to what had been.

'Happy birthday,' said her father. 'You are smiling.'

It was barely detectable, but Francis noticed it too; at least, it was a rehearsal for a smile.

'A lovely day for a lovely young woman,' said Mrs Davies, who had already bumped into Mrs Jones because both had tears in their eyes. 'You've come up a treat, and no mistake. You might be one of them there debutantes.'

'Oh, she is more special than that, Mrs Davies,' said Parks, giving his housekeeper a kindly stare. 'A toast to your future! To all of you who have helped bring life back to this old house. I had given up hope, but now …'

Everyone lifted their glasses, and the party began. Hendel could barely disguise his excitement. When he had taken Ann in his arms she had spoken to him. Only one word, but in time there would be more words, every word she might ever want to use.

'It is a miracle,' Parks told Rufus. 'You with your poetry and your clowning – you have shown Ann a world that was denied her. Indeed, it's denied to most of us. And you had no need to do it, when you might have been appearing on a stage in London being admired by hundreds of people every night.'

'Oh, that's baloney compared to this,' laughed Rufus, his hair more wild than ever, as if his hairdresser had been closed.

'It's only selfishness after all. I've only been amusing myself. It's Richard you should thank. He's a brilliant doctor. A fine person. Branlingham should cherish him. He cares about people. This is his moment.'

'Yes,' said Parks. 'He is a remarkable young man. When I first met him, I knew only that he was German. A countryman. What could be more reason for pride? He was – what is the word you use for this? Cagey? He was cagey about his background, and, perhaps naturally, I was suspicious.'

'You can be forgiven,' said Rufus. 'He's modest, you see. Quite unlike me! When he left Germany at the end of the war he worked for a society that helps refugees. He still does that work, quite voluntarily, not that he'd tell anyone about it. They don't want to lose him.'

'Then he is a true friend,' said Parks, looking across the room to where Hendel sat with Ann. 'A good man.'

'Look here, old chap,' said Rufus, his hand on Parks' shoulder. 'I think you'd better make your mind up that he may well be rather more than a friend before too long. And in my opinion, you'd make a great father-in-law.'

Before Parks had time to respond, Rufus flashed him a cloud-lifting smile and passed on to beguile Mrs Davies, bewitched by finding so glorious an example of the male species grinning at her. The sherry trifle she nursed gave a tell-tale wobble.

'Where's Nurse Dalton?' asked Francis. He had been looking around the room, and missed her.

'She's gone to get some more food from her car,' Gordon reminded him.

'Here she is now,' said Mrs Davies, waving to Nurse Dalton who was lifting trays of Mrs Jones' baking from the back seat. 'Can you manage, dear?' she called.

'Well, I could do with some help. Mrs Jones' cakes may be light as a feather, but the trays are heavy!' She chirped with her usual brisk manner. 'Perhaps Dr Hendel would come and help bring them in.'

Uncle Billy was close by, a drink untouched in his hand, but made no attempt to give assistance. Francis wondered what was wrong with him. Normally, he'd have been the first to jump up and lend a hand to anyone, but Billy didn't say 'Oh don't bother Dr Hendel. I'll do it.' It hardly mattered, because Hendel had already gone out to the car to fetch more of Mrs Jones's produce, and was bringing it back to the house.

'Perhaps you'll take them into the kitchen,' said Mary Dalton, and after three more excursions all the food had been transferred to Mrs Davies' domain.

Francis was coming back from the kitchen when Uncle Billy stopped him in the hall.

'Francis, lad' he whispered. 'I don't know what to do. I can't be sure, and I don't want to make a fuss, but …'

Hendel burst back into the hall, on his way outside to make sure that everything had been brought into the house.

'I'll set the plates out,' he said. 'I'm quite domesticated for a doctor.'

'You'll find plates and everything you need in the dresser,' said Mrs Davies, impressed that such an attractive young doctor was prepared to do things that she had always imagined were done by women. 'I'll leave you to it, then.'

Ten minutes later, the food had been moved into the sitting-room. Its distribution was a joint effort, with Richard Hendel, Mrs Davies and Francis passing round plates and napkins. Mary Dalton happened to be standing at the table where the feast had been spread, and passed Dr Hendel a plate with two sandwiches.

'That will be Ann's food,' said Hendel, reaching out, but, even as he touched it, Francis' hand grabbed the plate.

'What on earth?' asked Hendel.

'Do not eat anything,' said Francis, looking about. The babble of voices came to an abrupt stop, and all eyes turned to where he stood. 'Nobody must touch the food.' He held aloft the plate he had snatched. 'Especially from this plate.'

'What's wrong?' said Parks. 'What does he think he's doing?'

'You very rude boy!' cried Mary Dalton. 'Have you gone mad? Give it back instantly.'

'No,' said Uncle Billy. His face was white. 'I don't think we should do that ... Fräulein Bader!'

'In my experience,' said Francis, as if he'd had all the experience the world had to offer, 'it's seldom one thing that turns the key of a case. It's more a number of small things, things you didn't think significant, and then they come together and merge into something else.'

Rufus Wolfe and Richard Hendel sat obediently on the settee in the sitting-room of Red Cherry House, looking as if they were in the presence of an oracle. Knowing how much Francis loved having an audience – and goodness knows what theatrical tricks he had picked up from Rufus – Gordon braced himself for one of his cousin's more pompous pronouncements. They were rather less convincing to anyone who'd seen him swinging from the top of a lamppost.

'Somebody,' said Francis, pointedly ignoring Gordon who sat beside him, 'has braced himself for one of my pompous pronouncements. I'm afraid they are inevitable on such occasions, but I will keep the explanation as simple as possible.'

'Thank you,' said Rufus and Hendel simultaneously.

'This whole business wouldn't have come out without Gordon, and Uncle Billy of course!'

Uncle Billy almost blushed.

'Well … I recognised her, you see' said Billy. 'After all those years, I recognised her. I'd been thinking about that time in Germany only the other day, when I was turning out some stuff at Bundler's Cottage and I came across the camera. That brought her back into my mind. And then, there she was. I couldn't believe it, but … there she was.'

'In fact,' said Francis, 'I think most of the credit goes to Gordon and Uncle Billy, and Agatha Christie. I've been reading *The ABC Murders*. I know it might be more spiritually rewarding to be reading Verlaine or Rimbaud …' (Rufus winked at him), 'but I realised the plot of *The ABC Murders* was not unlike what's been happening in the village: a lot of seemingly random events. At the time, the church fête outbreak was thought of as a one-off, something that might happen anywhere now and again. There was no suspicion of deliberate wrongdoing. Then, there was the upset at the Bide-a-Wee Tea Rooms. Well, that might have been a coincidence. Then, there were the upsets at the Wedded Stoat wedding reception that made people sit up.'

'Or down', added Gordon.

'I think that was when I began to wonder: was someone in the village behind these gastric assaults? Of course, poisonings seemed too strong a description; after all, in all the incidents the victims endured a few hours of discomfort and then all was well, but that word kept flashing back at me: *poisoning*. What if the ultimate purpose was to do harm – serious harm – to *one particular person*? No one would suspect what was in effect a murder if a death occurred in the middle of such a lot of apparently sporadic incidents.'

'Just like in old Agatha's book!' exclaimed Rufus.

'Exactly. Then, rather than look for a motive, as would surely be the case if that person had been the only one to be affected, the one act the murderer intended all along just becomes one incident in a host of others. The reason for the murder gets lost in a fog.'

'*Murder?* But why?' asked Hendel. 'Mary Dalton had served the community well for many years. What changed her?'

'You did!'

'What?'

'Francis is being dramatic,' said Gordon reassuringly. 'He does that, you know, for effect. Actually, it wasn't so much your arrival as Dr Anderson's departure. All the years that he'd visited Hilltops, Dr Anderson kept Ann to himself. Every visit was money in his pocket.'

'Of course,' said Hendel. 'He made a great effort with his private patients.'

'Mary Dalton only began to visit Hilltops as the old doctor's regime drew to an end. Up until that time, Nurse Dalton and Ann had never met. It was only when Dr Anderson left that Mr Parks needed someone from the surgery to keep an eye on his daughter.'

'And that started this whole ghastly business?' asked Rufus.

'Perhaps,' said Francis. 'We can't be sure exactly what happened. It's possible that at their first meeting at Hilltops Mary Dalton recognised Ann, but I doubt it. So far as we know, she had only seen Ann once before, and that had been ten years ago in Germany. Ann had changed much in that time, from a child to a woman, and of course her health had suffered in the interim, so her demeanour had radically altered. When Mary Dalton – I should say Fräulein Bader – escaped from Germany and reached England, she made attempts to change her looks. She was a redhead, but dyed her hair black. I noticed the roots one day at the Bide-a-Wee.'

Rufus seemed puzzled. 'So it was Ann that recognised her as the woman who had taken her mother away?'

'Yes. But I don't think it was her dyed hair that gave her away. *It was the weather.*'

'The *weather*?' asked Hendel.

'It was a hot day at Hilltops, when I'd called to deliver one of Mum's corsets. Bader – as we should learn to call her – wore a long sleeved cardigan. It must have been uncomfortable on such a hot afternoon. When she pulled up her sleeve to reveal her wrist I saw Ann flinch. A little later, I could see Ann's face very clearly as you approached her, Dr Hendel. Just as you prepared to squat down beside her, you rolled back the sleeves of your shirt.'

'Yes,' said Hendel. 'As you say, it was an unusually hot day.'

'You rolled back your shirt sleeves, and I watched Ann's face. She had no words to say, but she stared at your wrists, the left as you rolled back your sleeve, and then the right. You probably didn't notice it, but from where I stood it was unmistakable. She was horrified.'

'My God!' cried Hendel. 'I don't understand.'

'It's simple,' said Francis. 'She was terrified of what your wrists might reveal. You see, she had just caught a glimpse of something tattooed on Mary Dalton's wrist. Ann probably didn't see the whole tattoo, because Nurse Dalton would have been careful not to expose it, but Ann saw enough to recognise it as the wrist she had seen on the day her mother was taken away. The day the woman at the door stooped down to the young girl child and stroked her hair.'

'Poor Ann,' said Rufus, who was wearing his heart on his sleeve.

'It was the moment when Ann realised that Nurse Dalton was Fräulein Bader,' Francis continued. 'And something in Ann's eyes told the woman she had been recognised. It was still highly unlikely that the truth would ever come out because Ann couldn't write or speak. The secret was safe enough, until a handsome prince on a white charger rode up and altered everything.'

Gordon turned to Richard Hendel. 'He means you,' he said. 'My cousin goes in for colourful language.'

'Dear old Dr Anderson had made tutting noises for years, but when you – somewhat against your socialist principles – began to visit Hilltops, Bader became aware of a gradual improvement in Ann's condition. She was still far from well, but now, something that could never have been foreseen, there was a glimmer of hope that one day Ann would speak again, and expose Mary Dalton for what she was, and that was something that Bader couldn't allow to happen. That was when she embarked on her plan of mild poisonings, always knowing that she would ultimately reach her one intended victim, the one person who would not recover. To throw suspicion on him, she dropped little insinuations about Dr Hendel into her conversations. Just before the fête she had him called away.'

'That's right. When I got to the address I'd been called to, miles away, the people said they had never rung the surgery.'

'She made it look as if you had somehow avoided the sickness. It gave the impression that you didn't care. And the same at the Bide-a-Wee. She made sure you and she had been having tea there that day, so you were implicated in being there just before the sickness broke out. Of course, when she apparently became a victim at the Bide-a-Wee there was nothing wrong with her; she was pretending to be ill.'

'Which is why she refused to go to the hospital with the others,' added Gordon, 'in case they discovered there was nothing wrong with her. Then, of course, there was that embarrassing business at the Wedded Stoat. She was always bustling about the village. Nurses are well known for being busybodies. Nobody would have taken any notice. While they were all in the church she probably got into the pub and contaminated the food. She was so trusted in the village that she could easily have got into the Wedded Stoat's kitchens at any time.'

'But that doesn't explain why Francis ended up on a lamppost and broke the world record for running the mile.'

'I'm sorry to say it, but it was my cousin's greed.'

'I beg your pardon?' said Francis.

'You simply couldn't resist a free chocolate, could you?'

'Several free chocolates, actually,' said Francis.

'There was a slight contretemps during the wedding feast. Nurse Dalton looked in at the reception. Of course, she'd doctored some of the food some time earlier in the day. She must have had great fun watching the afternoon's developments. Anyway, while she was there, her bag fell to the floor, spilling the contents. She gathered up as much as she could, but in the confusion I think a box of chocolates was picked up and found its way onto one of the tables.'

'I don't see what this has to do with anything,' said Rufus.

'I noticed Francis scoffing one chocolate after another, and the disastrous effect it had on him. I knew there must be a reason. I managed to retrieve the box and the one remaining chocolate that Francis – such greed! – had missed. I retained that chocolate for chemical analysis. My science master confirmed that it contained fourteen milligrams of methamphetamine, probably a branded substance called Pervitin, more commonly known as "The People's Drug". A letter to a pen friend in Germany confirmed my suspicions. The box bore the legend "Hildebrand's Chokolat", a confectionary sanctioned by the Third Reich that contained high levels of Pervitin. The chocolates had been on sale throughout Germany. Apparently, they were popular with housewives who found that after a few chocs they could get through the hoovering and dusting at top speed. And probably climb a few lampposts too.'

'But it wasn't the chocolates that were causing the sicknesses at the Wedded Stoat?'

'Oh no,' said Gordon. 'I think they were only for Nurse Dalton's personal use, probably to help her get through her awful plan. At least it explained why Francis was acting so strangely for a few hours, and suggested that someone with German connections might be up to no good.'

'And I am German,' said Hendel.

'Precisely. As is Mr Parks. I was confused as to what might be happening. Now, of course, it makes sense, but at the time I had no reason to link the chocolates to Mary Dalton.'

'If it hadn't been for you and Francis,' said Hendel, 'where would we be now? I dread to think of what might have happened.'

'My brilliant cousin!' said Francis. 'In all the incidents, Bader took care that her tampering with the food would lead only to limited suffering, until Ann's party gave her the perfect opportunity to deliver the one fatal dose to the person that had from the start been the intended victim.'

'What will become of Mary Dalton?' asked Rufus.

'Not Mary Dalton,' said Francis. 'Fräulein Bader. That is for the courts to decide.'

'Despite what has happened,' said Richard Hendel, 'I believe that people can change. Any of us may make decisions that we regret later in life. We can lose ourselves in dark avenues. There can be no doubt that Bader was haunted by the past, and it thrust itself back at her. The past does that. The day she was recognised by Ann, she saw the new life she had made for herself in ruins. She became the victim of her own past. In a footling way, I have done what I can to bring hope to people who have been frightened by life. Others do much more. I do not boast. But what I have learned of refugees, of those whose lives have struggled through repression and exploitation and unspeakable cruelty, is that there may yet be a light at the end of a tunnel.'

'Perhaps,' said Gordon, quietly.

'Oh, it is not for everybody, that light,' said Hendel. 'But with determination and faith …'

It was only when Francis snatched the plate that Uncle Billy knew. The one sandwich on the plate destined for that poor girl. Smoked salmon and strychnine. Fräulein Bader's face hadn't altered much. The hair, of course, was dyed. The woman he had known had red hair. Flaming, that's what people called hair of that colour, and it had flamed the day he and the other men walked into the camp.

What was a naval man doing there anyway? The soldiers called him their Jack Tar. They needed jokes, no matter how feeble. One night they danced a hornpipe for him, and he and the lads got drunk. Thinking of what they had seen that day, Billy couldn't find words to describe it. The politicians called it liberation. Billy had been seconded because of his skills with a camera. They needed men who would record the horror, so that people couldn't say it had not happened. The photographs proved what couldn't be denied. Billy remembered all the faces, the starved, the hopeless, the dead. Among them, he knew, was the face of Mary Dalton, defiant and calm, waiting at the gates of Hell.

He sat on the edge of his bed for a minute or two, took a deep breath and went into the kitchen to prepare his nephew's supper. Gordon was a growing lad, and needed his food.

Continuous Performance

Joan Pepcoe cleared the breakfast things by nine o'clock. She scrubbed the frying pan with a Brillo pad, completing the procedure with a generous application of Vim. She pressed the knitted dishcloth into a bowl of bleach and set the washing-up liquid in line with the empty milk bottle. Seeing the white scar at its rim, she held it to the light, turning it in her hand to check for imperfection. Five minutes later she was satisfied with its spotlessness.

By the time *Housewives' Choice* started on the wireless, there were already boxes she could tick on the wall chart. Charlie liked everything well organised. She had completed 'Breakfast table cleared', 'Crumbs and general debris', 'Washing up (Breakfast)', and 'Initial toilet inspection (a.m.)'. On the debit side, the chart reminded her that there was plenty still to do: 'Hoovering 10-11 a.m.', 'Dusting 11-11.30 a.m.', 'Skirting boards' (mercifully for alternate days), and 'Garden tidy'. She might have enjoyed being in the patches of earth front and back if she'd played some part in their design, not that she could see much beyond the limply embroidered net curtains that covered the windows of the little terraced house. Mottled light filtered apologetically into the small rooms, turning the people that walked past into vague outlines. Not that Joan was bothered. She no longer took much interest in the world beyond the garden gate. No one called except the milkman and now and again the postman, so it was a surprise when at 11.42 that Tuesday morning the doorbell rang. It was a moment or two before she connected the sound with having to move into the narrow hall and open the door.

'Good morning.'

The woman was smiling as she said it.

'A lovely one, too.'

She was not much older, not much taller, than Joan. Quite nicely turned out. Bright eyes that looked hard into her own. Joan wondered what to do if the woman wanted information or tried to sell her something. It would either be that, or to do with God.

'Are you from the council?' she asked, wanting to get that option out of the way. Something of that nature would be man's work, and would mean the woman coming back when Charlie was at home.

'Oh no, dear. Just a friendly call on this sunny morning. I like to deliver personally rather than popping it through the letterbox.'

She held out a leaflet. Joan read *"Pop along to the Tabernacle. Sing-a-Song-a-God."*

'It's on a Friday. You're new to the area, aren't you?'

Joan inclined her head, hoping it might cause a smile.

'I thought so. You'd be very welcome at the Tabernacle. We don't go on about God. We won't push him down your throat. We feel he either enters you or doesn't. But you're probably busy. Too much going on nowadays, isn't there? Been on your holidays this year? Anywhere nice?'

From inside the house the woman could hear *Housewives' Choice* dedicating 'Come Back to Sorrento' to a Mrs Rita Hicks of Surbiton. As she stood at the open door, a burst of sun made a sudden halo around Joan's head, the glare making her shield her eyes.

'Oh no. We don't travel. My husband doesn't care for foreign food. I bought a quiche once and had to pass it off as an egg and bacon flan.'

After leaving the house, Joan's caller dumped the rest of the Tabernacle leaflets into the first litter-bin she came to. The tree-lined avenue of shops around the corner was beginning to fill with people enjoying the spring weather. Ahead of her, a man stepped off the pavement to circumnavigate a huddle of shoppers blocking his way. She recognised him at once, although there was something new about the way he walked, springier, like the weather, jaunty. He paused to look in a shop window. She crossed the road, reaching the anonymity of a bus shelter. He went into the shop. The men's outfitters had a colourful exhibition of summery clothes in the window: beachwear, sandals, a short-sleeved shirt in poplin, a pair of sunglasses posed with bucket and spade. After a bit, an assistant appeared in the window, taking the shirt and a pair of gaudy Bermuda shorts from the display.

The man was carrying a paper bag with string handles as he stepped back into the street. His next stop was at one of the larger stores. The place was busy enough for her to tail him through the cosmetics, ladies' upholstery and childrens' toy department. In the photography section he made for a booth that advertised '*Xtra Speedy Passport Snaps*'. All right for some, she thought. Still, there was probably nothing in it, and people had their mind on other problems. Outside the shop, she noticed the placard for the evening newspaper, with '*Cinema Flasher at Large – Latest*' in heavy black type.

*

Sid Phillips knew that things were bad. He'd shared a pint with Harry from the Norvic, and Harry said there was no future in it, and Harry had been in the business over thirty years, so Harry should know. Never mind that the Norvic had installed Cinemascope two years ago, people still didn't come. They were down to one usherette at the Norvic, and she had to darn her own uniform. The Theatre de Luxe had even more problems: it was only a matter of time before it closed down, a victim of television and Teddy Boys. They'd already slashed the seats in the front stalls at the Theatre Royal, because that's what the newspapers said Teddy Boys did. The Cinema Palace in Magdalen Street had been done up ten years ago and renamed the Mayfair, as if that might lend an air of sophistication to the place, but no one was fooled. There were plans to build a bowling alley on the site.

No doubt about it. The outlook for the Bijou was grim. Sid was worried about his future, or what was left of it at 87 years of age. He'd been projectionist at the Bijou since 1932. His first film was *Murder on the Second Floor*, but he'd got the reels mixed up so that the murder victim came to life for the last fifteen minutes. No one had noticed, so Sid had gone on in much the same way for the next twenty-four years. Not that the Bijou showed thrillers any more. The Bijou had an ace up its sleeve: Westerns. They'd shown so many that Sid was surprised there wasn't a place outside the cinema to tie your horse to. John Wayne, Roy Rogers, Gene Autry and their like had been the life and soul of the Bijou for as long as Sid could remember. There had even been the Hopalong Tea Room that had once thronged with customers, but had been shut down, although patrons were still offered a cup of tea during the interval.

If the Bijou closed, it wasn't himself that Sid was worried about, but his daughter. He'd got Molly the job as cashier twenty years ago, after her husband had up and left her for another woman with not so much as a goodbye. Mr Brentwitch was only too pleased to have had Sid's recommendation. Molly had worked in a corner shop and counted the collection at St Oswald's on a Sunday morning, so she knew about money.

'It'll save us having to advertise,' said Mr Brentwitch, who liked the easy way of doing things. Mr Brentwitch preferred everything to run smoothly. 'Keep it in the family.' He'd given Sid a reassuring pat on the shoulder, as if they were related.

Mr Brentwitch's willingness to fall in with the suggestions of his staff made him a popular boss, but every emperor must fall. Last Christmas Eve, Mr Brentwitch had dropped dead of a heart attack in the foyer of the Bijou just before the late showing of *Cattle Queen of Hardman's Creek*. The fact that the Bijou had just been acquired by a faceless conglomerate was thought to be unrelated, but Mr Brentwitch's passing marked a change in the fortunes of the Bijou. The staff managed perfectly well during the rudderless few weeks that passed. Molly took over many of the managerial duties, as well as sitting in the cubbyhole that passed for a Box Office, and the usherettes pulled together to keep up a seamless attendance at the continuous performances that began at 1.30 in the afternoons and ran through until 11 pm.

Mr Pepcoe arrived in February. He'd been managing a Bermondsey cinema owned by the conglomerate, before being transferred. The staff heard that his wife had a history of nervous trouble, so it was probably sensible to leave London for the clear air of Norfolk. It soon became apparent that Mr Pepcoe was nothing like Mr Brentwitch. On his very first day he got the staff together in Mr Brentwitch's office and told them of his plans. His manner suggested that they would be unwelcome.

Mr Brentwitch had accommodated everyone's little ways, how Dorothy Dewhurst would never work Saturdays because she thought the morning matinees for the youngsters too common, and Sid insisting on playing all three verses of 'God Save the Queen' at the end of each day, and how Molly took it on herself to purchase the 'Parfum de Paris' from Woolies each month. Spraying the auditorium with the sickly stuff just before opening the doors and again around tea-time and at 9.30 in the evening was one of Molly's many rituals. She thought it added a dash of class to the place. Otherwise, Jeyes Fluid and Flit proved quite effective at getting rid of the odd cockroach. Sid thought it was a bit rich for people to call the Bijou a flea-pit. Fleas were about the only insects they'd never had.

It was the first screening at the Bijou of the new Western, *Cowpoke Lil*. Miss Simms' only reason for visiting the cinema was her wish to form an impression of the new manager, of whom she had heard mixed reports, and here he was, standing to attention in the vestibule, doubling as the sort of major domo that could still be seen outside the Theatre Royal, in frogged coat, epaulettes and peaked cap. This one, of course, was wearing a suit, and had brylcreemed hair.

'Welcome to the Bijou! You're just in time to catch the beginning of our main feature,' said Mr Pepcoe, bowing slightly as if Miss Simms might be of royal descent. His eyes met hers, as he huskily said '*Cowpoke Lil?*'

'Oh no,' she said, pursing her lips. 'My name is Simms. I've not come to see the films. A cup of tea and a bun.'

'I'm sorry, madam, but the Hopalong Tea Room has been closed for some time.'

'It's only half past three.'

'Closed permanently, madam.'

Miss Simms made a clicking noise with teeth that were not her own.

'There was little demand for it,' said Mr Pepcoe.

'What a pity! All the solid things of life are going by the board. As a sub-postmistress, I am concerned that it won't be long before the head of our Queen is removed from our postage stamps.'

'That will be an unhappy day, indeed,' said Mr Pepcoe, bowing even lower.

'However, the Bijou still provides sustenance. Our usherettes pass through the cinema at regular intervals with a range of refreshments. A Strawberry Mivvi, or an orange squash, or you may book a cup of tea for the interval.'

As he spoke, there wafted over Miss Simms the alluring mist of 'Parfum de Paris'. It caught at the back of her throat and smarted her eyes. Opening them, she saw the cardboard recreation of a fine specimen of manhood erected at the foot of the stairs that led to the circle.

'Ah', said Mr Pepcoe, who followed the line of her vision. 'That is a lifelike reproduction of the star of *Cowpoke Lil*, Tex Mandy. One of the most popular performers in Westerns. He has a natural talent for them, having spent much of his life in the saddle before Hollywood beckoned.'

Miss Simms could certainly see that wide open spaces had done Tex no harm.

'An essential training ground for the Western film,' Mr Pepcoe informed her. 'Of course he has to spend much of the film mounted.'

Molly Barlow in the box office nodded graciously as she handed Miss Simms her ticket.

'And how d'you take your tea?' she asked. She didn't trust Pauline or Dorothy to go out with the ice-cream tray, let alone take command of the box office in her absence, but today Molly had no choice. She had an appointment.

'Are you ready for the 4.30, Mr Saintsperson?'

'The last of the day! Yes, I think we can cope. One of the lost sheep, I think?'

'Found,' said Miss Gray, who smelled of peppermint, fresh as a daisy after a long day of handing her employer his instruments. She gently opened the door into the waiting room where the last of Tuesday's patients sat absently leafing through a year-old copy of the *Illustrated London News.*

'Mr Saintsperson will see you now, Mrs Barlow.'

Mr Saintsperson looked up from the desk at which he sat consulting her notes. The mention of her name ignited a memory. It was a pleasant sensation.

'Mrs Barlow.'

'Good afternoon,' said Molly. Knowing how impossible it was to have a conversation once a dentist got going, she imagined these might be the last words she would say to him. The surgery gleamed white around her.

Mr Saintsperson waved her to the chair.

'Quite a stranger.'

'Yes.' She couldn't avoid the childlike need to explain her time off for bad behaviour. 'Foolish of me, I know. I've been remiss.'

'Don't beat yourself up about it, Mrs Barlow. A visit to the dentist isn't everyone's idea of a knees-up. I've often thought of putting a notice in the window – 'Come In. We Don't Bite' – haven't I, Miss Gray?'

Miss Gray chuckled and said 'Yes'. It was the first she'd heard of it.

'You last saw us' – his eyes wandered over the notes – 'two years ago. How time flies. You will be delighted to learn that dentistry has since made rapid strides. Note the lack of sawdust on the floor. We no longer make false teeth from kindling wood or whalebone or wrench molars from the mouths of deceased hippopotamuses. You may also notice that you are sitting in a state of the art reclining examination chair.'

He pressed a lever that gently tipped her backwards, sending her feet high above her. She felt the top of her stockings tighten.

'And Miss Gray refuses to release patients until they have a smile the whiter of which you will not find in Hollywood.'

Molly kept her mouth closed. Was it really two years since she'd visited the dentist? Mr Saintsperson's hair had more silver in it. The creases in his face, very marked around the cheeks, made him even more handsome. Germanic, thought Molly, and that pleasing voice, like treacle overlaid with honey. You could imagine it saying all sorts of disgraceful things. Of course she hadn't forgotten the sense of humour, teasing and easy, that never forsook him. Miss Gray handed him a pair of surgical gloves. He twanged them awake. Molly, her field of vision constricted by lying prone, caught glimpses of his long, white fingers flexing in readiness. Lovely hands he had, very flexible as hands went.

'Do you still work at the cinema, Mrs Barlow?' he asked.

'Yes. The Bijou.' No wonder she sounded surprised. She'd expected to be incoherent by now.

'The Bijou, of course. My late wife was a regular patron. She was a great fan of the silver screen. She developed an inexplicable passion for Westerns. She became quite a regular customer of yours.'

Molly had almost forgotten her. Now, a person in a fur tippet came into her mind. Mrs Saintsperson. A nice woman, always a nod and a thank you and a remark or two about that week's feature when she bought her ticket. Hadn't she died? Molly had missed her coming in each week, and had read something in the papers. A death in hospital … Sarah Saintsperson: the wife of Cyril Saintsperson, dentist, a woman well known for her charity work. The face of her widower was directly above hers, slowly advancing.

'Now, if you're quite comfortable … Open wide.'

Molly had relaxed into the chair with a calm nervousness. There was no fear of the drill today. If he so much as mentioned it, she would delay by making another appointment, but a restless flutter remained. What happened next was so unexpected that she had to stop herself by laughing out loud. God forbid that anything in her expression or voice (not that she attempted to say anything after 'Open wide') should betray it, but the thrill of the man's face so very near, the warmth of his breath, his eyes somehow challenging hers not to look into them, the air tactfully exhaling from his nostrils … This wasn't what she expected, but out of the blue this dental check-up had reminded her of something that had long gone from her life. Except, she managed to think, that it had never been there. Cocooned in this silent frenzy, she tried to bring herself back to reality – a dentist was examining her teeth, a procedure underwritten by the National Health Service. Pulling herself back from the brink, she saw his face sway above her until she heard 'You may rinse now, Mrs Barlow' as he levitated her to normality.

'Much to my relief,' said Mr Saintsperson, proving that even dentists had bedside manners, 'and no doubt to yours, the good news is that the necessity for false teeth remains a distant nightmare. Heaven knows we see plenty of those here. How many sets of artificial gnashers have we ordered this week, Miss Gray?'

'Too many, Mr Saintsperson.'

'In the face of everything, you see that Miss Gray remains optimistic. "By Gum" seems to be the most appropriate response. Fortunately, two fillings should see your teeth fit for active service for the next six months.'

Mr Saintsperson's wide smile made it clear that this was a magnificent achievement on Molly's part.

'Only a minor decay, but what do we see ahead of us if we don't take care, Miss Gray?

'Could that be the Slippery Slope, Mr Saintsperson?'

'Exactly, Miss Gray. Mark her words well, Mrs Barlow. That woman is an oracle. Cut out the sweeties. It must be a temptation with such a plentiful supply in the cinema kiosk. And fizzy or highly sugared drinks. You might as well substitute prussic acid.'

He squelched off the surgical gloves and helped her from the chair.

'As Miss Lynn insists on reminding us, we'll meet again. Don't let it be before too long. Miss Gray will arrange your next appointment. Good-day.'

He held open the door into the waiting-room, the silver in his hair more exaggerated at the temples. Even as Molly waited for Miss Gray to find a mutually suitable date in the diary, Molly knew she was on the cusp of a dilemma. The last thing anyone wanted was frequent trips to the dentist, but … It wasn't the sweets. It was the Kia-Ora that had done it. She'd always known she drank too much of the stuff. If she kept on drinking it, she would soon have reason enough to make yet more visits to Mr Saintsperson. On the other hand, would she want him to be the person who fitted her with false teeth?

Francis Jones was easily bored, and his cousin appeared to have attended a master class in how to bore him. Gordon's passion for Radio Luxembourg was a source of considerable irritation to Francis, who much preferred the dramas on the Home Service, especially if they were mysteries, preferably by Francis Durbridge or Anthony Wilson. Things came to a head with the Ovaltineys. Because it was the second Friday of the month, Mr and Mrs Jones had gone to a cookery demonstration at the gas showrooms in Norwich. Gordon had cycled from Bundler's Cottage in Strutton-by-the-Way to spend the evening with his cousin, and burst into Red Cherry House with a huge grin, whistling a tune that Francis recognised all too well as the Ovaltineys' theme song.

'You'll never guess!' shouted Gordon triumphantly.
'You've become a Silver Star Ovaltiney,' yawned Francis.
Gordon's face fell, but picked up soon enough.
'How did you know?'
'Because nothing else could have sent you into such ecstasy. It's pathetic. You're a grown boy – well, a growing one – not some silly child. Not only should you be growing out of it, you should never have grown into it in the first place.'
'Sometimes, Francis, you are a complete misery.'

'Not at all. Mirth is constantly at my elbow. It's just that I think there's more to life than being obsessed by a malt-based beverage.'

'As a member of the League of Ovaltineys – and yes, I have just been awarded a Silver Star, which is just about the equivalent of being made a Field Marshall in the army – I will not allow you to underrate my achievement. As one of the Ovaltineys' songs tells us, "One little raindrop doesn't mean a shower".'

'Forgive me. I didn't know Sigmund Freud was writing lyrics nowadays.'

'Perhaps you're just not the clubbable type. And you're usually unbearable when there's nothing going on.'

'I must admit things have been pretty dull recently. We cleared up that Boudicca affair at Norwich Museum weeks ago, and the priceless amulet has now been restored to the people of Norwich, since when nothing exceptional has presented itself. Wish as we may, we could hardly expect a mystery to come knocking.'

It was at that very moment that there was a rasp at the door of Red Cherry House. Francis sprang to his feet. He didn't immediately recognise the woman. He'd glimpsed her once, hanging out washing in her back garden, wearing much the same housewifely uniform as she wore now, a beige blouse, powder blue cardigan buttoned almost to the neck, twill skirt and flat shoes. She and her husband had recently moved into one of the terraced houses along the street. Her face, almost grotesquely made-up and artificial in the half-light of the doorway, was somehow out of kilter with the rest of her.

'Sorry to trouble you,' she said, 'but I don't know what to do.'

'Come in, please,' said Francis. 'You've recently moved into Branlingham, haven't you?'

'That's right. Mrs Pepcoe. Pleased to meet you, I'm sure.'

'Mum and Dad are out at the moment, I'm afraid.'

'Are they? It wasn't them I wanted. I know who you are. I've heard people talk about you. You and your cousin, isn't it?'

'That's right. Gordon. Gordon, who is just about to offer you his seat and a cup of tea.'

Gordon shot up from the sofa.

'Oh no,' said Mrs Pepcoe, 'nothing for me, thanks. And I prefer standing. To tell you the truth, I couldn't keep still if I sat down.'

'Well, my cousin Gordon and myself are always here to help those in perplexity.'

Hm, thought Gordon, not if one of them is in the kitchen making a pot of tea.

'Oh yes,' said Mrs Pepcoe, apparently seeing the boys for the first time and looking from one to the other. 'It's the telephone.'

'I'm sorry?'

'You've got one, haven't you? A telephone? I heard this was the only house in the street with a telephone. I went down to the kiosk outside the Wedded Stoat but it's out of order and I don't know what to do.'

The cheek of it! Francis bristled and awarded Mrs Pepcoe a cold smile. The effect was startling. Tears welled in her eyes, and without warning her body crumpled. Gordon almost caught her in his arms. Her bird-like frame suggested the slightest pressure might crush her. Francis made way on the sofa and rested her against the cushions, while for Gordon tea-making now ranked as one of the emergency services.

'Our telephone is at your disposal, of course,' said Francis. 'My parents had it installed because in our line of work it can be a matter of life and death, and time is often of the essence.'

'You must think me very rude, coming here like this.' She scrunched a damp lace handkerchief, dabbing at her eyes and the corners of her mouth, smearing violently scarlet lipsticked lips. 'But I'm beside myself. Charlie hasn't come home, and I don't know what to do.'

Francis lifted an eyebrow at her.

'My husband, Charlie. On my special day, too. I don't know what's happened. He said he'd be home by the time I got back from Lowestoft. He ordered a taxi for me this morning to take me to the train station. He had me booked in for the salon at half past ten. Today is our wedding anniversary. Charlie had arranged for me to have a pampering session at 'Maison Clara' in the High Street. Pedicure, facials, a special hair-do, steam room, everything. They even did my nails' (she waggled painted fingers in the air) 'and this permanent wave. When I looked in the mirror at three o'clock I didn't recognise myself. They've done it nice, though, haven't they? I was home by half past four and the house was empty, and Charlie had said he'd be back.'

'Back from where, Mrs Pepcoe?' asked Francis.

'His work. He's manager at the Bijou Picture House in Westlegate. He's never been late before. He leaves the house every morning at 8.30 and catches the bus into Norwich, although the cinema doesn't open till early afternoon. But he's managerial, you see, so once he knows everything's up and running he's home by four, always. Except today.'

Gordon looked at his *Eagle* wristwatch. Knowing that it gained twenty-five minutes every day, he calculated that Mr Pepcoe should have been home six hours ago.

'And it's now well after ten,' Francis confirmed. He was already moving to the telephone. 'You don't think he may have gone for a drink with a friend?'

'Charlie doesn't drink. Doesn't agree with him. I'm partial to a small sherry, but Charlie won't allow it in the house. Besides, we haven't got friends,' said Mrs Pepcoe.

'And you've not contacted anyone or anywhere to find out where he might be?'

'I haven't got a telephone.'

'Right. Do you have the telephone number of the Bijou?'

'No. Charlie didn't think it was necessary. He wouldn't like me phoning him at work.'

Gordon came back into the room with a tray of tea as Francis was flicking through the pages of the *Evening News* and dialled a number.

'Hello. Is that the Bijou cinema? I'm enquiring on behalf of Mrs Pepcoe. Yes, the wife of Mr Pepcoe. She's with me now. Mrs Pepcoe is concerned that her husband hasn't returned home this evening. Is he still with you? To whom am I speaking? Mrs Barlow … No, Mrs Pepcoe hasn't seen him since' (Francis mouthed 'when?' at Mrs Pepcoe) '… since this morning at half past eight when he left home. Thank you.'

'What do they say?' asked Gordon.

'I'm speaking to the cashier, apparently. The cinema's just about to close. She's gone to have a word with the other staff to see if anyone … Yes? … I see. Well, thank you, Mrs Barlow. Goodnight.'

Francis put down the receiver and stood thoughtful and still by its side. 'She's confirmed that your husband followed his normal routine and left at his usual time.'

'Then where is he? What am I supposed to do? His dinner's

ruined. I did a toad in the hole. His favourite, just how he likes it, crispy batter but not too much of it, and the sausages turned half way through cooking, and a dab of Colman's on the right side of the plate so he doesn't have to unscrew the lid. I got the sausages nicely too, positioned with a two-inch gap between them in a straight line, otherwise he says they look unappealingly arranged. I didn't use the ruler either.'

Francis and Gordon couldn't think of a response to this, but Mrs Pepcoe had to be dealt with. Had she a relative or friend she could consult? (Not really.) Could her husband have decided on the spur of the moment to change his routine? (That was out of the question.) Did he keep a diary in which he might have made a note of an appointment? (He kept it locked in his briefcase.) Perhaps if she went home now, he might have arrived and be concerned because *she* wasn't at home. This idea seemed to register, and after finishing her cup of tea, looking into it as if it were the richest of gifts, she scuttled out of Red Cherry House, almost tripping along the street to her home.

'Which, incidentally, is called "Shangri-La"', said Gordon.

'Hardly appropriate, when the place sounds more like a regimental headquarters. The poor woman is lining up bangers with mathematical precision. Anyway, let's start telephoning the hospitals.'

As this was what people in similar circumstances did in films, Gordon didn't think it a very original idea, but the calls confirmed that no Mr Pepcoe had been admitted. Glancing at the clock, Francis decided it was time to take things a stage further and was about to contact the police when the telephone rang.

'Hello. Mrs Barlow? Yes … this is Francis Jones … Really?

... Are you sure? ... Yes. I understand ... Of course. Thank you. Goodbye.'

He replaced the mouthpiece with studied slowness.

'Well?' said Gordon, blood already running faster through his body.

'That was the Bijou. They've found Mr Pepcoe.'

'Whaaaaaaaaaat?'

Inspector 'Tod' Slaughter and Sergeant Cudd pulled up in the station's Wolseley at the rear of the Bijou as another police car arrived with Joan Pepcoe sitting in the back flanked by Francis and Gordon. Slaughter's roar of disbelief almost deafened Cudd, who was used to calming his superior's troubled waters. As if this business with a flasher going round cinemas wasn't enough of a headache without what was beginning to look like a suspicious death.

'Couldn't be helped, sir. When they sent the car for Mrs Pepcoe she insisted the boys came with her. She was in a state of near collapse. They have a reassuring bedside manner, those lads.'

'Not with me, they don't!' spluttered Slaughter, just managing to keep his eyes in their sockets. 'You *read* too much, Cudd, that's one of your troubles. It's my belief those two are turning into *teenagers* ... The older one thinks he's Hercule bleedin' Poirot and the young one's got carrot-coloured hair and more freckles than Anne of Green Gables. Now, where's the body?'

Slaughter's progress was impeded by a young constable who looked as if it was his first time in long trousers and insisted on seeing identification before letting him into the cinema.

'Only doing my duty, sir' said the constable, alarmed at the colour the inspector had turned. 'As a matter of fact, I thought I'd seen your face on the movies.'

Cudd gave him a warning look, in case he was about to explain that he was a horror movie fan.

Wanting to get into the cinema before the other police car emptied its passengers, Slaughter roughly pushed open the swing doors into the auditorium. The house lights were up, but did no favours to the place. The dim tinges of light in play when films were being shown perhaps lent the space a certain atmosphere, but Slaughter looked around at what was now disclosed as a dowdy dump sadly in need of redecoration. From the stalls, a woman walked up to him.

'I've done with the body,' she said.

Slaughter reared up on his heels.

'Thank you, dear. A very commendable bunch, you St John Ambulance volunteers, but you can slip off home now, ducks. Best to leave it to us professionals.'

The woman's face clouded.

'I am Harriet Wayworth. Chief Medical Officer for Norfolk Police.'

Slaughter's jaw dropped, wiping away the standard look of acute condescension he reserved for females. The woman's face, meanwhile, was bathed in contempt.

'He's been dead for between two and three hours. I'll have a more definite timing when we've got him back to the morgue. From an initial examination I should say you're probably looking at a poisoning, but it's impossible to know until we've done tests.'

Cudd smiled back at her. 'Of course. Miss Wayworth is the new medical officer, sir. Inspector Slaughter didn't recognise you, ma'am.'

'But I recognised *him*. I'd heard he was arrogant, ill-mannered, not overtly intelligent, misogynistic and clinically obese, and I am happy to confirm that diagnosis. Good night.'

Slaughter breathed in deeply as Miss Wayworth's high heels marched out into the vestibule.

'Better get a look at him.'

He lumbered along the aisle for several rows towards the body slumped back in its seat. He stopped, looked, and looked again. The light was dim, but he could make out the long black wig, the pink blouse, a garish scarf, rinsed in the perfume of powder and lipstick.

'Mr Pepcoe?' he whispered, but answer came there none.

Of course, Molly wished that Mr Brentwitch hadn't dropped dead just before Pearl and Dean, leaving the Bijou's staff to the mercy of his successor. Staff and patrons alike showed little enthusiasm for the new man. At the risk of seeming aloof, Molly made a point of standing aside from the usherettes' gossip, although she couldn't always ignore hearing it. It seemed natural to keep her thoughts about Mr Pepcoe to herself. She'd learned her lesson after telling Dorothy Dewhurst she'd seen the new manager in his office doing the football pools. The look on the woman's face reminded Molly of a shark that had just swallowed a tasty sprat. Molly shouldn't have let on about it, but the surprise of it had left her unguarded. Did people always look demented when they studied their pools? She hadn't put him down as a gambler, and couldn't have mistaken the look in his eyes as he lifted his face to hers when she walked into the office. They seemed to inflame with the intensity of several light bulbs, eyes that belonged to a demon, like something (and she regretted saying so to Dorothy) you might see at the pictures. It made you think, when you saw someone's eyes looking at you like that. It made you wonder what else might be going on inside their body. But it didn't do to let on to the usherettes.

Nevertheless, she knew that dad had known something was up, no matter how carefully she tried to hide her feelings. She'd felt the colour flood into her cheeks that first time when Pepcoe met the staff, and knew that dad was watching her like the benevolent hawk he was. It was clear that he and the new manager wouldn't get on. It was only a few days later that she noticed how dad had lost the spring in his step, and didn't even bother to get the reels in the wrong order.

As an employee, Molly admitted she personally had no cause for complaint. Mr Pepcoe was consistently polite, and could even seem considerate. Only last night he'd almost embarrassed her with an unexpected little act of kindness, reaching below his desk and producing a bottle of Kia-Ora.

'A symbolic thank you,' he said, 'for all you do in keeping everything running tickety-boo. A very modest thank you, but meant. This is for you, and you alone.'

She didn't know what to say. If the circumstances had been different, his gift might have seemed flirtatious, but that was out of the question. Perhaps it was what some might call a romantic gesture. Afterwards, the sheer idiocy of the presentation appalled her, leaving her ashamed that she had stood so childlike and helpless before him, taking the Kia-Ora into her hands as if it was a string of pearls. She was back in the box-office kiosk before she came to her senses and remembered Mr Saintsperson's warning. Pepcoe's gift of the Kia-Ora was nothing like a kind thought; from the dental point of view, he might as well have given her poison. She put the Kia-Ora on the ledge below the box-office counter, alongside her handbag and keys.

*

'*I* couldn't believe my eyes when Pauline called me over.' The elder of the two usherettes seemed to be hugely enjoying the scandalous exit of Mr Pepcoe. 'Really, I don't know what things are coming to, what with that dreadful man going around exposing himself to all and sundry. We each have our own little domain at the Bijou. I'm naturally more Dress Circle than Pauline. Of course, you get a nicer class in the Dress Circle, although they've been saying that the flasher prefers doing it upstairs. But when I heard Pauline call out "There's a woman in the stalls, I think she's a gonner" naturally I went down. And there she – I mean, *Mr Pepcoe* – was.'

Slaughter had first tried interviewing the two usherettes together, but found them uncooperative, perhaps because they had heard him refer to them a little too loudly as Pinky and Perky. Francis knew better. He had set up a sort of informal HQ in the remnants of the Hopalong Tea Room. Of course, it was Gordon who made consoling cups of tea while Francis asked the questions under the watchful gaze of John Wayne and others of the cowboy fraternity who stared down from photographs along the wall.

As Pauline Moody was now being interviewed by Slaughter, Francis' first interviewee was Dorothy Dewhurst. Solidly built, with no discernible waist, thick legs and a manner that suggested she'd just popped out of a garden party at Buckingham Palace, Dorothy was still in her uniform but had lopsidedly put on a felt hat in preparation for going home. Between giving the impression that she strongly disapproved of being in the same building as a dead man in woman's clothing, she sucked at the hot tea with relish, smacking her lips as she replaced the cup in its saucer.

'When you think of what the Hopalong used to be,' she

sighed, as if recalling a heavenly vision. 'Mr Brentwitch would be horrified to see it in this state. We used to do a lovely teacake with really succulent currants.'

'Another cup, Mrs Dewhurst?' asked Gordon, waving a teapot in her direction.

'Think of the scandal! I shall be considering my resignation. After 32 years ... I know one shouldn't talk ill of the dead but the rot set in the day Mr Brentwitch departed this life. Mr Brentwitch tipped his hat, gave his seat up for ladies, was repulsed by crudity of every description, whereas likely as not Mr Pepcoe was sat in his office doing the football pools instead of attending to the needs of the Bijou. Mrs Barlow told me she'd seen him filling in the coupons. Quite shocked she was.'

'You were not an admirer of Mr Pepcoe?' suggested Gordon through the steam of the urn.

'I didn't take to him from the beginning. Sweet as pie when you met him, but ... wandering hands. I said to Pauline, that man goes on more of a roundabout route than the number 12 bus. And no care for the Bijou. No care at all. Mr Brentwitch used to make us stand guard at the exits at the end of each day so the customers couldn't escape before "God Save the Queen" had run its course, but Pepcoe ... he'd go home before Roy Rogers had got Trigger out of the stable. No idea of organisation. He must run rings about that poor wife of his, not that she's ever been near or by. All talk if you ask me, but no sense of organisation at all. Take last week. Pauline ran out of Kia-Ora, had to take out her tray just with choc ices and a few tubs. Sheer bad management on his part. Mr Brentwich was never short of a lollipop. Pauline and Mrs Barlow had quite a set-to about it. She insisted they'd just had a new supply of Kia-Ora come in. Our patrons were gasping for it during that hot spell. It only turned out that Mr Pepcoe had stored it in the manager's room when it had always been kept in the Box Office where Mrs Barlow could keep an eye on it. He'd have been out on his ear if Time and Motion had investigated.'

'Did you recognise any of the clothes Mr Pepcoe was wearing?' asked Francis.

'No. I thought they were very last year. That dress did nothing for him. With that hair colour a pastel shade would have been more becoming. The shoes were all wrong. The scarf should have been colour co-ordinated. No eye for fashion.'

'You had no idea that he was sitting in the stalls?'

'No, because of keeping an eye out for the Flasher, Pauline and I were mostly upstairs where we thought he was most likely to … well, you know … *show himself*. In case of confrontation, I've brought my husband's tin hat from the war.'

'And what precautions did you take?'

Mrs Dewhurst heaved her bosom to regimental attention.

'I did what any good usherette would do. I put a new battery in my torch.'

Like Dorothy Dewhurst, Pauline Moody was still wearing her usherette's uniform when Francis and Gordon sat her down in the Hopalong, but the effect was different. Her costume bulged at a bust that struggled for fresh air, and the hem of the skirt was several inches higher. She almost winked at the boys as she crossed her legs, revealing an extraordinary amount of stocking. Gordon slopped the tea in its saucer as he handed it across.

'This place should be condemned,' she said. 'I mean, no one's going to be coming in here when they're likely to get done in in the two and sixpennies. I read about you two in the papers. Boy detectives! Can't be worse than that pig of an inspector, can you? Giving me the soft touch … cup of tea and a smile and I'll forget you're giving me the Third Degree. So, what do you want to know, boys?'

'I believe you were the person who discovered the body?' asked Francis.

'That's right. Busybody Barlow shifted herself out of Control Station Bijou and asked if any of us had seen our lord and master since he'd bunked off early this afternoon. Just when we were getting ready to close she had a phone call asking where he was.'

'Yes. It was me that telephoned,' explained Francis.

'I do the final check of the lavs last thing before closing. Some people say they can't hear the end of the films because of me unleashing the waters of Babylon. I try to time the flush just right; adds a touch of mystery to the proceedings. I told Barlow that Pepcoe had gone home and why couldn't we close up and go home ourselves, because the place was empty except for a woman I'd seen in the stalls when I popped down there. Funny thing is, I hadn't seen her come in. One minute she wasn't there and next minute she was. It's dim in there anyway, and the torches are rubbish. And Mrs High and Mighty Barlow said there couldn't be a woman in there because she'd not had anyone buy a ticket. Anyway, she must have gone back to the phone and told you Mr Pepcoe wasn't here.'

'She did.'

'Then she must have thought better of it and come back and done another recce. She would have had a fit if someone had got in without paying. And that's when we had a good look at the woman and recognised him under that wig.'

'And otherwise the cinema was empty?'

'By then, yes. Except for Dolly Dewdrop who was still in

the circle. We called her down. So she sails in like Lady Muck at a fish-stall and looks at the body with that look she's always got, as though she's never had cod with her chips. And yes, she says, that's Mr Pepcoe all right.'

'A shocking experience for you, Miss Moody. An appalling end to the day.'

'Not really. After watching *Cowpoke Lil* three times round it perked me up a bit.'

The following afternoon Inspector Slaughter called a press conference. Harriet Wayworth's report on the post mortem revealed that Pepcoe had died from arsenical poisoning. But why was he sitting in the stalls at the Bijou dressed as a woman when everyone thought he had left the cinema as usual earlier in the day and returned home? His wife was as mystified as anyone when a locked suitcase was discovered in Pepcoe's office. Cudd forced it open, revealing assorted items of light, summery menswear, a blindingly colourful pair of Bermuda shorts and a one-way aeroplane ticket to Spain and a passport. Unable to explain any of this, Slaughter sidelined the affair at the Bijou, and turned the press conference into a statement about the flasher, who was said to still be making the rounds of the local picture-houses.

Later that day, when Cudd brought in the *Eastern Evening News*, Slaughter swelled with pride at the full front page coverage, with a prominent photograph of himself standing on the steps of Norwich Police Headquarters. Slaughter had seldom seen a policeman look so magisterial.

'Well, Cudd, wouldn't surprise me if I didn't hear from the Chief Constable about this, eh? My goodness! They've gone to town on this one. Just the thing for a flasher case – full exposure! This is the sort of thing that leads to promotion.'

'The station will miss you if you go,' said Cudd, without making it clear if this would be a good or bad thing.

'Look at that headline! Bloody hell! They didn't use lettering that big when Neville Chamberlain met Hitler! Read it out, Cudd.'

Nestling as deeply as his girth would allow in the swivel chair behind his desk, Slaughter cupped the back of his neck in both hands and stretched his legs in expectation of a job well done. Cudd coughed and read.

'Following the discovery of a man's body last night at the Bijou Cinema in Westlegate, Inspector Edward Slaughter of Norwich Police today identified the body as that of Charles Pepcoe, who had recently joined the staff of the cinema as manager. Owing to the suspicious nature of the discovery, the body was removed for medical examination. Meanwhile, Inspector Slaughter advised the public to be on the look out for a man known to be exposing himself in public, whom he believed to be involved in the case. He stated that "This miscreant, who we are referring to as the cinema flasher, is said to be specialising in Cinemascope. On no account should this man be approached, and the public should not take the matter into its own hands. We do not yet know the size of the problem. Although the flasher works with great speed, this is far from an open and shut case. In the meantime, anyone seeing a suspicious looking man in a raincoat should contact Norwich Police immediately."'

Cudd paused. Slaughter looked up at him, scratching one of his chins. 'Well? Talk about good coverage! Nothing wrong with that.'

'It rained yesterday,' said Cudd. 'We've already had 485 calls.'

*

Pepcoe's death had come at the end of a troublesome day for Sid Phillips. He had run the final reel of the film backwards, with the sheriff and his posse doing reverse turns on horseback. Tired and dispirited, he slipped away from the Bijou, leaving his daughter to switch off everything in the projection room before the police arrived. He'd reached home before they discovered Pepcoe's body, so hadn't heard about it until Molly called round this morning. He couldn't believe what had happened last night at the Bijou, although he wasn't altogether surprised that someone might have taken a dislike to the new manager. He wasn't too fond of Pepcoe himself, although he'd never considered murdering him.

Molly opened the door to Francis and Gordon when they arrived just before lunch.

'We've had all the nosey parkers hereabouts wanting grisly details about what happened,' she said. 'I'm just off to get dad some shopping. He'll talk to you. No upsetting him, mind. It's really shaken him up. He's in the living room. I don't think he knows what to do with himself.'

Sid thought that the tripe merchant Slaughter or Sergeant Cudd had arrived to question him again. They'd come round just after breakfast wanting to know the ins and outs at the cinema, although he didn't know what to tell them. No one liked Mr Pepcoe, but it was one thing to step into a shop doorway to avoid meeting someone, quite another to do them in. It was a relief when Sid realised the callers were Francis and Gordon, who often put their heads around the projection room door to say hello after the Saturday morning matinees.

'Has Inspector Slaughter been to see you?' asked Francis.

'Man's a fool. Kept going on about some idiot who's going round exposing himself in cinemas. I told him, who in their right mind'd do that in the dark? Asked me what I knew about Pepcoe.' Sid pulled down the corners of his mouth in disgust. 'Pepcoe! Only been here for a week before he said how tiring my work must be at my age and didn't I want to spend more time on my allotment.'

'Did you?'

'I hate bleedin' allotments. He wanted me pensioned off, plain and simple, or better still packed off without a penny. Complained about the films getting muddled up. That's my style, I told him. With me, it's an art form.'

'Have you any idea who might have wanted Mr Pepcoe … out of the way?' asked Gordon.

'Well, I didn't do it, if that's what you're getting at. The funny thing is, I'd made up my mind that yesterday was going to be my last day.'

'You meant to retire?'

'Not officially, no. Leave him in the lurch. No notice given, leave him up the creek without a paddle. As a matter of fact, I feel like a new man. Tonight'll be the first time in years I don't have to suffer "God Save the Queen". Bloody awful tune.'

The old man's words were harsh, but the boys could see his eyes filling with tears. When he looked up from the floor his voice was gentler.

'Truth is, boys, it's not me that I'm worried about. It's Molly.'

'Your daughter?'

'My *only* daughter. The only person I've got in the world now, since her mum died. What's going to happen to her, eh? It's a pound to a penny the Bijou will close. There can't have been more than a handful of people through the doors this last week, and this publicity'll put the tin hat on it. It's all right for *me*; I'm living on borrowed time. Whoever did Pepcoe in has done me a favour. Given me that little shove I needed, when I can say enough's enough. But for Molly ... She was down on her luck when I persuaded Mr Brentwitch to take her on as cashier, and it was the making of her. She lived and breathed the Bijou, spent every minute of the day there. If it wasn't for her the place would've fallen apart years ago. She's never had what you might call a happy life, see, never met the right person, not like when I met her mum. I knew the day I clapped eyes on her that we'd be together for ever. It was three years ago next month we lost her.'

Sid looked to the mantelpiece where a silver framed photograph of bride and groom, themselves wrapped into the porch of a church, stared out at what they hoped would be a bright future. His voice caught at the edge of a word, faltered, and struck up again.

'Had a bit of a do, did Molly. There was a man, years ago, that she fell for. Mum and I never set eyes on him. She was putty in his hands. Dominated her, he did. They moved away, lost touch. Broke mother up something terrible. "He'll dump her," she used to say, and mum was always right.'

'So Molly came back home?'

'Yes, and I got her the job at the Bijou.'

'That must have given her something to live for,' said Francis.

'I think over the years she's forgotten him, never looked at another man. She's always been impressionable. Gets swept off her feet, not that you'd think that to look at her. That's why I've been so worried. The day Pepcoe arrived to take over he called us all into his office. I was watching her when she come into the room and met him for the first time, and my heart sank. It was horrible. There was something about Pepcoe I didn't like, but I could see he was a charmer to some women. Men can tell, you know, about other men. He could wind the women round his little finger if he wanted. There'd never been any of that with Mr Brentwitch. Molly had always been happy working with him, stable, you know. But she's one of these people who can form very sudden passions for someone, as quick as if it was a flash of lightning. And I watched it happen that day Pepcoe arrived, standing there smooth as anything in his London suit with his smarmy smile and his put-on manners. I could see he was just the type to tip Molly over the edge again.'

'So, you didn't like Mr Pepcoe, while your daughter …?'

'No doubt about it, Francis. I think she was infatuated with him from that first moment. So far as Molly was concerned fate had sent her a new man.'

'And do you think Mr Pepcoe realised this?'

'No idea, and it's a bit late to try asking him now.'

'She'll go down for it,' said Slaughter. 'It's that Barlow woman.'

'Is it?' asked Cudd. Sometimes he wished he had more faith in his superior's opinions.

'It's murder sure enough. Straight down the line murder. Hardly worth the trouble of a trial.'

'I daresay you're right, sir,' said Cudd without conviction, 'but I fancy Francis and Gordon will have theories of their own.'

Slaughter's face turned puce. 'Theories? She poisoned him, simple as that. The only thing I can't get straight yet is what this flasher had to do with it.'

'Ah, now, I think you may have a point there, sir. I don't think as he did.'

'What? He'll strike again, you mark my words, and when we get him he'll reveal everything.'

'Not so sure about that, sir. Don't really know if we'd want him to reveal everything, anyway. Perhaps he's been tapping his barometer, seeing how the weather's warming up. Men have stopped wearing raincoats. I mean, he'll be more conspicuous now, won't he?'

Slaughter squeezed a pimple on his nose, pinched his eyes and took a hard look at his sergeant.

'So, Cudd … what do you suggest we do?'

'How about a newsflash?'

'Well,' said Gordon, 'Inspector Slaughter seems to have sewn everything up. If all goes to his plan, the phantom film flasher will soon be in his hands!'

'A somewhat unfortunate turn of phrase,' suggested Francis.

'And Mrs Barlow about to be banged to rights for murder! Who would have thought it?'

'Who indeed? Not me, for one. In fact, I shall be calling on the inspector this afternoon to apprise him of certain theories and facts that he seems to have overlooked. He seems to have misunderstood the relationship between Molly Barlow and Mr Pepcoe.'

'What do you mean?'

'It was Sid telling us how he'd been in Pepcoe's office the first day he met the staff at the Bijou that alerted me. Sid was watching his daughter's face, and looking at Pepcoe he recognised a type … a type of man that Molly was attracted to. No wonder Sid was concerned. He didn't want Molly's life turned upside down again. He hated the idea of the possible emotional upheaval if Pepcoe was the sort of man Molly might fall for *again*. Of course, Sid's fear was that Molly might be about to make another mistake with another man, the sort of man she'd married before. And this time it would have been complicated by the fact that Pepcoe was a married man. But what Sid didn't realise is that Pepcoe wasn't the *sort* of man she'd married before – he *was* the man she'd married before!'

'You mean Ronnie Barlow? Pepcoe and Molly had been married?'

'Yes, the husband that his father-in-law had never set eyes on, the husband who'd simply abandoned her. Sid was correct in seeing "that look" in Molly's eyes, and it set me thinking. What if Molly was falling again not for a *new* man but *for the same man* … She hadn't seen him for years. Had no idea what had happened to him after he'd walked out on her. And it wasn't only Sid who saw the change in her when she and Pepcoe met. Pepcoe, alias Ronnie Barlow, saw it too …'

'Well, he could hardly have missed it,' exclaimed Gordon. 'Think what a shock it must have been to have his ex-wife walk back into his life.'

'You can forget ex-wife. They'd never divorced. Pepcoe had remarried. He was a bigamist. Not a good thing to be when you bump into your legal wife.'

'But he knew enough about Molly to know at once from the look in her eyes …'

'That she was still in love with him … exactly! A more balanced personality might have had a hardened opinion of her lost husband, but Molly, as Sid told us, was highly impressionable. Nevertheless, it must quickly have occurred to her that life at the Bijou could never be the same. It was one thing that Ronnie Barlow was now calling himself Charles Pepcoe, quite another that he had a new wife, a woman who presumably knew nothing of Molly's existence. And this was the man she was now going to have to work with every day.'

'So, what did Pepcoe do?'

'He did the most cowardly thing. He pretended he hadn't recognised her. He acted as if nothing had happened, as if he'd never set eyes on Molly before. Treated her just the same as he treated Mrs Dewhurst and Miss Moody.'

'The swine! While Molly kept on loving him from afar?'

'You have a sickening turn of phrase at times,' said Francis. 'Perhaps. Momentarily. But she couldn't fool herself altogether. Molly Barlow may be emotionally unstable, but she's not stupid. The screw began to turn when Pepcoe made it clear that he wanted rid of her father. That couldn't be allowed. Sid had done everything he could for her. I think more and more she wanted to challenge Pepcoe, but she knew that might bring down the whole house of cards at the Bijou, and her life with it.'

'It was a terrible situation for her, living a lie like that.'

'It wasn't of her own making. But there were developments. Ronnie Barlow was an addicted no-good gambler. Throughout his time with Molly I suspect he squandered his money on horses that didn't run fast enough. He put money on the dogs, too.'

'How do you know?' asked Gordon, squinting at his cousin.

'That sort always ends up putting money on dogs. It was only natural that he should also do the football pools, always hoping for that big win that would alter everything, open the door to a new life on the Riviera. Yachts and glamorous hussies. And when Molly went into his office one day he didn't bother to disguise the fact that he was doing the pools. It's something he would have done when they were living together. If he'd had any feeling at all for her, he wouldn't have let her see him doing it at the Bijou. There could have been no doubt in his mind that Molly would simply have accepted the fact. He was confident enough of her continuing love for him that he could blatantly present himself to her as the man who had been – and still was – her husband.'

'What a cruel thing to do.'

'Molly knew him well. She could see that nothing had changed about the man who had abandoned her. But Ronnie or Pepcoe or whoever he really was had pushed her a little too far. She was so upset that she told Mrs Dewhurst she'd seen him doing the pools in his office He was beaming, excitable, unable to concentrate on the simplest thing. You see, Molly suspected he'd had a substantial win.'

'But how could she prove it? If he marked his form with an "X" to show he wanted no publicity, no one need ever have known except the pools company.'

'Oh, I don't think Molly wanted to prove anything,' explained Francis. 'She didn't want to bring him down. Even after the way he'd treated her and her father, she still had feelings for him. But she began to wonder about *Mrs* Pepcoe, the wife he never mentioned, the wife who never set foot in the Bijou, the woman whom nobody had ever met. The invisible woman, in fact. And she decided to meet her.'

'How could she manage that without Pepcoe knowing?'

'It probably wasn't difficult. Just making sure she visited the house at a time when she knew Pepcoe was at work. She probably called at the house on some pretext – collecting jumble for the church bazaar or some such – and a simple chat would have told her as much as she needed to know.'

'What *did* she want to know?' asked Gordon.

'Was Mrs Pepcoe happy, or was Mr Pepcoe making her life as miserable as he had made Molly's? Molly suspected he might have come into a fortune on the pools, and she wondered what difference that would make to him. Perhaps he was thinking about walking out on Joan just as he'd walked out on Molly. And I think Molly perhaps began to suspect that Ronnie Barlow – or Charlie Pepcoe if you prefer! – knew that she was beginning to alter her opinion of her ex-husband. Her rose-coloured spectacles were starting to dim over, and Pepcoe must have been concerned about the situation. Perhaps Joan had mentioned the fact that someone had come to the door one day – after all, think what an event that would have been in Joan's humdrum existence. What if Molly exposed him?'

'You mean, like the flasher?'

'Oh, do be serious. Anyway, Pepcoe decided to get rid of Molly once and for all.'

'I think I see! The Kia-Ora!'

'Yes. One new thing he'd learned about Molly since coming to the Bijou was that she absolutely loved the stuff, couldn't get enough of it.'

'Ah, the Kia-Ora probably acts as a sort of emotional crutch to compensate for the lack of sexual satisfaction.'

'Steady on, Gordon. I know you came second in biology last term but there are limits. So, Pepcoe gets hold of some of the Kia-Ora and puts arsenic into the bottle. Generously makes Molly a gift of her favourite drink to take home.'

'Yum yum. And free too!'

'None of Pepcoe's fingerprints on the bottle, of course. He didn't know that on the same morning Molly's dentist had threatened her with dentures if she didn't stop drinking the ghastly stuff. So that night, the night before Pepcoe meant to make his escape, she put the poisoned bottle of Kia-Ora in one of the nooks of the Box Office. Pepcoe didn't know. He was sure she'd have drunk it as soon as she got home, or even before, but the next day, Molly turned up for work as she always did.

'All that nonsense about the phantom flasher – probably a very great deal more of a phantom than anyone realised – played into Pepcoe's hands. He'd organized for Dorothy Dewhurst and Pauline Moody both to be on duty in the Dress Circle that night, on guard in case the worst happened. He knew the exact timings of the film that was showing, knew precisely at what times the soundtrack would be at its noisiest. An especially loud sequence, duration about five minutes, would begin at around 9.30 that evening, when Cowpoke Lil rounded up twenty thousand stampeding cattle. This he knew to be the exact time at which Molly always did her third round of the day of the auditorium with the "Parfum de Paris".'

'He was a calculating beast!' said Gordon.

'Oh yes, everything was worked out in cold blood. He arrived for work as if it were any other day, and told them he'd be leaving at his usual time. Of course, he didn't mention that he'd got his wife out of the way by booking her in for a beauty treatment at Lowestoft.'

'Molly heard him leave, didn't she?'

'She thought so. What she in fact heard was the door of his office being locked. She was probably doing something else at the time, not fixing her eyes on what her manager was up to. What she heard wasn't Pepocoe leaving but Pepcoe *locking the office*. No one else had a key to his office. And he'd locked himself inside it. He knew where the staff should be that night, the usherettes patrolling upstairs because that was where the flasher was thought most likely to be operating, and Molly in the Box Office until she went to spray the "Parfum de Paris" at 9.30. He'd brought female clothes, and changed into the wig and blouse and scarf and coat as the time drew near. He knew exactly the spot where Molly would spray …'

'Yes…. just where the Teddy Boys had their picnics …'

'And he knew the stalls were empty. He slipped unseen into the auditorium through the pass door when Molly went into the storeroom to fetch the scent. And he waited for her to appear.'

'And then?'

'Oh, I think there can be no doubt that he meant to kill her, and then catch the night train to London. He was leaving the country the following morning, and didn't plan on ever coming back. Mr Pepcoe was looking forward to a life of Riley, with no encumbrance, no wife and no ex-wife either.'

'And how did he mean to silence Molly Barlow?' asked Gordon. 'Strangulation, I should think. Remember the scarf.'

'Yes, and Mrs Dewhurst said it didn't go with the rest of the costume.'

'I don't think the scarf was a fashion statement. So long as it was long enough to go around Molly Barlow's throat it was stylish enough for his purpose. My theory seems to fit snugly with what transpired. When Molly walked into the darkened auditorium, Pepcoe tried to overpower her. On screen, Cowpoke Lil and her posse were going hell for leather for the hills. Such a noise as you've never heard! I don't suppose Pepcoe expected Molly to put up much resistance, but slowly, slowly, her attitude towards the man she'd once been so madly in love with, had changed. She fought back. In the confined space, Pepcoe may have lost his footing for a moment …'

'No wonder,' said Gordon. 'He wasn't used to wearing high heels.'

'The post mortem revealed a cut to his head. The edges of those old fashioned steel encased seats are horribly sharp. The shock of the impact floored him, and I think at that point he collapsed. It was Molly's natural impulse to have a care of him, despite everything she had been through.'

'She was still in love with him!'

'Well, love can be a very silly thing. She tried to rouse him, but there was no response. I suspect she detected a pulse, but his breathing was irregular. It alarmed her. She couldn't, wouldn't, let him die. She called for help, but on screen Cowpoke Lil and her compatriots were involved in a hugely noisy shoot-out with the bank robbers who did cattle-kidnapping as a hobby, and Molly's voice …'

'Faint with shock, obviously,' said Gordon.

'Exactly. She couldn't be heard. All she knew was that she had to revive Pepcoe. She couldn't get into the manager's office because he'd locked it. It was no good going into the Hopalong because the water in there had been turned off when the Hopalong had officially closed. She'd given Mrs Dewhurst the job of locking up the kitchen every night, so she couldn't access that either. But she'd put the Kia-Ora that Pepcoe had given her in the Box Office, and anyway the Box Office was nearer to hand than anywhere else.'

'So, she ran to the Box Office, retrieved the Kia-Ora that Pepcoe had given her …'

'The *poisoned* Kia-Ora,' said Francis. 'She knew how refreshing it was, you see. She'd always loved it. It had been one of the happy discoveries she'd made when she'd begun working at the Bijou. She lifted the Kia-Ora to Pepcoe's lips.

The sweetness would bring him round.'

'But it didn't,' sighed Gordon. The full horror of Francis's suggestion sent a shudder through him. 'It killed him.'

'That's right,' said Francis. 'Molly Barlow poured poison down her husband's throat. Technically speaking, Molly Barlow killed him, but in the eyes of the law I think – if there is any justice in this wicked world – you will find that Ronnie Barlow, alias Charles Pepcoe, killed himself.'

The airport was busier than Joan Pepcoe could ever have imagined. She'd pinched herself when she woke that morning, too early because she'd exhausted herself with the packing and lay awake wondering what she'd forgotten.

She couldn't have been more than twelve when her mum and dad took her for a week's holiday at Cleethorpes. Mrs Freebody took in your meat and fish and turned it into evening meals, although you had to be out of the boarding house by eleven o'clock each day, and a notice in the bedrooms warned against anything untoward. They'd never had much money, but dad worked all the hours God sent, and they couldn't afford foreign holidays. And then she'd met Charlie, who'd never so much as breathed the word 'holiday' as far as she could recall.

He'd been handsome when she met him. That's it, she thought, that's me settled for life, and when he said it was best she got right away from her mum and dad and the rest of her family she didn't need convincing. Charlie had a knack of getting his own way, and she'd wonder about it sometimes, whether she'd done the right thing, and then he'd smile again, and the doubts flew out the window until the next time he gave one of those lop-sided smiles when you thought it was the least likely thing his face would do. Very nice nails, too, as if they'd been polished, and a voice like a snake charmer when he wanted. They'd been happy at times, hadn't they? No one could take that away from her, but she supposed now there might be different kinds of happiness, something you learned about as time went by.

Funny how things worked out for Molly, too. She'd had such hopes of Ronnie Barlow, so much love she felt for him, and then he'd gone, turned into Mr Pepcoe who pretended he'd never seen her before in his life, and won the pools. Not a silly amount either. In fact, a *very silly* amount, really, a fortune, more than she could ever have imagined.

Joan had almost fainted when the representative from Littlewoods told her that in what he called 'the circumstances' she'd be getting all the money. After all, it wouldn't do Charlie (or Ronnie, for that matter) any good now.

Joan's bags were already swallowed by the aeroplane. She could see it, the terrifying girth of its wings, through the big plate windows of the waiting lounge. Excitement and fright flushed through her now and again, but they said that Spain was lovely this time of year. The fear of being quite alone in the world, the feeling she had lived with for so long, hovered somewhere at the back of her mind, clinging to the last.

'Come on, Joan. They're boarding. We don't want to miss it.'

Joan got to her feet, took Molly's hand. Joan held it tight for a moment. 'It's good to have a friend,' she said.

Molly felt much the same, but, exciting as the prospect of this escape was, she was already looking forward to her reunion with Mr Saintsperson.

The appointment was not dental.

Seeing is Believing

Eastern Evening News,
March 21st 1957

Norfolk Constabulary has expressed regret that it allowed a criminal whose identity was known to the public to evade justice.

On Tuesday at Norwich market, Roger Ryland (35), who had escaped from Mousehold Prison, asked P. C. Paul Hawkins for directions to the railway station.

Passers-by, recognising Ryland from images published in this newspaper, formed a crowd, waiting for the constable to arrest him.

Housewife Brenda Place told our reporter 'We were amazed that the two men seemed to be enjoying a joke, before the policeman saw off Ryland with a cheery wave. I was one of several people telling the policeman he had let a wanted man go free, but he insisted the man looked nothing like the pictures he'd seen. I wonder sometimes why we pay our rates. I didn't like the look of the man at all. I didn't like the look of the escaped criminal either.'

This morning, Norfolk Constabulary issued a statement that appears to vindicate the constable's inaction.

'We have been assured by an expert in the field,' said Chief Inspector 'Tod' Slaughter, 'that each of us does not necessarily see the same thing when looking at an image. May I remind your readers of that little phrase "in the eyes of the beholder"? In this case, P. C. Hawkins' visual reading of Ryland's face was very different from that of members of the public who witnessed the incident. P. C. Hawkins will be retrained in facial and bodily identification.'

Slaughter threw the newspaper across his desk. He was reasonably confident that Hawkins might just about distinguish between Brigitte Bardot, Jayne Mansfield and Sabrina, but he wouldn't swear to it.

'*Turn* it round.'
'Round?'
'The other way. Bottom to top.'
'How will that help?'
'It might.'
'Does it?'
'Twist it a bit more this way.'
'Does it, then?'
'Not that way. The other way.'
'Now do you see it?'
'No. Put it back how it was.'
'Is it sideways?'
'Not from here it isn't. It's upside down.'
'Not from here it isn't.'
'Try squinting. That sometimes works.'
'Sometimes. But not now.'
'It's there! There!'

'*Where?*'

'*There!* Don't tell me you can't see it!'

'Tell me what I'm supposed to be looking at and I'll tell you if I can see it.'

'What, *there?*'

'Where are you looking?'

'*There! There!*'

'Oh, oh … ooooooooh. My goodness. Yes, I can see it! That's the mouth, isn't it?'

'The *mouth*? That's a *nostril!*'

'What?'

'A *nostril.*'

'It's only got one nostril? There's nothing about that in the Bible.'

'The *left* nostril. The other one's there, on the right.'

'Yes. There it is!'

'Where? … Well? *Where?*'

'Would you believe it! It was there a moment ago.'

'Goodness knows. I can't see the one on the left now. Both nostrils have completely disappeared.'

'Up there! Where the snow's got a dent in it.'

'That's an eye, isn't it?'

'An eye? How's that an eye? If it is, it's got a terrible squint.'

'Oh, I give up,' said Doris Jones. 'The Yorkshires are done, anyway. Put the paper away, George, or we'll all be in the madhouse. And stop looking so smug, just because you're the only one who's seen it. I'm plating up. My Bramleys don't like to be kept waiting.'

Sunday lunch at Red Cherry House was never a calm affair. *The Billy Cotton Band Show* was no aid to digestion. Francis wondered at the vulgarities his family enjoyed. The ritual of Sunday newspapers depressed him, too, at least the ones that found their way to Red Cherry House, the *News of the World* and the *Sunday Pictorial*, although he wasn't above getting a vicarious thrill, a whiff of a wicked world beyond reach of the sleepy village of Branlingham, from flicking through them. Today's *People* had struck an ecclesiastical note.

> Can *you* see the "Face in the Mountain"?
> *This photograph of a mountain range in Switzerland hides a secret, the discovery of which has changed many lives. Will you find the face of Jesus hidden among the rocks?*

Francis scorned to give the matter any attention, and sat quiet as a tomb while his mother and father and Gordon and Uncle Billy bickered and shifted the paper this way and that in the hope of making out anything that looked remotely like a face, but snatched up the paper as soon as he and Gordon were left alone in the parlour.

'I suppose it's as clear as the nose on his face to *you*?' said Gordon.

'It might be if I could *see* the nose on his face, which I can't, and I have no intention of wasting a Sunday afternoon with such vacuous nonsense. Dad says he can see it, but I suspect that's his best chance of shutting mum up. When you consider how many families throughout the country are at this very moment being rent asunder in this hopeless pursuit … The gutter press has a great deal to answer for.'

'Oh, take your foot off the gas,' groaned Gordon, using a phrase that he imagined might be in the vocabulary of teddy boys. 'But I suspect you're the one person who *needs* to see it. And you wouldn't help anyone else to see it either, just keep it to yourself. Smug, I call it. Like that face you pull when anyone so much as mentions bingo.' Obligingly, Francis pulled the bingo face. The summons to lunch sounded louder and final, and once seated at the kitchen table all thoughts of seeing the face in the mountain were forgotten as Mrs Jones set down the heaving plates, roast beef with gravy to die for, plump potatoes frizzled and lathered in goose fat, vividly bright vegetables, gleaming sprouts and Yorkshire puddings born of alchemy. Then, for what Uncle Billy, much to Francis's disgust, called 'afters', Mrs Jones' golden-pastry Bramley apple pie, scalloped at its edge, accompanied by a generous jug of custard, in the presence of which everyone knew better than to mention Birds.

Floored by the frazzled steamy warmth of the kitchen and the enormous portions, the afternoon followed its usual course. Anyone looking into the windows of Red Cherry House at three o'clock that Sunday afternoon would think they'd stumbled on the palace of the Sleeping Beauty, where the inhabitants had lapsed into a hundred year's sleep, but today Uncle Billy had left to visit a friend in hospital (gammy legs), while Mr and Mrs Jones had loosened restrictive clothing and succumbed to an hour's snoring. Downstairs, irritated by the fact that he still hadn't identified 'the face', Francis was at his most restless. Gordon sat glaring at his cousin as if defying him to so much as glance at the photograph. Into this sleepy enclave came a knocking at the door.

'Can I help you?' asked Gordon, seeing a disreputable visitor who might have emerged from a wild wood.

'Master Jones?'

'Well, one of the master Jones, yes. The one sitting comfortably by the fire is my cousin Francis. He's the one people generally ask for.'

'I see,' said the stranger. 'Well, either or both will do nicely.'

Francis jumped up and extended his hand.

'Gordon, don't let our visitor stand on the cusp. Come in, sir. What brings you to our neck of the woods? I have often wished that my way of life was more peripatetic. The Romany way has much to recommend it. I suspect it may account for your robust complexion, the air of naturally belonging to wherever your caravan has rested. Some tea to warm you!'

It seemed to Gordon that the man sitting opposite his cousin was no stranger to the life of the road. Francis had welcomed him warmly, almost pulled him into the sitting-room of Red Cherry House, where he now sat nursing a cup and saucer and stretching himself in the direction of the fire brisking in the grate.

'Is your encampment close by?' Francis enquired. 'The working horse is such a tireless servant. Gordon, some sugar lumps for our guest's faithful old friend!'

The stranger lifted his hands in protest. His nut-brown fingers were encrusted with rings around which strange creatures writhed. There were looping golden rings in his ears, and a gaily-coloured scarf knotted around his neck. The scent of moleskin was overpowering.

'Would I be right in assuming you are not of the Raggle Taggle dynasty?' asked Francis, who hadn't taken his eyes off the man since he'd walked in. 'Roumania, perhaps? One of the great fatherlands of the noble gipsy, with a rich history of culture and mystic expertise.' Francis's eyes burned with startling intensity. 'I would be most interested to learn more of that country's gypsy lore from a man to whom such wonders are second nature.'

The gypsy had lifted the tea-cup to his lips, but paused, and slowly replaced it in its saucer.

'I think we both know that I do not have such information at my finger-tips' he said.

Francis laughed heartily. 'Oh, your impersonation is very good.' His soft smile hadn't taken the penetrating sharpness from his eyes. 'Very convincing, in fact. You could easily pass as a member of the Muranian gipsy chorus in the local amateur operatic society's production of *King's Rhapsody*, although a clay pipe, tambourine, and a hedgehog on the roast would not have gone amiss.'

The unshaven man gave a wry smile.

'I suspected you would see through me at once. So, what they say of your skills is true! Old habits die hard. I have spent so much of my life pretending to be other people that it is easier to be other than what I am. You know who I am not. But do you know who I am? I am no longer sure that I know myself.'

'Well?' said Gordon, not without a show of impatience. 'Who *are* you?'

'An impostor of some sort,' replied Francis. 'And don't bother about those sugar lumps, Gordon. It may have escaped your notice that our Romany visitor is wearing bicycle clips.'

'Oh, dear,' said the man, holding out his legs. 'That's the sort of careless mistake I'm too often making nowadays. So, you have the advantage of me.'

'More advantages than you might imagine, sir. I have seen you before, I think. On Tuesday, you were in the gardens at Norwich Castle, painting a scene in oils. The smock and beret singled you out. Your perspective on that church spire was quite wrong, by the way. On Wednesday I saw you dressed as a rosy-faced farmer in plus fours leaning at the door of the Rat With Pickle, a dubious public house frequented by those forever breaking the law and those forever trying to enforce it. It is usually impossible to differentiate. On Thursday, it was you, I think, in Jarrold's tearoom, a most attractive female mannequin in a fashion parade of the latest rainwear.'

'Promoting pixie hoods! I ask you!'

'You might well smile, Gordon' said Francis sternly, 'but something tells me this is no laughing matter.' He settled more comfortably into his chair, and Gordon felt the atmosphere almost breathe a sigh of relief. 'Now, sir. Let us begin afresh. We have established that you are not of the Romany. That is a disappointment to me, for the Romany are a brave and ill-used people. I know who you are *not*, despite your obvious adeptness at impersonation, but I have no idea who you *are*.'

'The bicycle clips! Such a silly slip-up. It's little more than a habit, nowadays, this need to disguise. In my line of work, it was always expected of me. One day a Spanish businessman, the next a Peruvian diplomat, one week a beggar on the streets of Seville, the next a Russian billionaire luxuriating in a suite at the Savoy. It has been a life, if not of happiness, then of extremes.'

'Do watch the cycle clips the next time you do the Romany gypsy,' suggested Francis. 'Your work is clearly varied. If I were to hazard a guess as to your occupation, I would put you down as a spy.'

The man winced. 'Oh, such a short, unkind word. *How* unkind of course depends on which side I am working for.'

'And what can a spy be doing in Branlingham?'

'Don't be daft,' cried Gordon. 'You've come to see us, haven't you, sir?'

Pulling the coloured scarf wearily from his neck, the visitor smiled at Gordon. For the first time, he seemed to relax.

'Yes,' he said, his voice softer now. 'This is where I needed to be. I have heard so much of the boy detectives, and the strange affairs you have solved, mysteries far beyond the comprehension of the official authorities. Who else could have solved the astonishing business of the Bensonian Differentiator? Believe me, the government of this country understands all too well what might have befallen the world had you not intervened to prevent global catastrophe. They speak of it still at MI5.'

'Steady on!' said Gordon, who liked to keep Francis' feet on the ground. 'We only did it with the help of a mermaid.'

'Precisely!' shouted the man. 'The British police would never have dreamed of involving anything so subterranean. Not even the finest Secret Service agents recognised the threat posed by Professor Drakananoff.'

'Our Russian friend! Ah yes ...' sighed Francis, with that faraway look that most people assumed was modesty. (Most people would have been wrong.) 'But in your line of work you must have been involved with some extraordinary events?'

'One or two, perhaps, barely worth mentioning ... The Sudcombe Branch Affair. Does that mean anything to you?'

Francis sprang forward until his face was only a few inches from his visitor's face. '*Sudcombe Branch?*' he whispered. 'Then ... heaven's above! ... Are you the man that ...?'

'Yes! I see you know something of it. My name of course never appeared in the press in connection with it. It is, anyway, a name that I try to keep to myself. My mother was a great reader of literature, including the novels of Henry James, which she devoured avidly but carelessly. Thinking Peter Quint to be the hero of one of his works, she bestowed his name on me. It is a cross I have borne throughout life. My siblings similarly suffered from her misreading of fiction. My younger brother Vlad was born soon after my mother read a novel by Bram Stoker. We don't mention my sister Goneril.'

'But Mr Quint, it's an honour to have you here. The Sudcome Branch Affair! To think I am sitting with the man who confronted the most devilish mind of his generation!'

'Perhaps one of you wouldn't mind explaining what you are talking about?' suggested Gordon.

'Mr Quint brought a master criminal to justice, Gordon. Sudcombe Branch was the pseudonym of an arch villain whose despicable activities were known the world over, although, when you sat next to him on a London bus, you would have thought him the most ordinary and unexceptionable of souls.'

'I never sat next to him on a London bus,' said Gordon.

'And Mr Quint is the man who rid the world of him!' exclaimed Francis. 'The confrontation between Sudcombe Branch and this gentleman is renowned as one of the most thrilling in the history of crime. Inevitably, it has been compared with another, more widely known, confrontation, at the Reichenbach Falls. I cannot recall for the moment where your brush with Sudcombe Branch took place, Mr Quint. The Dolomites? The Alps? Mount Everest?'

'Cromer Cliffs. I tussled with that miserable, morally exhausted menace to mankind for two hours on the cliff tops by the links. It was an epic struggle. At last, finding in myself some super human strength of purpose, I cast him over the edge. Still, he would not go. He clung on to life, even then, hanging upside down from the cliff by his feet as he was. Medical records have consequently proved that his toe-nails had the strength of tungsten steel, identical to those of the Totally Indolent South American Lower-Slung Striped Sloth.'

'But, at last, he fell!' hissed Francis.

'Yes. I was at my wit's end how to finish it. Try as I might to lever those evil toe-nails from the cliff-fringe, I could not do it. He might yet by some fiendish trick have heaved himself back on to terra reasonably firma, and then I remembered … I had in my pocket a bag of mint humbugs which I meant to enjoy as I roamed the Norfolk countryside. I moved out of Sudcombe Branch's sight, emptied the humbugs upon the ground, blew into the paper bag and burst it above his toes. The effect was stupendous. The shock sent him down, down …'

'And so ended the fearful career of Sudcombe Branch!' Francis whispered.

'It may be,' said Quint, 'although there are chilling moments when I fear that his terrible influence moves among us still.'

He stirred, seeming to recollect himself.

'But that is not why I am here. I have reached an age when certain things need to be faced, questions to be answered. There is the itch I am unable to scratch. The symphony I am unable to finish. The book of which I have lost the page that will explain the plot. The sign at the crossroads that gives no directions.'

Quint reached into the pocket of his tattered donkey jacket and withdrew a leather wallet. Gordon saw how tenderly he felt within its compartments before extracting something from its recesses.

'A photograph,' said Quint, handing it to Francis.

Francis looked down. 'It's half a photograph,' he said.

'Yes,' said Quint. 'And I want you to find the other half.'

There were times when the feeling of the world about you altered on the head of a pin. It happened that evening when Francis stood at the door of Red Cherry House as Peter Quint walked into the street. In tune, the trees waved violently, sending fistfuls of leaf in whatever direction the wind fancied, the air buzzing with energy. A bird that had stayed up too late struggled to make itself heard. The sky seemed to know that something was up, cream-puff clouds appearing as if from nowhere, dancing across a background of inky vermilion. The sort of night when you didn't need wings to fly if only you could first get off the ground, when the most unrealistic things that only happened in books became everyday. Francis breathed in the April sweetness. He felt sixteen again. And then remembered that he was.

The spell broke as he turned back into the room. His cousin had a disconcerting ability to put on a face intended to bring Francis back to earth.

'Well,' said Gordon, 'you've gone and done it this time!'

'Really! I don't know where you get these barrack room expressions from.'

'Sometimes you think you're invincible. You get carried away. One word of flattery about your brilliant detective mind and you think you can conquer the world.'

'Nonsense.'

'I can read you like a book,' said Gordon. 'You're not the only sensitive boy this side of the Wash. I watched you standing there, staring into the evening. I felt the shivers go up and down your spine.'

Francis didn't respond. The sensation had passed, anyway.

That extraordinarily serene but menacing nightscape would have changed by now. He made a mental note not to turn his back on his cousin again.

'You're worried that I'll fail,' said Francis.

'Not at all. I'm worried that you'll let that sad old man down. I know you can't resist a challenge, but this … Does the word "impossible" not come into your vocabulary? This is beyond a needle in a haystack. It's half a photograph, for heaven's sake.'

'Well?'

'Well! I suppose at this very moment someone somewhere in this great big world may be looking at the other half, wondering where this half is.'

'In that case, why not wait for them to contact us?'

'You may be a bright spark, Francis, but you've no common sense. We know nothing whatsoever about that half of a photograph. We don't know where it was taken, or when. We have no idea who took it, or why. We only know the boy in the picture is Peter Quint because he says it is. And that's the only thing we know.'

'How old does he look to you?'

Gordon looked hard at the image of the boy.

'He looks, maybe … ten. Sixty years ago, perhaps.'

'At least. What else?'

'It looks like summer. He's wearing shorts and he's smiling. If it was winter, he'd be shivering. The open-necked shirt, ankle socks, white … sandals … And his eyes … looks as if he's screwing them up against bright light.'

'Yes. Whoever was holding the camera would have had his back to the sun. Our first shred of evidence. It was summer, about sixty years ago.'

'Case pretty well sewn up, then,' said Gordon. 'And he's standing on some steps, concrete steps, with some sort of porch, an entrance to somewhere or other, just visible at the left hand edge of the photograph. The lettering on the porch … carved into the stone by the look of it … "ING" … A building? A place?'

'It's a possibility. The letters are enormous. The word must have been important enough to make it essential that it was emblazoned in such huge letters.'

'And on the left of the photograph, where it's been ripped, that looks very much like part of a hand, and … isn't that the edge of a suitcase?'

'My goodness, I think you're right, Gordon. And it looks like a small case, too. A suitcase for a child?'

'So, we can make some sort of initial guess as to what the missing half of the photograph might show. Someone holding a travelling case for a child.'

'A good enough reason to take a photograph,' said Francis. 'Peter Quint was going somewhere, perhaps. But I'm disappointed that you've missed something of prime importance.'

'Like what?'

'Cloud formations. No two are ever the same. Each is unique. All we have to do is find out at what time of day sixty years ago this particular commixture of weather manifested above somewhere in England possibly ending in ING, and the case is all but solved.'

Having made this dramatic statement, Francis subsided into the depths of the sofa and hid his head in his hands.

'It pains me to say it,' he groaned, 'but you're right. It's hopeless.'

'What an attitude!' spat Gordon. 'So, you're giving up? At last, Francis Jones admits he can't move mountains. Or see faces in them, for that matter!'

'What can we do? I should never have promised that poor unhappy man, never have raised his hopes.'

'No, you shouldn't. You'll never learn, will you? There are certain mountains that even you can't climb!'

'Oh, no more mountains today, please!'

'But we can keep trying, can't we? Never give up. You might as well adopt it as our motto. If we can look him in the eye and at least say, we did our best.'

Francis half-sighed, half-smiled.

'That may have to be enough.'

'Sir.'

It was the end of Tuesday afternoon Photography Club at St Basil's Grammar. Francis had timed his arrival to coincide with the departure of the last of its members. Mr Rollinson was gathering papers in readiness for the next lesson of the day when Francis put his face around the door.

'Jones? Are you lost? Or have you realised the error of your ways? Do you wish to rejoin the Photography Club? We can't be doing with lapsed members.'

Francis had left the Photography Club because 'Roley' Rollinson took him for geography, and had never inspired Francis to want to learn the first thing about rain forests, tectonics, tundras, geysers and glaciers and the accumulated wonders of the earth. Obviously, he would make photography just as boring.

'I wonder if you'd take a look at this, sir.'

'It's half a photograph, Jones.'

'Yes.'

'And you don't have the other half?'

'No, sir. That's just it. That's why I thought, with your expertise when it comes to photography …'

'You never show much faith in me when I'm introducing you to the delights of geography. Frankly, it's very hurtful. In your line of work – you're expected to become some sort of super-human detective when and if you grow up, aren't you? – a smidgen of knowledge about the universe may come in handy some day. Quite apart from which, we've missed you.'

'Yes, sir. I'm sure you're right, sir. Please look at the photograph.'

'Where's the other half?'

'That's it, sir. No idea. What can you tell me about it? Anything. You're the only person I can ask, and the best.'

'I can confidently confirm it's half a photograph.'

'But I remember you saying "Sometimes the most interesting thing about a photograph is what's missing."'

'My goodness! Did I say that? You must have been amazed that I said something interesting … But I'm not sure it's particularly relevant in this case.'

'I think it is, sir. And there *is* something missing, isn't there? I mean, there's probably something missing in this half of the photograph, as well as the fact that the other half *is* already missing, and we don't know what may be missing from that half either. Then, there's a sort of mark on the back. Even that's not complete, of course, the rest of it ripped off when the photograph was torn.'

Rollinson turned the photograph in his hand. The name imprinted by a rubber stamp had all but worn away through time, but Rollinson's eyes widened at the sight of the vague shapes surrounded in a circle.

'See that, Jones?'

Francis peered at the foxed back of the photograph.

'What am I looking for, sir?'

'That shape. It's as good as a signature. Can you make it out? It's a swan.'

'Is it? It doesn't look like a swan.'

'It does when you know that's what it's supposed to be. Part of a swan, anyway. The wing. Look.'

'Yes, I can make it out now. Does that help?'

'It might. I think I've seen that mark before. I have a friend in Sussex who has an unhealthy knowledge of photography. It's almost a disease with him. There's an outsize chance, and there's not the slightest reason I should put myself out for such an ungrateful boy, but …'

'Jones.'

'Sir?'

'That photograph you brought in the other day. I spoke to my friend in Sussex. He recognised the swan.'

'He did?'

'It's the emblem of J W Swann, a portrait photographer who set up shop in Shoreham around 1889. In his modest way, Swann was one of the pioneers of photography. He even experimented with colour, without much success. My friend thought this was a studio portrait.'

'Really?'

'If you look carefully, you can see that the steps could be part of a canvas backdrop, as could that porch.'

'It doesn't explain the "ING", though, does it?'

'No, but Swann wasn't known for outdoor photography.'

'So the picture was posed? With a travelling case? Doesn't that strike you as a little odd, sir?'

'It doesn't make much sense, certainly. Not much hope of finding anything more about it, anyway. James Wentworth

Swann shut his studio shortly before the 1939 war. He'd tried to break into the picture postcard trade, but couldn't make a go of it. Beyond that, there seems little information that will help you.'

'What happened to his studio? He must have had a great number of photographs.'

'He destroyed them. Apparently, he insisted on examining each image, before deciding its fate. He went through every photograph, one by one. It took months.'

'And destroyed them?'

'In a way, yes. He tore each of them in half.'

'You can't be serious? What am I to make of that?'

'Well, it rather looks as if your half of a photograph is only one half of many thousands of photographs.'

'Which can only mean that the needle is hidden even deeper in the haystack.'

'There is something, however … When the picture postcard trade failed to provide him with a new career, Swann left Shoreham. He moved to Norfolk, settled in Wymondham. My Sussex associate is pretty sure that he's long dead, but there was a daughter who may still be around. Who knows? It might be worth a try.'

Francis was grateful that Mr Rollinson had taken so much trouble, and tried to look excited at the prospect of this possible lead, but wasn't sure he hid the despondency he felt inside. He didn't see much point in trying to contact the woman. He could already see the incredulous look on her face when he showed her the photograph; the *half* of the photograph. It wouldn't be worth the price of a stamp to send her a letter.

*

'*You've* asked Mr Quint to meet us here?'

Gordon's eyes popped. The Bide-a-Wee Tea Rooms may have been a second home to him and his cousin, and Beryl Sanders was thrilled to have the boys sitting in her bow window with a cream tea ready for demolition spread before them, but never before had they used the Bide-a-Wee as a suitable location for meeting a British secret agent.

'Yes. Morning coffee. Any objection? We have to tell him face to face that we've failed.'

'*We've* failed?' squealed Gordon. 'Don't drag me into this. It was *you* that told him finding the other half of that silly photo would be easy as buttering bread.'

In the circumstances, both boys assumed a grave aspect as Peter Quint, now dressed in everyday sober wear, tinkled the bell at the teashop entrance.

'Boys! Boys! What a delight to see you again. You can't imagine what new life you've stirred up in me. Now, let us begin on our splendid tea. We are quite ready for you, my dear!'

Beryl was certain that this was someone of infamous repute.

'The biggest, plumpest and most moist of scones, my dear, laced with fresh strawberry conserve and ladled with Devonshire cream. And tea – steaming hot mind you! – in dainty cups.'

How painful it was for the boys to have to wreck every hope of this poor man! It was better not to delay it. Francis had begun to explain, when Quint put his hands over those of the boys and grasped them warmly.

'My dear young friends. I have come to apologise. That silly photograph! I never should have presented you with such an impossible problem. How could there be any resolution to such a mystery? It was foolish and selfish of me. I am an old man. Forgive me.'

Gordon shot a glance at Francis, who was doing a pretty good imitation of the Sphinx but kicked Gordon under the table.

'No apology necessary, Mr Quint,' said the Sphinx. 'But please, let me return the photograph to you.'

'Thank you.' Quint reached out to take the white envelope. 'Let us speak no more of the matter.'

Francis held fast to the man's gaze.

'There is one question I would, however, like to ask. *Why?*'

For one moment, he and Quint froze, Francis extending the envelope and Quint waiting to take it.

'I wondered if you would ask,' said Quint. 'At our first meeting, I expected you to ask me that.'

'I didn't feel then that I needed to know, or wanted to. I do now.'

'Will knowing make any difference?' asked Quint, smiling as he placed the envelope beside his napkin.

'Who knows? Half a photograph. It seemed such an insignificant thing to be concerned with. Perhaps before we part you owe us some sort of explanation.'

'The fact is, I haven't looked at that photograph for years. It has been out of sight but always in my mind. So much has been lost as I've moved constantly from place to place, country to country. The past has fallen about me, emptying the pockets of memory. Perhaps you noticed, when I first handed it to you, I did not even look at the photograph. I did not need to. It has worked its way into me, but the image is … incomplete. There is what is missing. That is what I require before I can rest, before I can begin to understand why it means so very much to me.'

'And you really have no idea why it is so important to you?'

'If I can find the other half, it may confirm what I have always suspected. It is like the jigsaw that you complete but from which one, just one, piece is missing. You know the piece exists, you know it will complete your satisfaction, but without it the job is not done.'

'And you can remember nothing about this photograph being taken? Or why it should seem so vital to you?'

'None. My childhood was not happy. At an early age I was removed to an orphanage. Because I could not cope with remembering the unhappiness I endured, I erased the memory, as I eradicated all memory of my early years.'

'As if you had no childhood?'

'Exactly. Every fact about it has vanished. The photograph is the only proof that I ever had one.'

'And the other half …?'

'Just think what it might tell me, what it might help me to understand.'

'So,' said Francis, settling back in comfort in readiness for some sort of explanation, 'when would you say your life started?'

'Oh, I can tell you that. When I met Dotty,' said Quint. 'That was when. When I met Dotty. The only person who ever loved me.'

To his surprise, Rosemary Pullman replied to Francis' letter. Her father had died some years before, but she still lived in the house he had bought in Wymondham. She would be pleased to see Francis if he cared to come, perhaps for Saturday morning coffee.

There was a look of surprise when she opened the door to two boys, but one glance at them restored her confidence.

They could smell the coffee, already set out in the parlour of the little house that slanted steeply along Chandler's Hill, with any number of internal steps taking you from one room to another. Mrs Pullman discreetly drew their attention to the outdoor privy should they have need of it. That settled, she welcomed them into the house, where order and peace ruled.

'How can I help you?'

'I'm not sure you can,' began Francis, before explaining the puzzle Peter Quint had presented them with, and handing her the photograph.

'The name means nothing to you, I expect?' asked Gordon. 'Peter Quint?'

Mrs Pullman paused thoughtfully as she took the photograph. 'I don't think so. It doesn't ring a bell.' She turned the picture in her hand. 'It's definitely one of father's. That's his stamp. Where's the other half?'

'That's the problem,' said Gordon. 'This would have been taken at Shoreham, would it?'

'Possibly. That's where dad had his studio. He was well known in his day, you know, got his name into books. The studio finally closed up in the late 1930s. Business had boomed in the early days – we're talking turn of the century – but he got into all sorts of schemes that didn't work out. He thought the picture postcard trade would make his fortune, but the money trickled away. My mother had always wanted to come back to Norfolk where she was brought up. We moved in here just in time to hear Neville Chamberlain declare war with Germany. I was washing the doorstep when I heard it on the wireless. Never liked the man. I think it was the moustache. Hitler had one as well, didn't he? You'd think he'd have shaved it off in the circumstances.'

'So, you're sure this would have been taken in Shoreham?'

She looked over her spectacles and brought the image into better focus.

'Like I say, possibly. Dad was among the best studio photographers, no doubt about it. If they wanted pictures of a Lord Mayor's do, or any big occasion, they asked Dad, but it would have been the exception for him to have taken a photo like this outside the studio.'

'Did he continue his work in Wymondham?' asked Gordon.

'That was the idea. He set up business opposite the Market Cross. Mum worked there as his assistant. She blossomed here. She'd withered in Shoreham. They did all they could to get the new studio up and running, but it never really took off. It made dad ill; changed him altogether. Finally, he decided to close the business down for good. So bitter about it, he was, kept saying what a failure he'd been. We tried to help him through it, but it had told on him. He was never the same. He got so he never wanted to see another of his photographs ever again.'

'I heard that he destroyed them all.'

'That was the worst thing of all. It was a madness with him, insisting that he examined every single photograph he'd ever taken and then tearing them apart in his hands. He swore he'd never let anyone set eyes on his work again.'

'But this surely can't be the only fragment of his work left?' asked Francis. 'If, as you say, he destroyed everything else?'

'Come with me.'

The boys set down their coffee cups and followed the woman up two steps into a darker, almost subterranean space and down three steps into a room from which all sound seemed to have been excluded. The floor was covered with cardboard boxes, the shelves along its walls groaning with canisters, files and papers.

'You see,' said Rosemary Pullman, 'dad didn't so much destroy his work as ruin it. There are no negatives. We've not been able to find any. What you see here is half of everything. One half he destroyed, the other half he kept. I had a man come from the local film society. He reckoned there were something like twenty thousand images here.'

'You mean, twenty thousand *halves* of images?' Francis almost whispered.

'I'm afraid so. I suppose there's no reason to keep them, is there? Not really ... What point is there? They're of no use to anyone. To tell you the truth, I don't want them here any longer, but if I were to get rid of them ... it would be getting rid of *him*, wouldn't it ... getting rid of his life's work, of everything that had meant anything to him? I'd lose dad all over again.'

Talk about a wasted journey! The only result was that the boys felt they should now be of some service to Mrs Pullman, perhaps offering to sort through the archive and get it into some sort of order, but they knew such an idea was ridiculous. The truth was that she could tell them nothing useful about their half-of-a-photograph and had no idea who the boy in the picture might be.

Their getaway felt uncomfortable enough, made worse when Gordon at the last moment said that he needed to make a visit. Francis knew this would mean standing at the back door of the house for at least another two minutes with their hostess as they gazed vaguely in the direction of the row of outside lavatories at the bottom of the hill. And perhaps even having to whistle.

'I'm sorry I couldn't be more helpful,' said Mrs Pullman. 'It's funny, though … It's only just occurred to me. Yes, that's definitely one of dad's. But you've only got half of it.'

'Yes.'

'Well, don't you see, it must be the other half of one of the photographs that dad destroyed. So, how did your Mr Quint get it? It's odd, though … For a moment I thought the boy in the photo was our Michael.'

'Michael?'

'My late baby brother. He'd have been about that age. Something about the eyes.'

The sound of Gordon flushing the lavatory echoed up Chandler's Hill.

'Michael stayed in Shoreham when the rest of the family came up to Norfolk, moved out of the shop and got a place of his own. He'd always loved it down there. He was Mum's bright-eyed favourite, and always sporty, archery, rowing, some really quite rare sports. He did well at lancing, too. He was a lovely boy. He died young.'

'Oh well,' said Francis, praying that at any moment Gordon would reappear. 'I think we just have to accept that this is one studio portrait that will always remain a mystery.'

A second alarm of the pulling of a chain and the unleashing of a mini-Niagara was followed by the sound of a metal latch clanking into place. Gordon closed the privy door behind him and began walking up the slope towards the house.

For some reason, Mrs Pullman waved to him as he approached.

'Oh, that isn't part of a studio portrait,' she said, still smiling towards Gordon. 'There would be no reason for dad to pose anyone like that. No. That photograph wasn't taken because a customer wanted to put it on the mantelpiece. That picture was taken for a reason. Some sort of occasion.'

'It was all that coffee,' Gordon explained as they boarded the bus home.

'Highly embarrassing,' said Francis.

He'd seen her name on the posters at Dredgeworth, that scummy little seaside town where he was supposed to be breaking the record for uninterrupted piano-playing in that lumber-room at the top of a narrow flight of steps off the market place. He could play well enough, although he'd never had a lesson, and this piano marathon lark was quite popular at the time. The agent who'd hired him came in every hour to make sure he hadn't collapsed at the keyboard and went outside to chalk up how many hours he'd been playing. It ran into thousands. People would clamber up the stairs, lured by the ragged strains of some popular tune, and there he'd be, still hammering away, his fingers bandaged and bloody, his eyes watery with fatigue, and the legend '*MAESTRO PETER QUINT: Playing now for 1,200 hours non-stop without sleep!*' on top of the piano. He hadn't, of course. There was a buzzer that the man on the door downstairs pressed when any punter paid his money to climb up and see the tireless musician, so he got periods of rest, and most nights he snatched a bit of sleep before it was time to pour new red ink over the bandages.

The trouble was, to all purposes he was still Peter Quint, and something told him – he who had never and would never be content to be himself – that he would always be happier being someone else. That was what Dotty recognised at once. Dotty Broadwater, comedienne-soubrette and a regular in Dredgeworth summer seasons. In the West End, she'd understudied Phyllis Monkman in *The Co-Optimists* concert party so she knew her stuff, and meant no one to forget it. Her photograph outside Dredgeworth Floral Pavilion may have time-travelled back thirty-odd years, it might as well have been a photograph of her daughter, except she'd never had one and never regretted it either. Dotty may not have noticed because she was short-sighted, as well as out-of-tune as was obvious to anyone who sat through her vocal selection from *The Arcadians*. She had never been beautiful, but at least the portrait had been taken before crow feet took root and her hips started swelling, her feet in agony from shoes that would have given a fairy blisters. She'd borrowed them from Jessie Matthews when they were chorus girls, and had never given them back. In reflective moments, she wondered how Jessie had managed all these years without them.

As principal comedienne of Grenville Pittock's Danglers, the self-proclaimed premiere concert party of the South Coast, Dotty was loved by audiences and kept at arm's length by her theatrical colleagues. In the absence of the pierrot's supremo Grenville Pittock, it was Dotty who hired and fired at Dredgeworth, kept the corps de ballet (Phyllis and Elspeth and the 'musical' boy Roy who wore more make-up than Phyllis and Elspeth between them) up to scratch, and kept a sharp eye on the takings. She also kept a professional look out for any young man who might catch her eye.

She had no idea what Peter Quint was doing in that dreary has-been of a coastal resort, and would hardly have believed him if he'd told her the reason: that evening he was beginning a piano marathon in the town. Quite good timing, as it happened, because it was a matinee day for the Danglers, and the woman in the box office told him the show finished at 4.30, and he thought he'd need a drink then. Somewhere around the second verse of Dotty singing 'Moonstruck', he noticed that the woman on stage caught his eye. It was quite by chance that they met again in the Miramar Café. It was convenient for the Floral Pavilion artistes and the Danglers had a ten per cent off hot food arrangement with the management.

'I thought it was you,' Dotty said, waving a teapot at him from across the tables. She wore sables, and even more make-up than Roy. Her voice was metallic. When she opened her mouth, for the first time he saw how chipped her teeth were. Not that it mattered; she had what people called a winning smile, as if the limelight had never been switched off.

'All on your ownsome? Come and keep me company, dear.'

Hermione Baddeley. That was who she reminded him of. Hermione Baddeley in *Brighton Rock*. The same sort of natural warmth, common and perfumed and always with that suggestion of sexual readiness, but nice with it. A woman who never looked dressed without a fur tippet, probably composed of rabbit.

'Don't be shy, dear.'

Or Olive Sloane, now that he looked closer at her. She was another. He recognised the type, or thought he did. How wrong he was to be proved! The staff at the Miramar were used to her theatrical ways. One of the waitresses almost winked at Dotty, which didn't ease his embarrassment, but he went over and sat at her table.

'I wouldn't say you're good-looking, dear,' she said. She ordered a plate of mixed fancies, without ever quite taking her eyes off him. 'No. I wouldn't describe you as an Adonis. Still, it's an interesting face. It stood out this afternoon, among all those fish-heads. Hardly worth keeping the curtain up, was it?

Couldn't help recognising you from your photo in the market square. What do you want to get mixed up in that business for, dear? That marathon piano-playing lark's no good, you know. Do your health in before you know what's what. You really *can* play the piano, I take it?'

Oh yes, he assured her. He'd once had hopes of being a concert pianist, but what hope of that with his background? Whoever heard of an orphan out of an orphanage becoming a concert pianist? She asked his name, having forgotten the name under the photograph in the market square.

'Oh dear. Well, it's different, I must say. How would you like to be a Dangler? Our present pianist is being transferred to Grangeley Cove for the rest of the season. Ten bob a week more, not that he's worth it. I couldn't believe it. You've seen what we can do. It's better in the evenings. More pep. We tend to hold back a bit at the matinees. No use killing yourself when they're sat there like dummies, is there? Mind you, I think we'd have to do something about your name. A "Q" on the bills never looks good. In the West End, of course, with you at a grand piano, I could see the name Peter Quint striking quite an upper-class note, but it's too intellectual for concert party work in a dump like Dredgeworth.'

She peered at him skew-ways, holding her saucer at an angle to get it out of the way. 'You look more of a Percival to me. Or a Basil. The sort of name to which a diploma in piano-playing could be inscribed.'

He'd never felt the least like a Percival or Basil, so was almost relieved when the next week's posters introduced him as 'Cuthbert Cunningham, Pianistic Expert'. Dotty supervised the rehearsals as he accompanied the rest of the artistes. The younger members of the company were in awe of their mature leading lady; stories of her legendary appearances at Grangeley Cove and understudying in London were testament to her talents. In the concert party world, a season at Grangeley Cove was tantamount to the London Palladium, but as August dwindled into September, the excitably carefree mood evaporated. The spectre of unemployment descended on the once cheerful Danglers. A blowsy wet wind blew in from the sea, thrashing out the canvas from deckchairs in the open-air auditorium of the Floral Pavilion.

Dotty had stopped singing 'In the Good Old Summertime' and substituted 'Warm Yourself Up With a Drop of Old Ireland' to even less public acclaim. Funny, that. Thirty years ago it had been a sensation when she sang it at Grangeley Cove. The dull ache of the final two weeks of the season played out, the illusion of theatrical magic tarnishing at the edge. Pierrots hated September because it was time for them to part, to go to whatever tatty boarding house or third-rate theatre fate had decided for them. The bite of autumn spelled disillusion.

On the last day, between the afternoon and evening show, Dotty and Peter met for their final tea at the Miramar, which – in sympathy with the brave pierrots – was also closing, the season having reached its fag-end.

'First time I saw you, I said you'd got a good face,' she said. 'A chameleon, that's what you are. And you can play that piano. My goodness, you can. And you've got a brain. Something going on upstairs with you all the time.'

That was when it happened, when the great change began. She'd never wanted to be a soubrette, she told him. So far as she was concerned, Jessie Matthews could have those bloody shoes back whenever she wished. She leant across the table, her face so close that for the first time he saw the cracks landscaped beneath the layers of Leichner greasepaint she didn't remove between shows.

'You may have wondered why I'm here,' she said. 'In this dreary town. When I could be somewhere better.'

Quint presumed she was referring, as she frequently did, to the rather more West Endy Grangeley Cove, or perhaps Phyllis had been on the blower, beseeching her to stand in again.

'Being a Dangler is useful,' she whispered above the chocolate éclairs that had been ordered as a farewell speciality. 'I work the coastal towns,' she said, her voice growing softer by the second. 'It's government work, dear. Submarines. There's a fleet of them a mile or so out from the shore here. Nobody knows, you see. Goes without saying, they have to have a contact on land.' She relaxed back into her chair, fixing him with a smile he'd not noticed before, piercing, analytical. She wondered why she'd bothered to drop her voice. No one had ever thought her capable of saying anything of the least interest, so why would they eavesdrop?

'You're sharp, dear. You can change your face. It's a skill. There's opportunities for the likes of you, and they're recruiting. My people are interested if you're interested.' She took a card from her handbag and passed it to him. 'Don't be long, dear. I need to be in at the half.'

She bid a tearful goodbye to the waitresses, and with a merry cry of 'See you all again next year, luvs,' she swept into the street, as great a theatrical star as somewhere like Dredgeworth, which didn't deserve her at all, deserved. Quint watched from the Miramar as she strode the length of the promenade towards the Floral Pavilion, its posters proclaiming the summery arrival of Grenville Pittocks's Danglers already consigned to history. He saw her pause by the sea wall. What was she dreaming of?

The submarines? Those great grey steel mammals sleeping deep, suspended and waiting, humming fathoms down, beneath the waves?

He dreamed of Dotty that night, a sea-drenched Brünnhilde, assuredly a valkyrie but now unmistakably in the costume she wore when she sang 'In the Shade of the Old Apple Tree', her brawny legs across a submarine that throbbed across the ocean floor, her breasts brave ensigns, heaving with the swell of the ocean. She seemed to look back toward him, beckoning him on.

He rang the number on the card the very next day, and was invited to an office in Whitehall. When they gave him the job he realised that nobody had so much as mentioned Dotty, the only person he had ever loved when he had been Cuthbert Cunningham, whom he had last seen skimming the ocean floor.

'The truth of it is, we'll never know what Quint wanted to see in the missing half of the photograph,' said Francis.

'What he *needed* to see,' replied Gordon.

'But without the missing half, the fragment that survived stared out at him, unexplained.'

'Different, perhaps, if he'd had someone in his life. Then it wouldn't have mattered so much, do you think?'

'Perhaps. I see what you mean by "someone". There was no shortage of people, people he knew … He had plenty of people in his life. He had an extraordinary career peopled by all sorts of, well, people. Sudcombe Branch, for one. He had Dotty Broadwater. I think she meant far more to him than he realises.'

'No, I mean, like, a partner for life.'

'Oh, *that* … it's not given to everyone, is it? For all we know, we may not find one either.'

'Do you want to?'

'I've never thought about it. I'm not sure I want to.'

'Why not?'

'It would be giving something of yourself away, wouldn't it?' suggested Francis. 'Something you could never get back.'

'Is that a bad thing? There are things about ourselves we might want to give to someone else. If they wanted them! Do you think that's what held Peter Quint back?'

'I don't know. He may have no more idea than we have. He has been looking for *something*. But do any of us know what that something is?'

'Must you be so philosophical on a fantastic weather morning like this? Look at it! The sun has got his hat on, there's birds' nests to be discovered and eggs to be identified, and I'd really like to get on with my pressed flower album, and …'

'The more I thought about it,' Francis interrupted, 'the plainer it became. How many of us know the essentials we are missing? Oh, money, perhaps, or a place to live, or what we think of as success, but I mean the essentials of the soul. Perhaps we don't realise what's missing, only know that it's not there. And when something that was missing turns up, couldn't that be the one thing that makes life complete? Or at least gives us hope.'

'You've lost me. Is this Sigmund Freud, Carl Jung or Francis Jones?'

'It's all of us, you, me, the people in the street, everyone.'

'Just make it simple, Francis.'

'I found the other half.'

'*What?*'

'*I found the other half.* We've been through such torments trying to think of an answer to this problem, and we never properly understood one thing. Peter Quint didn't know what the other half of the photograph showed. All he knew was that it was missing, and that something on the face of that small boy, still staring out into the future after all those years, told him this had been perhaps the happiest or most meaningful moment of his life. And perhaps that happiness was because of who was standing next to him. Quint could tell us nothing about those years, except that he'd been placed in an orphanage. Because the photograph was taken by Swann, we can assume it was taken in Sussex, perhaps in Shoreham. Swann's daughter told us little beyond how the family had moved from Shoreham to Norfolk, but there was something else. She mentioned a brother. A baby brother, about the same age as Quint.'

'That's right. Michael. Good at what we'd regard as unusual sports, if I remember. Fencing, wasn't it, and lancing …'

'Exactly. The sporting type. That was what threw me. Mrs Pullman said her brother had done really well at lancing. Of course, when she said that, she mentioned it in a list of sports … But it was the *place*: Lancing. Lancing College.'

'Next door to Shoreham!' said Gordon. 'You mean, it could explain the "ING" lettering at the back of the photograph?'

'And while you were closeted in that privy – I jolly well hope you locked the door – she said that Quint's photo couldn't have been a studio portrait. It must have been some sort of *occasion*. The child's suitcase suggested as much, if you remember. She said there had to be a reason that the photo was taken.'

'Oh, come on!' groaned Gordon. 'You're not seriously suggesting you know why it was taken? I mean, if you know why, presumably you know who's on the other half of the photograph. Which means you've solved the mystery! That would be extraordinary.'

'It would. And I haven't. The answer – the other half – may well be somewhere in that archive Mrs Pullman has no hope of ever sorting out. What, after all, would be the point of archiving tens of thousands of half a photograph?'

'Then it's just as hopeless as I warned you it would be from the beginning.'

'Perhaps not. Remember what Mrs Pullman said about Peter Quint? Something about him reminded her of her baby brother, the one who died. The other day, I went back to see her.'

'Without me?'

'You were cataloguing a fossil,' said Francis. 'So, while you were otherwise engaged, I asked her about her brother Michael. I got the feeling, that first time she mentioned him, that it was a painful recollection. He too had at one time been put into an orphanage, when he was almost the same age as Peter Quint. The reasons are unclear. In those days, children ended up in such places for all sorts of reasons, often unexplained. What is clear is that he was the son of J W Swann, photographer. When he lived at home, he sat for many portraits in his father's studio.'

'Then she presumably still has some of those – at least *half* – of those images of him?'

'Yes. In fact, there was a handful of family photographs that Swann didn't destroy, presumably because he had an emotional attachment to them. It was one thing to tear up his lifetime's commercial work. He probably would have little remembrance of who most of his sitters had been, and it was all long ago by the time he started destroying the archive, but why would he destroy the very photographs that told *his* story, the history of his own family? He couldn't bring himself to do it. And

Mrs Pullman was good enough to show me one or two of the family portraits. Of course, there had been no real reason why she would have thought of showing them to us when we made that first visit.'

'Francis, you're not telling me you found the other half of Quint's picture?'

'Amongst that family collection was a picture of Michael. A nice looking lad, with such a look of contentment about him. He had been a clever boy. At the time, Swann's studio in Shoreham was doing well, and he could afford to send Michael to Lancing College, giving his son the chance of a good education. What happened then is unclear, but Michael died a few years later in the orphanage. It may be that Lancing College will be able to tell us more.'

'Interesting enough, but how does that help us?' asked Gordon.

'See for yourself.'

Francis produced the photograph as if he were a conjuror at a variety theatre. 'Well?' he said. 'What do you make of it?'

Gordon stared at it for a few moments, turned the photograph this way and that, brought it close to his eyes, as if divining himself back through time. 'So, this is Michael Swann, right?'

'Yes, that's Michael. What else can you tell?'

'Well, for a start it's a complete photograph – I mean, it's not been torn in any way.'

'Exactly. But look at Michael's hand, right at the edge of the photograph.'

Gordon looked, closer. He looked up at Francis, then down again to the portrait.

'His hand ... it's ... it's reaching out, isn't it? The tips of his fingers are off the edge.'

'Precisely. Almost as if he were holding something in that hand, something that isn't in this photograph but was there at the moment the photograph was being taken.'

Gordon gasped. 'Francis, you can't mean … is this the other half of the photograph? Is that Michael Swann's hand reaching out to hold the other side of the suitcase that Peter Quint was holding?"

'Possibly, and possibly not. There's nothing identifiable in the background, nothing that convincingly matches up with the background against which Peter Quint is standing in his picture, but even so …'

'All right,' said Gordon, pausing to scratch his head, 'but none of this proves anything, does it?'

'Turn the photograph over,' said Francis.

The writing was copper-plate. A fountain pen had left its message there in purple ink.

'Well,' said Francis, because Gordon had turned to stone. 'Read it out.'

'*Where is the other half? The half I've been missing all my life.*'

'Are you OK?' asked Francis. He moved to Gordon, put his arm around his shoulder, squeezed at the back of him. 'I thought you'd cut up like that. You'd better pull yourself together. We're meeting Mr Quint in half an hour.'

'But what are you going to tell him? What *can* you tell him? Nothing proves anything.'

'I'm not sure he needs to know everything. He needs to know enough to make a difference. I think this may be the other half of Quint's photograph, the half that's always been missing. At some stage, this separate print was made, making it a solo portrait of Michael Swann.'

'And this is Michael's writing?'

'It may be.'

'Then ...' Gordon hesitated. 'They must have known each other, Michael and Peter? At least they must have met? And the words ... What do you make of them?'

'It's more a case of what Peter Quint will make of them. He maintains that he remembers nothing of his childhood. Perhaps this photograph and these words will bring something of it back.'

'So, you're going to give him that photograph?'

'Oh, no. I promised Mrs Pullman I'd return this photograph to her,' replied Francis. 'You know, Gordon, I really think you should seriously consider joining Mr Rollinson's Photography Club at school.'

'What? You said he was one of the most boring people imaginable, and swore never to darken his Photography Club again.'

'We can all make mistakes. I can assure you that I have the highest admiration for that most remarkable man.'

'You don't say?'

'Through the magic of his art, Mr Rollinson has managed to merge Mr Quint's half of a photograph with this portrait of Michael Swann. According to him, the match of the two was quite remarkable – the two photographs meeting, as it were, in the middle, with the two boys standing side by side. There will, however, be another figure in the photograph I will be handing over. Mr Rollinson proved to be a much less dull fish than I thought. He is theatre mad, and has through the years used his free time to explore light entertainment of all kinds; what we might call the lower orders, touring variety, music-hall ... and pierrots. Over this time, he has taken and collected thousands of photographs of many an actor, singer, acrobat, red-nosed comic and leading lady, among them no less than Miss Dotty Broadwater of Grangeley Cove fame. By a miracle of photographic chicanery, Dotty is now to be glimpsed in the background of the photograph, standing behind two young boys, smiling with maternal love down on them both.'

'Well, I never! You're just about to hand that poor old man something he could never have imagined – the other half – the bits that have always been missing.'

'I would have put it rather more eloquently than that, but basically that's spot on. Oh, and by the way, Mr Rollinson has also managed to transplant Michael Swann's words onto the reverse of the new photograph.'

Gordon read '*The half I've been missing all my life*'.

'What can it mean, Francis?' he asked. 'I still don't know what it *means*.'

'I don't know what Michael Swann meant when he wrote those words, as I think he must have done. I only know that they are the very words that Peter Quint might well have written on the other half of the photograph, the half that is lost. Those eight words were enough for both of them, all they needed to express something we can only guess at.'

Francis was standing with his back to the window of the sitting room at Red Cherry House. Just as he said those words again – 'The half I've been missing all my life' – the sun sent out a glow that framed his head with a sort of light. Celestial, almost, Gordon thought. A shudder went through him. He was lost for words. It was just as well that at that moment Peter Quint knocked at the front door. Gordon got up to open it, and the old man walked in.

The Kiss of Venus

When and how had Francis and Gordon's Uncle Peter grown moustaches, bought a beret, moved to France and become Oncle Pierre?

Branlingham woke one day to read of his appointment as curator at one of the great art galleries of Paris. Could this be the brother of Doris Jones, an impeccably dressed young man who every morning sat ramrod-straight on the top floor of the bus into Norwich and by 9 am was in position at the haberdashery department of Chamberlins department store? Surely not the same!

Some thought young Peter precious, from the way he wore kid gloves and spats, and walked with a silver-topped cane although there was nothing wrong with his knees, and sported a fedora bought from Marshall and Snelgrove's summer sale, and cultivated that extraordinary moustache that perked up at the edges. More darkly, some called him bookish. Blodwyn Williams at the library couldn't keep up with his demand for esoteric literature. Miss Simms had just snapped up the latest Denise Robins when she saw him strolling out of the library with Oscar Wilde under his arm. The fact that he made no attempt to conceal it stirred her moral unease.

'Oh dear!' said Blodwyn, who had just bitten off half of

her first Wagon Wheel of the morning, 'He forgot his other book.'

Miss Simms gazed with horror at the volume in Blodwyn's hand: *Renaissance Nudes of the Great Masters.* Blodwyn caught Miss Simms' expression.

'I know,' she said, flicking through the pages with half a wicked eye on the gaping postmistress, '*and* there's double page spreads.'

Miss Simms made no secret of the relief she felt at Oncle Pierre's emigration.

'Less fun, though,' Blodwyn replied, waving a Wagon Wheel in Miss Simms' direction. 'Peter – I mean, Pierre – read interesting books. He was a man of passion.'

'I feared as much,' sniffed Miss Simms.

'A passion for *knowledge*. It wasn't only paintings and statues of classical male nudes …'

'So I should hope. Some of those sculptors didn't know when to stop chiselling.'

'Peter had a real passion about all sorts of things, about life itself. Once he got something in his head he'd explore it to the full. Wild plants – he went through book after book about them, and fungi, mushrooms and all that, there can't be a book about them he hasn't read. I know I'm Welsh and all that, but he had a craze for the architecture of Arabia, and the pantomimes of Joseph Grimaldi, and Victorian workhouses. He was amazed that some were still in operation. Outraged, he was; wanted them closed down immediate. He got angry about people, properly riled at what he saw as injustice. And capital punishment. Now, that was something that really got him going. I mean, I know I'm Welsh and all that,' (she gazed at her Wagon Wheel as if she might see her reflection in it) 'but you could sense the loathing. He said he was thinking of writing to the papers about it and all. Book after book he consumed as if there was no tomorrow.'

'Well,' said Miss Simms, who had heard quite enough, 'he can't have had much to think about if he had time for all that reading.'

When Uncle Peter moved to Paris he left his library to Francis. Mrs Jones was nonplussed by the number of crates arriving at Red Cherry House, but Uncle Billy rose to the challenge by building shelves and two handsome bookcases of elm that showed Peter's books to advantage. Francis was overcome by so much knowledge staring him in the face. The impossibility of digesting it! He had approached his uncle's collection timidly, touching a volume here, half prising a book from a shelf there, tapping his index finger at the exposed edge of a spine, and, at last, opening it …

This happened sooner than he might have imagined. The book was one that Francis had often seen his uncle consulting, about Victorian painters, for whom Uncle Peter had a particular fascination. For Francis, the moment had an almost religious significance. These books, so prized by his uncle, were now his, his inheritance the awesome responsibility of having to read them. Francis felt himself not only their caretaker, but custodian of everything they contained.

The book fell open at an illustration. He knew this picture. So, on opening the very first book of Oncle Pierre's collection, it was as if Francis had bumped into an old friend. The caption read: 'Edward Poynter's *A Visit to Aesculapius*, painted 1880'.

Yes, this picture was one that Peter had pointed out to Francis in one of their visits to a London gallery. Aesculapius, the Greek god of medicine, was receiving Venus, who had made an appointment with Aesculapius' receptionist because she'd pricked her foot on a thorn when out hunting. The painting commemorated a simple moment. In fact, Francis couldn't see the point of it; it was hardly apocalyptic. Thankful for his having removed the thorn, Venus kissed Aesculapius. Not that you'd know any of that just by looking at the picture. Of course Uncle Peter had spun a ten minute explanation around it. Francis remembered little of what he'd said except to note that the kiss was chaste, but had gone away convinced that not everything in life was what it seemed.

'Prisoner at the bar! You have been found guilty of a most heinous crime. In fifty years on the bench I can recall none more calculated to make the blood run cold. Throughout these proceedings, you have shown not one atom of remorse, seemingly insensible to the tragedy you have brought down on the head of those doomed to cross your path. It is my duty to ensure that the verdict of the twelve good men and true of the jury – a jury that has unflinchingly determined to see justice done – is carried to its awful conclusion. Is there any reason why sentence of death should not be passed upon you?'

'Yes. I didn't do it! And women sit on juries too, Hector.'

Judge Postgate's eyes snapped open.

'Silence in court!'

The thin, wrinkled mouth tightened at the corners, the veins standing proud through his neck.

'I didn't do it, Hector, and you will do yourself a mischief if you carry on in this way.'

Hector Alaric Postgate blinked. He had imagined himself in session at the Old Bailey, informing a convicted criminal that he would shortly be meeting his maker, but when the fog cleared he saw it was his sister who had come in from the garden. She wore the gloves she used for pruning. A sheath of yellow roses lay in a trug.

'Albania? I didn't hear you.'

'Jen's laid tea. I'm sure we could do with a cup. It's been one of those interminable Sundays, the sort you think will never end. A Tony Hancock day.'

'The Persian yellow!'

'What, dear?'

'Your early season roses. *Rosa Foetida*.'

'Yes. Beautiful, but too full, too sensual.'

Her voice had a suggestion of triumph in it. Until Jen had arrived, the chalky soil of the garden had yielded the weediest of specimens, azaleas and camellias giving up the ghost against the odds. The bursting richness of the roses stood for so much more.

'Last night's rain has battered them,' she said, fondling the froth of petals. 'They won't last long, but they'll cheer up the dinner table. You know all the Latin names, don't you, Hector? Just as you've never forgotten the names of those who've appeared before you in court.'

'Ah. More than one Rose, I fancy,' replied her brother, steepling his fingers together. 'I recall a Marigold, and once a Marguerite in a smash and grab job in Hatton Garden. And a Lily. A woman of the night, naturally. In the way of things, they mostly were named after flowers. Mayfair Lily came up before me regular as clockwork. And often as not a Myrtle.'

'You're not quite awake, Hector. It doesn't do to sit in the sun too long. I'll bring the tea.'

It wasn't the first time she'd heard him passing sentence. A moment later and he'd have been reaching for the black cap. The thought made her shudder. There had been signs in the past, but now there was no doubt: his mind played tricks on Hector Alaric Postgate, the 87-year-old retired judge whose appearances had instilled fear, and sometimes loathing, in those who sat in court.

Albania went into the kitchen, tilted the flowers into a bowl, filled the kettle and switched on the radio. It was *Grand Hotel*. The palm court melodies lightened her mood for an instant as she waited for the water to boil. A note was propped up on the table.

'*Mrs Timson – I'll be a bit later in the morning. Tea is in the larder. There's shortbread left from yesterday. Jen.*'

Tiredness washed over her, her legs dead weights. How long would Hector be staying? Last time it had been a weekend, which had been strain enough. This would be a longer visit, but how could she refuse when he invited himself? He had no one. Never having married, and being obliged to live the life of a judge, friends had to be so carefully chosen that he had none; certainly nobody who would put up with him for two or three months while renovation was carried out at his exclusive London block of apartments. She was his only relative. The mere idea of being in some sense responsible for him made her stomach clench.

It wasn't as if she had ever been particularly close to her brother. As a boy, he had been their parents' preference; little beyond a decent secretarial job in the city and, hopefully, a husband, had been expected of her. Her marriage (a satisfactory one, that had ended in her partner's death six years ago) had prised the siblings even more apart. Her husband made no secret of the fact that he felt uncomfortable in Hector's presence, as if he had committed a crime for which at any moment he would be sentenced. On the rare occasions her brother visited, she was caught between the two men, her dissatisfaction with both heightened by seeing how each behaved in the other's presence. Agreeable on some levels as her marriage had been, she felt less constricted when her husband died. The house grew dustier. Unsteady piles of books sprang up in the untidiest corners. Plain food vanished from her diet, replaced by those she had longed to try. She was no longer the social wife, presiding at cocktail parties, and spending too much time at the hairdresser. Her hair grew rangy, wild as the garden that sprung with nettles and uncontrollable daffodils in the spring. She rather enjoyed the change, the shame of letting herself, ever so slightly, go.

As it turned out, she never used the shorthand learned at secretarial college – Hector, of course, was up at Cambridge – because a husband presented himself before she needed a job. At the height of his success, there had been a housekeeper and a maid and a man who came in from the village once a week to garden. All long gone. Now, she was lucky to have Jen, who had put a note in the post office window seeking part-time domestic work.

Dependable local woman seeks part-time work as home help. Good cook and experience as gardener

Miss Simms drew Albania's attention to it, at the same time suggesting that there might be a question mark as far as the advertiser's suitability was concerned. Where had this woman come from? Nobody knew anything about her. She had dyed hair, and dressed in a fashion that by Branlingham standards was considered racy. There was a son, but no sign of a husband. Was she *quite*? One had to be so *careful*. Miss Simms' lips pursed, suggesting various improprieties.

'Do you mean she's *fast*?' asked Albania, although she didn't know what she meant, but by then a customer had come into the post office, lifting her eyebrows at catching the word. Miss Simms changed colour and turned to the perforation of a twopenny stamp.

John Scott took a taxi from the railway station to his appointment in the centre of Norwich, making for Grapes Hill in search of a tall chimney. 'You can't miss it' the woman on the telephone had said. The taxi dropped him at St Miles' Bridge. It was mid-day when he climbed to St Benedict's Street on his way to the city centre. The rain began just as the bus to Branlingham showed up. Seconds later it was falling steadily, and began pelting shortly after. At Branlingham, he made the mistake of getting off the bus at the wrong stop. By the time he reached the door of the Wedded Stoat, the rain was slanting off his hat into his shoes. He shook his dripping coat in the porch and wiped his eyes, feeling like a retriever that had been through too many puddles. He seemed to be the only customer in the pub.

'Look what the storm's washed in,' said the girl behind the bar. 'What do drowned rats drink?'

'Whisky,' he replied.

'You'd best dry out by the fire. You're soaked through.'

'It's a good step from the bus stop.'

'Take off your coat and I'll dry it.'

'Thank you.'

'We're more Salvation Army than public house. Practically a registered charity. There'll not be many through the door today. You're not local.'

He didn't know if this was a statement or question. She

took his hat and coat into the private quarters and called back, 'I haven't seen you in Branlingham.'

'It's my first visit.'

'Not your last, hopefully,' she said, resting against the bar and taking a long look at him. 'I remember the first time I clapped eyes on it. Wasn't impressed.'

He'd thought much the same when he'd noticed the pub, but there was a limit to how much driving rain a man could walk through. He'd almost sworn, turned around and headed off. What madness had brought him here in the first place?

'Not always as quiet as this, then?'

'Business isn't brisk. You wouldn't think before the war the village had four pubs, would you? Bell's?'

He hadn't asked for the double she poured.

'You can wake up the jukebox if you like. Create a party atmosphere.'

She smiled, brought over the whisky and went back through the bar. He was sitting so close to the fire that steam waved from his trousers. Before he was scorched he got up and went to the jukebox where flashing lights cried out for attention. He pressed Lonnie Donegan 'Don't You Rock Me Daddy-O' and went back to sit at the table. Why Lonnie Donnegan? He couldn't stand skiffle, but today everything had gone cock-eyed. Even the discs in the jukebox seemed to be mocking him. There was no way he was going to listen to Russ Hamilton singing 'We Will Make Love' or Pat Boone crooning 'Remember You're Mine'. Not now. Not today, with soggy feet and hair plastered to his head, and then the disappointment of finding the pub nothing like he had thought it might be.

No chance. He sighed, waggled the liquid in the glass, drained it in two gulps. There were faded sepia photographs along the walls. Just by where he sat was one of a haycart carrying people dressed in mediaeval costume, men ridiculous in floppy velvet hats and women wearing wimples. A placard on the float read '*Olde Times. Branlingham Festival of Britain 1951.*'

'Any chance of a top-up?'

When she came back to the table he noticed her properly for the first time. Attractive in a not very spectacular way, with a look halfway to a smile that altered her face. She had brown hair that smelled of geraniums when it brushed by him. She didn't speak, but took his glass and looked down at him for a moment before crossing to the bar. He stretched his legs, and went back to staring at the photograph, at the people happy to be small fry in a great national celebration. If he was to think of the past, he needed that second whisky. The trouble with much of the past was that it was always retrievable.

He met Pat in 1951, the summer of the Festival of Britain. She was sitting at the next table in Lyons' Corner House on the Strand, reading a leaflet about the exhibition, sticky-fingered from balancing a cup of tea and a toasted teacake. She was planning to go to the Southbank that afternoon, and before he knew it there they were, walking towards it together over the Embankment Bridge. An apparently enchanted space that seemed to have been put there expressly for them, the exhibition swallowed them up. Pat was looking forward to the Guinness Clock and he to the Sea and Ships Pavilion in the Dome of Discovery. He'd always wanted to be a sailor, going off on voyages around the world, happy to call nowhere home. He couldn't remember if it was on that first date that he told her he was a clerk in a travel agency. They wandered through the exhibits and saw themselves on television. In a strange way it cemented their relationship. Being seen together on the screen left them feeling strangely disembodied, but also established them as a couple.

They had coffee at the Fairway Café by the Station Gate entrance. Someone at the next table overheard Pat talking excitedly about how they mustn't miss the Guinness Clock and explained that it wasn't in the Southbank exhibition at all, but in the Pleasure Gardens at Battersea. It gave John the chance to console Pat, and a reason for arranging another meeting. They married the following year.

She couldn't have children, which mattered because she longed for them, and got tearful if she saw mothers and babies together. It was best to avoid meeting a pram. It was partly because of this that Pat seemed to want things: washing machines, hoovers, a radiogram, the latest face powder, a television (although no one he knew had one), a smarter living room suite than the one he'd inherited from his parents, a new dress or shoes. He worked overtime to raise funds, but there was always something else, more modern, that Pat desired.

He supposed that was the reason he started sitting in pubs. It wasn't for the drink, which he barely liked. There were always other men, many of them there for variations of the same reason, to strike up a conversation with, so there was nothing unnatural when one of them began asking questions, if he'd like to earn a little money on the side. It was official work, he said, important government work. He couldn't promise anything, but he had heard that John was a steady, reliable sort of chap. It was in his blood, the man said. It turned out the man had known his father, and – well, like he said with a wink, these things were in the blood.

John took the job, accepting that it would be only intermittent work; they would let him know when he was wanted. There would be what they called a trial period. The man behind the desk smiled in a rueful way when he'd said that, adding that it was essential he learned the ropes. When they wanted him, it meant being away from home for a night; sometimes two, if there was a distance to travel, or more if there was other work to do in another part of the country. He would be kept busy enough.

This was difficult to explain to Pat, who grew to suspect another woman. She turned out his pockets for clues, sniffed at his clothes for unknown perfume. Eventually, she put down the cooling of their relationship to these days and nights he spent away from home, but the truth was that the difficulties had started long before that. He foolishly passed his absences off as occasions when he was sent to check out some hotel or other on behalf of the travel company for whom he worked, but in the street she'd met one of his colleagues who said he'd never heard of such an arrangement.

'*Are* you driving?'

The girl had a nice voice. Incisive but kindly.

'What?'

'I hope you're not driving.'

'No. I'd better be off.'

He stretched his arms and looked around the room. No one else had come into the bar.

'Well, you're welcome to sit and think,' she said. 'I thought you might have asked me my name. It's Bess.'

'John. John Scott. Well … it must be near closing time.'

'Nothing's spoiling. I'm leaving at the end of the week, anyway. Moving on.'

'You too?'

'What?'

'Another job?'

'Dunno. I used to enjoy working here. Decent regulars, and some tourists in the summer months. There was a garden where you could sit out. It's a mess now. It'll be four years come September I started. Now look at it.'

'What went wrong?'

'Landlord. Jim couldn't stay off the booze. Lovely bloke, but the temptation. Family hold back, I used to tell him, but it was no good. It's got so out of control that the regulars stay away, and the brewery isn't happy. Jim went awol couple of weeks ago. I hope he's all right, not somewhere in a ditch.'

'Poor beggar. So, Bess holds the fort. When that gets around, you'll have coach parties lining up outside.'

'You'll be lucky. Somehow, I don't think the Wedded Stoat's got much of a future. The brewery'll be putting it up for sale before you know what's what.'

'Why's it called The Wedded Stoat? What's that about?'

'It's a local legend. Time was, this was a row of workmen's cottages. Story goes that one of the old boys who lived here was leaning on his gate watching the world go by when he heard a rustling behind him.'

'A rustling?'

'Well, I suppose he must have been drinking. He turned round, and there in his porch were two stoats stood up proud as Punch beside one another, with a bit of muslin twined round one of the stoat's heads.'

'The blushing bride?'

'Something like that.'

'And that's how the place got its name.'

He seemed to relish this thought, rolled it around his mind, stood and drained his glass dry. Bess fetched his coat and hat. The rain had slowed. Outside, grass gleamed, green refreshed with silvery blades.

'That's probably where the two stoats were standing,' said Bess. 'Right where you are now.'

She stood beside him, closer than any woman had been since he couldn't remember when. Since Pat.

'You're not going without paying, are you?'

'Put it on the slate.'

'You've got a cheek.'

'Put it on the slate.'

He had a crooked smile, turned and opened the door. The brightness blinded him for a moment.

'I came direct from the brewery. I'm your new landlord. I take over next week. Bess is a great name for a barmaid.'

Lost for words, she watched him give a backward wave as he walked a little unsteadily into the street.

Miss Simms had been right about the woman who called herself Jen: no one knew anything about her, or where she came from. The sort of woman around whom rumours buzzed like bees around a honey pot. Despite Miss Simms' best efforts, all she knew was that the woman had moved into lodgings in a house on the Strutton road, a mile or so out of Branlingham, with her 15-year-old son Jimmy. Miss Simms knew only that there was no husband, and wasted no time in spreading this titbit at every opportunity. In the circumstances, she might have expected the woman to be a model of modesty, but this woman wasn't one for hiding her light under bushels. There was her hair, for a start; bright red, and straight out of a bottle. Miss

Simms had noticed that gangster's molls on the covers of lurid American magazines had hair just like it. Her face was painted, too; she had never seen such thick lipstick, and the woman was no spring chicken, 55 if she was a day, mutton – although Miss Simms would never have been so coarse as to use the phrase – dressed as lamb. It was a wonder she could walk in those high heels, and bracelets and bangles and charms tinkling on her wrists as if she were a Christmas tree on manoeuvres. There could be no doubt. The woman was *common*.

On such a freshly minted morning, Percy Grainger seemed the natural choice for whistling, and Francis' first choice was 'Molly on the Shore'. He and Gordon were making their leisurely bicycling way to Reepham, where Mr Hartfield, their recently retired English teacher from St Basil's, was delighted to welcome them to his bachelor's thatched cottage. He had thought of Francis as one of his most promising pupils, although he didn't know where the boy's exceptional talent would take him. He had never taught Gordon, but knew him as a sporty and dependable lad, selflessly devoted to his older cousin. Naturally, Mr Hartfield was eager to learn of some new mystery that the boys were involved with.

'Nothing much at the moment, sir,' said Francis despondently.

'Just village life going on as usual, really,' added Gordon. 'Dead boring.'

'Oh, come, now,' said Mr Hartfield as he poured three generous glasses of ginger pop. 'Beneath that apparently dull façade there must be all manner of things going on that defy explanation. As a fan of Mrs Christie you will know that Miss Marple was a sharp observer of ordinary people going about everyday life, but she perceived things, seemingly of no consequence at the time, that subsequently came in handy for solving the most perplexing mysteries. Why did Mrs So-and-So not wear her new hat to church that Sunday? Why did her husband change the habit of a lifetime by suddenly turning left at the top of the road on his way to work instead of right as he had for thirty years? Why on the second Sunday after Easter did the vicar's wife's steak and kidney pudding have not one ounce of kidney in it when it was known throughout the county as her speciality dish? Such apparently innocent incidents, but to the mind of a detective …'

'That's quite so, sir,' said Francis. 'Well, let's see. There is a newcomer to Branlingham, a Mr John Scott who has taken over as landlord at the Wedded Stoat.'

'It's a public house,' added Gordon. 'Fallen on hard times.'

'There's a barmaid, Bess, who was planning on leaving the pub, but she's decided to stay on. Then, a retired judge from London is staying with his widowed sister Mrs Timson.'

'That's right,' said Gordon. 'And one of my school pals, Jimmy, has a mother who's been helping Mrs Timson around the house. I've heard Miss Simms at the post office talking about Jimmy's mum as if she's a scarlet woman.'

'Well, there we are!' exclaimed Mr Hartfield. 'And when these characters meet, that's when your fun will begin!'

After looking through Mr Hartfield's recently acquired books, and fortified with hot tea and luxuriously buttered muffins, the boys waved goodbye to their host and set off for the nearby village of Salle. The day continued as springy as it had begun, so they whistled Grainger's 'Shepherd's Hey' as they pedalled between the sun-dappled hedgerows, although Francis said he didn't suppose many shepherds had ever heard of it. The moment that the magnificent tower of St Peter and St Paul's church came into view never failed to thrill them. What would the landscape of East Anglia be without these massive monuments to man's clinging belief in faith? The beacon of Blythburgh church was just as potent, and one of the highlights of a train journey from Norwich was that moment when the great cathedral at Ely came into view, rising with magisterial mystery out of the surrounding marshes, straining at heaven itself in its exclamation of majestic beauty.

Well wrapped against the abiding cold of the wool church of Salle, Gordon was busy with his heelball on a brass-rubbing of the long-departed Thomas Rose (his wife, inexplicably, was laid to rest at the opposite end of the building, pointing in the opposite direction), while Francis made copious notes about the intricate design of the misericords. Decorated with sunflowers, roses, lilies, hawthorn and pomegranates, the carvings were testament to some forgotten craftsman's skill and patience, an artist sprung from the native soil who at the end of a long day shuffled back to his pauper's cottage, unaware of the heritage he had left to posterity. Francis was on his knees admiring the work when a verger appeared from the organ loft.

'How wonderful to see that these old churches still attract the young!'

'Good morning, sir,' Francis replied. 'This is such a special place. My cousin and I come here often.'

'Not that we *believe*,' said Gordon, unnecessarily, Francis thought. 'I mean, we might believe, but we're not sure we do.'

'No problem,' said the verger. 'Many people that come here are non-believers or doubting Thomases. But these places have aesthetic as well as religious attractions.'

'That's it,' cried Gordon. 'Jolly good brass-rubbing, never mind the other stuff.'

'Gordon isn't quite such a non-believer as he makes out, sir. You couldn't find a more faithful friend, so there must be something in him.'

'I have no doubt of it. I often wonder myself.'

'Wonder?'

'About faith. We all have need of it, I think, in whatever direction we turn, even if that turn is inward. And perhaps a place like this, designated to our calm, allows us to at least think of the world and the part we play in it. It's a forgiving church, if you can stand the temperature.'

'It's such a lonely building,' said Gordon, 'I'd be amazed if it ever had a full house.'

'I agree,' said the verger. 'You must remember it was built as much to show the wealth hereabouts that came from the wool of sheep as for the benefit of the poor of the parish, who were anyway very thin on the ground. Then, of course, they were thin because in summer they survived on gruel and berries from the bushes. In winter they left the hovels they couldn't afford to heat to attend services here, where it was probably colder than if they'd stayed at home. Somewhat ironic for a wool church, don't you think?'

'But it was an important part of the community, wasn't it?'

'Undoubtedly. The church owes its existence to the patronage of the Boleyn family. And if Mrs Strickland is to be believed, the Boleyns have never quite left it.'

'Mrs Strickland?' asked Gordon. 'Does she do the flowers?'

'A Victorian authoress. She wrote a number of volumes about the queens of England. Rather too many volumes, in my opinion. Her account of what happened to Anne Boleyn is still a popular talking point in these parts.'

'What did happen to her? I know she was supposed to walk the Bloody Tower with her head tucked underneath her arm …'

'Really, Gordon! That's not Mrs Strickland, that's Stanley Holloway.'

'It's a grisly tale, whoever tells it,' the verger continued. 'Over four hundred years ago Henry VIII had his wife Anne Boleyn accused of high treason and immoral behaviour. A jury that included her own uncle and her one-time fiancé sentenced her to death. She was beheaded on Tower Green four days later, and her decapitated remains interred in the Chapel Royal of St Peter ad Vincula in the Tower of London. According to local legend, under cover of darkness, on the night of her execution, her maids broke into the chapel, stole her body and brought it back to Salle, the true home of the Boleyns. Who knows?' He peered vaguely around the vast building. 'Perhaps she is laid here, under an anonymous tombstone as some insist, although it seems unlikely.'

'Perhaps that is what she would have wanted,' suggested Francis. 'After all, she was a person for whom faith was important. It was vital to her. This would have been a coming home for her.'

'Yes. She forgave her executioner at the moment of death, you know. She absolved him from the dreadful deed he was about to commit. The act of forgiveness … who knows which of us will be called to attempt it?'

'Such a bore,' said Albania, 'but I must stir myself.'

The letter from her late husband's solicitor was unexpected. A matter of importance had arisen; would she telephone to make an appointment? Albania disliked London, and wondered about the right shoes and whether she might invest in a taxi from Liverpool Street to the solicitor's Bloomsbury office. The meeting would probably last only a few minutes, but how much more convenient if it could have happened before Hector came to stay. She would need to leave the house early in the morning, and travelling fussed her. If it had to be done, she might as well make a day of it – she had so few treats now – have lunch at Fortnum and Mason and go on to a matinee before catching an early evening train back to Norfolk.

The only problem was that her brother must be left alone for the day. He treated the house as a hotel and his sister as its general manager, apparently unsure of where particular rooms or facilities were located. Not for the first time, she counted her blessings that she had Jen to call on. Could Jen supervise in her absence? If her visit to London could be arranged for one of Jimmy's school days, when he would be away after breakfast and had football practice before returning home in the early evening, it might be managed.

'Hector is really no trouble,' said Albania, hoping to convince herself and Jen at the same time, 'and he'll want only a light lunch.'

'Don't worry,' Jen replied. She got on with people, and imagined Hector, whom she had yet to meet, as a mirror image of his sister, reflecting her easy attitude to life.

On the morning of Albania's London visit, Jen let herself in by the back door. Albania had left a plate of ham and tongue covered with a damp teacloth, and an assortment of salad vegetables waited cool in the larder alongside a dish of cold rice. Jen had brought apricots from the greengrocer, setting them in a saucepan with a dash of water and muscovado sugar. She had once been at a lunch where poached apricots were served, and thought them the height of unostentatious luxury. When the time came to serve, she took a tray into the dining room and was surprised to see Albania's brother already seated at the table unfolding a napkin and staring grimly ahead.

'Lunch is ready, Mr Postgate,' she said, realising what a silly thing it was to say in the circumstances.

At least, she thought, he knew where to go for his food. She put up a hand to primp her hair against her reflection in the window. She was sure she looked younger than her years, although some were unsubtle enough to think she was her son's grandmother. Mrs Timson's brother was not at all what she had expected. For the merest second, she waited in the doorway before approaching the table. Hector Postgate seemed oblivious of her presence.

'Where is Albania?' he asked. 'My sister, Albania.'

A heaviness around his eyes suggested he had been dozing or had sleep-walked into the room. The face was gaunt, his cheeks folding back as if jowls had once hung there. 'My sister, Albania,' he repeated, more wearily.

'Mrs Timson has gone to London for the day.' She tidied his knife and fork about his plate. 'She'll be back this evening.'

'London!' exclaimed Hector. 'How extraordinary! That is where I have come *from*. Had I known that was her destination, I would hardly have bothered to travel from London to see her. It seems utterly pointless that we should have been travelling in opposite directions, like ships passing in the night. Counsel should have informed me of this.'

'I'm Jen. Your sister asked me to come in to see to your lunch.'

'Jen?' He paused as he lifted a napkin to his mouth. 'What sort of name is that? I see no reason for the abbreviation of font-given names. Does some shame attach to your parentage? Why are you not called Jennifer? Or Genevieve? I have never held with fore-shortening in any walk of life and do not intend to change my opinion at so late a time. Why do you not answer to Jennifer if that was the vicar-given name bestowed on you?'

'Because I'm not Jennifer,' she answered, startled at the speed with which he had irritated her. 'I'm Jen.'

He made no response, as if he had never sought a reply. She poured a glass of wine and set it at his right hand. As she replaced the bottle on the table, he looked up at her. A waft of medicinal mouthwash went by.

Returning to the kitchen, Jen sat by the oven, listening to the soft bubble of the simmering apricots. She hadn't expected this. The house had always been so welcoming to her, and now this.

'Why don't you move in here?' Albania had asked her a few days earlier. 'You and Jimmy would be much more comfortable than in that boarding house, and Jimmy would have a room of his own, and there's the garden, it's perfect for a boy to mess about in. It's not charity,' she said, expecting that Jen might accuse her of it. 'I'd expect a rent.' Even then, Jen knew that Albania's idea of rent would be an absurdly small amount of money. 'The place would come alive again,' said Albania, 'and we'd be doing each other a good turn. And the garden needs you! You awoke it, the prince bringing back the Sleeping Beauty to life with a kiss. What is it you do with plants? They breathe and grow at your approach. '

'Oh, I couldn't do that.'

'Why ever not?'

'You know nothing about me. What about those things they say about me in the village?'

'Oh, you know about that, do you? Do you suppose I'd pay any attention to those old biddies tittle-tattling? Well, you can always tell me what you think I ought to know. Come to that, you know nothing about me. They probably say the most dreadful things about me, too.'

Jen turned down the gas under the apricots and spooned them into a china dish, with a jug of cream as accompaniment. She hovered at the oven, unsure she should put her head around the door of the dining room, but the soft clatter of cutlery had stopped minutes ago. When she collected his plate and settled the table for the next course, it was almost as if he were noticing her for the first time.

'Jen,' he said, now starting off on the same tack as before. 'It hardly seems a proper name at all. I recall now that Albania – she is my sister, you know, I the elder by two years – Albania informed me you would be here today. She thinks highly of you, although the provenance of the post office window seems doubtful.'

'Your sister has been kind to me,' said Jen.

'Trust must be earned. I hope you will not disappoint her.'

'I hope not. I think perhaps we all of us disappoint at one time or other, don't we? We can none of us help it.'

He leaned back in his chair as if to concentrate the better on her face.

'I see you are a student of philosophy,' he said. Jen thought he might as well have said 'What a remark for a servant to make!' but she smiled on.

'Albania has never been much of a philosopher, not having had to think for herself. Her late husband – did you know him?'

Jen shook her head.

'Her late husband was a most unsatisfactory creature, self-contained, bound in his own small world to which in turn he bound her. He was handsome. Oh, very. One could see the attraction. Oh, yes. I hoped that Albania might have changed after he abandoned her.'

'Abandoned her?' said Jen. 'I understood that Mr Timson died.'

'Death or abandonment. It comes to much the same thing. I have spent my life listening and sorting words and making of them what I may.' He clenched the side of his chair and pulled himself up to his full height as if addressing the court. 'Telling counsel for the defence to speak more clearly, instructing counsel for the prosecution to use language more easily understood by the ill-educated accused in the dock, selecting words that will resonate with those in the court-room gathered to hear my comments when sentencing.'

'Were all the accused ill-educated?'

He looked up. Her voice had an unaccountably sharp edge, but the slight smile could still be traced.

'You were a judge, then? Albania had not told me you were a judge.'

'Retired, alas,' he said, and sank back a little, his body growing visibly slighter.

'It must have been lonely work. The judge sits above, doesn't he, looking down on the rest of mankind? You have viewed life from somewhere outside it. You must have seen a deal of badness in your career?'

He took a long sip of wine, and looked at her clearly, once again as if for the first time. 'I have seen more than many,' he said, 'and less than most. You have the air of someone who has seen a good deal yourself. I am wondering if Jen quite suits you as a name. We grow into our names. Being called Hector has kept me quite apart from certain sections of society that might in other circumstances have been more welcoming. If I had been a Bert, a Sid, a Frank, a Don … what would have become of me?'

'How do I address a judge?' asked Jen.

'I didn't intend that you should regard me in an official way, but … Judge Postgate would be acceptable in this situation. In court, of course, you would address me as "My lord".'

'Judges carry a posy of flowers when they arrive at court, don't they? To ward off the stench of the unwashed populace?'

'That is as tradition has it,' replied Hector, as if he had no responsibility for such antique goings-on.

'When you think of all the lives …' said Jen.

'Yes. They have passed before me, as they do before every judge, in an endless stream.'

'And you have decided what will happen to them.'

'Nothing of the sort. I was uninvolved in their fates. The eternal looker-on. I decided very little, and did not hold myself responsible. People are the architects of their own destiny. I was merely the instrument through which the law exercised its power. An instrument blind to the easy sway of sentimentality and to the wayward nuances of proof. Now … changing times. I no longer sit, of course. I find myself unmissed by the world I once looked down upon and which looked ever up at me. Having been among such clamour, I find myself quite isolated.'

'Did you never marry?'

'I never did. Nor did I fall in love or prey to any romantic entanglement. The idea of such an association never occurred to any woman of my acquaintance. Albania, on the other hand … I don't think her husband liked me, but oddly enough, I miss him. Such a good, strong fellow in his way. Set up, you might say. Blue eyes that took something from you when you looked into them. Robert ... If he were here, I think we would have things to say now, a shared outlook as we passed into old age. We would have things to say to one another. Things of moment. He was not a Cambridge man, but in his way he had a quiet charm about him. Couldn't stand the fellow, of course, but perhaps, in time, we might have been companionable.'

'Companionship is a good thing,' said Jen. 'There's poached apricots with cream to follow.'

Albania found the street in Bloomsbury without difficulty, although she'd left her *A-Z of London* at home. As expected, her meeting at the solicitor's was punctual and crisp. Old Baverstock, the senior partner, escorted her to the door when they had finished, having insisted on getting her a taxi to Piccadilly. She was relieved to clamber into it, in such a daze as she was. The waiter at Fortnum and Mason showed her to a table shielded from the hubbub of the room, and could not have been more attentive or friendly. It was as if he instinctively knew she had just been told that she was penniless.

'I'm going to the theatre,' Albania told him as she settled the bill and pressed a generous tip into his white hand. It was dangerous information to give out. She regretted having done so almost at once, sensing the pity the young man must feel for her. She thought he might be an out of work actor.

'I'm sure you will enjoy your afternoon, madam,' he sighed, and gave her such a look. Why couldn't she have had someone like him all her life? She thought: twenty years ago, he and I might have been lovers, she waiting in a room for her waiter to appear, a prelude to an afternoon of delight, stroking his smooth skin, although she suspected he was probably more interested in men than women. And if such a man could not have been her lover, why not her son? It wouldn't in the least have mattered that he was a waiter or dustman or building site labourer, not if he'd been there to listen and sometimes care and attempt an understanding of her.

Another taxi took her to the Strand. Albania's immediate instinct when she walked into the vestibule of the Savoy Theatre was that she wished she was at home, not faced with the tedious return journey to Norfolk, but the embrace of D'Oyly Carte's old playhouse wrapped around her: the attentive attendants, the softness of the furnishings, the unexpected intimacy. Until the overture struck up she had forgotten she was seeing a musical. The curtain rose to reveal a girl sitting by a well and singing about how exciting it was to be up so early in the morning. The plot was footling, but something about what she was watching alternately lifted and depressed her in a way she found impossible to explain. Having decided not to order the matinee tray of tea and Fuller's fruit cake that would be passed along the row to where she sat, she spent the interval in the bar, pecking at a gin and tonic, experiencing a mix of despair and joy that threatened to embarrass her.

Jen had gone by the time she got back to Branlingham. Hector had fallen asleep in front of the television, despite the efforts of Pearl Carr and Teddy Johnson to beguile him with a selection of cockney songs. She tiptoed into the kitchen, took off her hat and burst into tears.

Within a few weeks of John Scott taking over *The Wedded Stoat*, Branlingham remembered its existence. The first thing he'd done was to give the pub a fresh lick of paint, inside and out. The windows were cleaned, the woodwork scrubbed, the faded velvet curtains replaced with a floral cretonne. Softer lighting gave off a cosy glow that the old fluorescent tubes hadn't managed. The gas fires that had hissed in the public and snug bars were ripped out; now, logs burned, pulling faces in the embers. Inspired by the changes, Bess suggested they should start doing food, Sunday lunches with beef and roast potatoes like her mum had taught her to cook when she was two parts of nothing. Old customers came back, and newcomers enlisted.

Bess got on well with the new landlord. He wasn't at all the sort you'd expect to be a publican. He went about things in a quiet but determined way. Didn't drink much, either, joking that he'd had quite enough the first day they'd met, blaming the whisky she'd given him for his deciding to take the Wedded Stoat on. Bess saw herself as a boatswain's mate, waiting and willing at his side.

'Never thought I'd see this place come back to life,' she said. 'You're the brewery's golden boy.'

He was drawing a pint, smiled, didn't answer. He rang the till and looked up at the clock. It had been a tiring day. Another twenty minutes and he could call time. He went through to the back to begin locking up.

'Good evening.'

Bess turned. The voice startled her, something about the edge on it. Silly to imagine, but it was as if an icy feather had fluttered down her spine. The plump, pasty-faced man wore a camel coat that bulked out an already fleshy body. He wore spectacles, through which she noticed green-freckled eyes that might have been gazing up from a neglected pond.

'Mine host not about?'

'Not at the moment,' said Bess. 'It's near closing. What can I get you?'

He asked for half a pint of ale, but not for one moment did he look directly at her. She was certain he wasn't local. It was a warm evening for the time of year, but a woollen scarf was tucked in at the neck of his coat, and he carried woollen gloves. Perhaps he had left home early that morning when the day was colder.

'Cheers,' he said, almost to himself as he looked around the room and wiped his mouth with the back of his hand. 'Nice place.' His cheeks were puffy, his eyes dredging up deep from the watery depths.

'We like it,' said Bess.

'Yes. Old-ee world, isn't that what they call it?' His teeth were on show then, too big for his mouth. 'Classy.' He took another swig and said 'Have one for yourself.'

Bess thanked him but declined. Jen had been sitting with a friend in the snug for an hour or more when she came through to where Bess was serving and ordered two more Babychams.

'You must be celebrating!' said Bess.

'Well, two old school friends,' said Jen. 'We haven't seen each other for years, so it's nice to catch up. This place has improved, hasn't it?'

'New landlord,' said Bess.

'Oh!' said Jen. 'Is that a twinkle in your eye?'

As if on cue, John appeared with a bar towel in his hand. Bess tipped her eyes in his direction and smiled at Jen. 'See for yourself.' Jen looked towards John for a moment, lifted her eyebrows in understanding to Bess, and went back to the snug to be with her friend.

'Landlord about?' shouted Camel Coat.

'John ... Gentleman to see you.'

Bess was relieved to break away to another customer. John had come back to the bar to call 'Drink up, ladies and gentlemen'.

He seemed to stop for a moment, as if taking a look about and then catching sight of Camel Coat. Bess was serving the last round when she saw John cross over to where the latecomer was sitting, at the further end of the room. Camel Coat stood when John approached him, but they didn't shake hands before they both sat and began talking. Bess took an unexpected pleasure in going over to collect Camel Coat's tankard.

'Could you drink up, sir?' she said. Icicles might have been forming at the windows. 'We're just closing.'

'Well,' said Camel Coat, taking the hint, putting on his gloves and using all his teeth again, 'mustn't hang about, eh? I'll drop in again, Jack.' Opening the door into the street he turned at the last moment and called 'G'night, all.'

When the pub had emptied and Bess had emptied the ashtrays, washed up and tidied the room, she wheeled her bicycle to the front of the pub. Jen and her friend were standing in the road. John came out from the pub and looked up at the stars, clearly set against an ink-black sky. Jen gave her friend a goodnight kiss before walking from her in the opposite direction. John was smoking a cigarette, and waved to Bess as she set off home. Hoping the feeble beam of the lamppost was keeping her invisible, Jen turned back towards where John Scott was standing. He had an expression on his face she couldn't fathom. She thought it might be a trick of the light. Shivering, she pulled her coat closer around her shoulders and walked away to where the light from the lampposts weakened.

'*It* was called *Free as Air*,' Albania explained. 'A musical.'

'Good God. What on earth possessed you? I abhor musical comedies,' said Hector. 'The haunt of the homosexual.'

'What on earth do you mean by that?' asked Albania. 'Really, Hector, you have the most extraordinary views about life.'

'As if anyone in reality breaks out into preposterous song at the least provocation. That you should have wasted your money on such nonsense!'

'I rather enjoyed it. The story was quite appropriate as it turned out, as if they'd written it especially for me, as if they'd known I was coming.'

'What are you talking about?'

'It was all about being content with what you've got, the free air, letting the grass grow under your feet, getting away from the wicked world, not worrying about what may be or what tomorrow will bring.'

'Its attitude strikes me as utterly irresponsible. Sentimental claptrap for silly women and nancy boys. You seem to exist in a world of make-believe, Albania. You can have no idea of how wicked was the world I inhabited. I could never have pretended that life is a musical comedy. Yours apparently verges on the creed of that Frenchified fop Voltaire.'

'What are *you* talking about?'

'Voltaire's philosophy. The belief that the only thing that matters is chopping your wood and making your garden grow.'

'In that case I think I might like Voltaire.'

She eased off her shoes, aware that a blister was starting. The room seemed stale after the bustle of the theatre and railway station, and a deep, sullen silence yawned. Hector folded the newspaper he had almost been reading.

'Do you very much mind being alone, Albania?'

She looked up. It was an unusual enquiry, coming from her brother, who had never shown the slightest interest in what her feelings might be.

'Do *you?*' she asked, hoping to avoid an answer.

'When I was judging ...' he began, and Albania had a sudden image of what else he might have judged had he not elected to do it in a courtroom: geraniums at a local flower show, mince pies at a W.I., or a line of young women, each hoping to be crowned a Beauty Queen, at a minor seaside resort. As things had turned out, her brother's judgements had had rather more devastating results for the individuals concerned.

'When I was on the bench,' he continued, 'I was not so aware of having nobody – what is that dreadful phrase I have lately heard? – "in my life".'

'Even as a child, you had no friends.'

'There were chums at prep school, and later at Cambridge.'

'Chums? What a vocabulary you have. But nobody ever came to play, did they? Our childhoods were tidy. We grew up thinking the world around us was just as controllable, that everything had its proper place. Emotions were something that bothered other people, in a place from which you and I were excluded. I can't recall mother or father ever suggesting that life might be an adventure.'

'I blame Noël Coward for the moral slackening. Musicals, indeed. A playground for inverts.'

'Oh, dear, more of your homosexuals! You are ludicrous, Hector. You see a man in a silk dressing gown and put the wrongs of the world on his shoulders. I sometimes wonder if you ever had any understanding of how the world goes round. You learned of justice from books, you stayed in chambers when you should have roamed through woods. You distrusted the plaintiffs, had implicit belief in anything the police said, noted every fine legal point made by barristers, and took a glass of sherry before putting on your wig. Perhaps two glasses if you were about to don that appalling black cap. In what way were you equipped to understand ordinary people? I'm not sure you have ever exposed yourself to the common herd. It frightens me to think of the moral predicaments you were constantly faced with. Doesn't it make you wonder? There must have been occasions when you doubted the decision of a jury, when you were convinced that they were wrong. And then there was nothing you could do, was there, but to reach out for that frightful cap? Doesn't any of that torture you now?'

'You know nothing of the processes involved. Your comments are unfounded.'

'And should no doubt be struck from the record,' she said.

She hadn't meant to upset him. They had never quarrelled, even in childhood, when she had disliked him more than she disliked him in old age. In later life she never felt close enough to him to make any remark that might be construed as personal or critical. For his part, he had thought much about his sister and her marriage to a dull man, and how she had buried herself in the country when she might have played a greater part in his own life and made something of the talents he knew she possessed. But he remained silent.

'I'm sorry,' she said, and meant it.

'Don't you suppose that I have considered such things? I have pondered them deeply at times. Meanwhile, Albania, I will not persist in asking if you, too, feel alone. As a matter of fact, I had made up my mind to ask … to make you a proposition.'

'What's that?' she asked, feeling the distance between them widen again.

'You must know how alone I am. You clearly understand that. I have always considered you a person of some feeling. And

I think you too may feel alone, Albania. This house,' and his gaze took in the whole place in a movement of his head that seemed to his sister to encompass the thickening dust, the cobwebs, the unsteady mounds of books, the dead flowers, the cushions that had long ago lost the oomph of their stuffing, '… this house is getting too much for you.' He gave the sort of smile she imagined a doctor would one day produce when delivering fatal news. 'Have you considered that we might pool our resources?'

'What?'

'It would be a simple matter. A merging, with two possible solutions, either of which I am prepared to discuss. You come to live with me at Braithwaite Mansions, or I come here to live with you.'

Albania felt her stomach dip, the earth slipping beneath her feet.

'And what is your verdict?' she asked.

On Tuesdays, after closing the post office, it was Miss Simms' routine to visit her elderly mother, whom nobody in Branlingham had set eyes on in years. Miss Simms gave the impression that this ancient dame was in the pink of health, sustained by her daughter's weekly egg custards, delivered, by hand and on foot, in a pyrex dish.

Her route took Miss Simms past the Wedded Stoat. Being Gospel Hall, she had never been inside it. She averted her eyes as she approached, but drawing closer she heard voices that floated from the side of the building. Carefully balancing her dish, and checking that she was unobserved, she turned the corner into a concealing spot in the shade of a burgeoning tree. The voices were clearer now, and she had a direct line of vision through an open window.

Of course, she knew the new landlord by sight. There was Mr Scott now, sitting with his back to her in a Windsor chair. Crouched beside him was the common woman, the one who called herself Jen. Miss Simms' eyes widened in disbelief. The woman looked up at the landlord, slowly lifted her arm and, with enormous slowness and care, brushed a strand of hair from his forehead. She was smiling up at him. Miss Simms recognised it at once. It was the smile of a Jezebel.

'I forgive you,' said the woman.

It sounded to Miss Simms as if the landlord was quietly crying.

'How can you?' he croaked. 'I can't forgive myself. How could I expect you …?'

Miss Simms wished he didn't mumble so. Her egg custard quivered. That might have been the end of the drama, but an even more shocking development rooted her to the spot. The woman was gently pulling down the man's head and lifting her mouth to his. She kissed him full on the lips. Fearing that her mother's gift might curdle, Miss Simms turned tail and fled. Within a few hours, most of the village had heard that Branlingham's merry widow was having a torrid relationship with the new publican at the Wedded Stoat. Miss Simms had seen it with her own eyes.

Francis' first thought was that it reminded him of the picture Uncle Peter had so much admired, Edward Poynter's painting of Venus rewarding Aesculapius' kindness with a kiss; the kiss of Venus. But what had Miss Simms heard about forgiveness? What possible reason could there be for Jen to forgive the landlord of the Wedded Stoat?

*

Hector noticed the worsening tremor in his hand as he placed the glass of water on his bedside table. He and Albania had said their goodnights pleasantly, but he had been shocked by her outburst. In the charged atmosphere of the courtroom, there were countless occasions when tempers frayed, and things said that were better unsaid. ('That is an intolerable remark, and Counsel for the Prosecution will refrain from making such statements. I shall instruct that it be struck from the record of the court.') As judge, of course his own remarks had never been questioned, except no doubt by the more ignorant segments of the general public or those he sent down, of whom he knew little and cared less. But was Albania so naïve as to imagine that in the recesses of night he never doubted himself?

He could not confess it. More than once in that long career his heart had lurched when a jury returned a verdict that came as a surprise – no, more than that – a shock. At such moments, and they had been more frequent than anyone imagined, he became, merely and utterly, the powerless vessel through which justice worked. The innocent pronounced guilty, the guilty declared innocent: he had seen it all, and could do nothing either way.

He never forgot those unfortunates. There had been the case of Anthony Brett, as cold-blooded a villain as ever stood before him, whom he was obliged to send from the court a free man. Hector had never forgotten Brett's horrible smirk when the jury found him 'Not guilty'. The evidence should surely have directed him to the gallows. On the other side, what of Bernard Hopkirk, his blameless life ruined by being found guilty of a murder of which Judge Postgate was convinced he was innocent. For all he knew, Hopkirk was still rotting in hell, robbed of his liberty and ultimately his life by the conniving of the prosecution and the susceptibility of the jury. Then, there had been what the gutter press named 'The Camberwell Poisoning'.

It must have been fifteen or sixteen years ago. There was nothing particularly remarkable about the characters involved, beyond the fact that they were of the sordid type. It was no more or less disgusting a matter than many he had presided over. The victim was a Betts ... Charles Betts, or was it Harold? An insignificant, ill-educated creature if the opinions of those known to him were to be believed. The accused was his wife ... not a Myrtle or a Rose, but something leaning in that direction ... the name he couldn't recall, but Mrs Betts' face came now and again into a foggy focus before once again fading away. Both the Betts were in service, he a gardener-cum-handyman, she a housekeeper, at one of the grander houses in a leafier part of Camberwell. Much of the court proceeding had been tedious. Judge Postgate rarely got through a trial without awakening a juror who had dozed off. This sometimes occurred during nit-picking over medical evidence, which Hector considered unentertaining and invariably overrated. The Betts trial was particularly trying, with conflicting forensic reports on which nobody reached agreement.

Hector had made every attempt to make sense of the fine points around the victim's death, most unusually caused by hederin poisoning. In the evenings, he consulted transcriptions of old cases and medical texts, but nothing clarified his perception of what had happened, although the bare facts were easily grasped. On the day of his death, Betts had been cutting hedges for his employer. Throughout the day his wife brought cups of tea and, when the work was done, leant a hand sweeping up the debris. In the early hours of the next morning,

Betts complained of burning in the throat and was taken to the local infirmary, where he later died in agony.

There was never a doubt as to his wife's guilt. It was the old tale of unfaithfulness. Betts was a brutish husband. The defence pointed to marks on his wife's body that, weeks after his death, were proof of his ill-treatment. Trapped in an unhappy and violent marriage, Mrs Betts, twenty years younger than her husband, had turned to an eighteen-year-old groom, a fellow-employee, for consolation. In court, letters written to her teenage lover described her troubled and sexually excited state of mind. Hector had watched the jurors as the correspondence was read out; their faces, though blank, made no secret of their contempt for the loose conduct of the woman in the dock. In one devastating passage, she wrote that she would do anything that would propel her into her lover's supple arms. Much depended on whether the jury could be convinced that the unfortunate woman had deliberately and with malice aforethought planned to rid herself of her coarse husband. Could it be (the defence argued) that his death had been no more than a tragic accident, for which his wife was in no way responsible? How could any court of law (argued the prosecution) conclude anything other than that the sole intent of this adulterous woman was to murder the man to whom she had been unfaithful, so that she might sleep illicitly beside her adolescent Romeo?

Names, faces, verdicts, sentences crept through the cluttered passages of Judge Postgate's mind. In this case, of course, there had been no doubt. He had been unsurprised when the jury returned to the court barely twenty minutes after retiring. Guilty, as he had assumed. Judge Postgate discharged them in his usually condescending manner, as if assuring them that, despite being persons of no significance, they had made the correct decision. Not, of course, before he had passed sentence on the wretched defendant.

It was inevitable that he should feel a natural repugnance that a woman should be sent to the scaffold, but the three-cornered black cap was placed on his head.

'Ivy Veronica Betts …'

Camel Coat became a regular at The Wedded Stoat. His visits were short, and usually around closing time. He'd look around and say 'Jack about?'

John Scott got to disappearing as the evening went on, but Camel Coat couldn't be avoided. Bess noticed John's face when he caught sight of the man each night, a mixture of disappointment and fright. On one occasion John was distant and cool. He'd no sooner come into the bar to help speed the last customers home before Camel Coat beckoned.

'Jack! Another one in here.'

Without speaking, John fulfilled the order, taking the glass into the snug where Camel Coat was waiting. Tonight, he sat alongside him. Bess kept an eye out. It wasn't what landlords generally did. It wasn't etiquette, and she knew the other customers wouldn't like it. She was irritated that John had left her to cope alone: the pub was still busy half an hour off closing. Between serving drinks, she looked into the snug through the hatch that connected it to the public, and listened. John was sat in front of the shove halfpenny board with Camel Coat at his side. She heard him say 'There's a better game than this, Jack' and, laughing, he pulled a pencil from his breast pocket. When someone called for service, she went back to the pumps.

The two men must have stayed in the snug for a good half hour, until Camel Coat came back into the public, ordered a brandy and soda and lit up a Craven A. He got into a muddle with paying, foraging in his pockets. Bess noticed how much he sweated, and when his fingers touched her hand she hated their plump clamminess, as if she'd fondled a juicy slug. After a bit, John came back from the snug, passing Camel Coat sitting at the bar. Camel Coat almost grabbed his arm as he passed.

'Already looking forward to a drop tomorrow, Jack,' said Camel Coat, lifting his glass in salute.

The last customer gone, Bess was tidying up for the night when she saw the train ticket under the stool where Camel Coat had perched. London to Norwich, Second Class. Kicked almost out of sight was a scrap of paper. She picked it up, unscrunched it to reveal a pencil drawing. It looked like an insect upside down on a coat hanger. Turning it over, she saw a list of place names and dates. None of it meant anything to her. She screwed it up into a ball, throwing it and the train ticket into the waste-paper basket.

It was a starry night, calm and balmy. A breeze tickled the air with the soft zest of a South Sea island against a sky that might have been tropical. Bess decided to walk home rather than use the bicycle. She called her goodbye up the stairs to John, but there was no answer. She strolled back into the darkened bar and called again, but there was no answer. On her way out, she brushed against the waste-paper basket. She straightened it where it had toppled over. The scrap of paper she had screwed up earlier had fallen out. She picked it up now, keeping it in her hand rather than replacing it in the basket. Something about the drawing, that upside-down insect, reminded her of something or other. Goodness knew what the list of dates and places meant. If she called at Red Cherry House she might take the paper to Francis Jones. People said the boy was bright, and could explain the inexplicable. It might be worth a try, although Bess couldn't think why. Perhaps it was the feeling that something at the Wedded Stoat wasn't right. That was it; something wasn't *right*. She snuggled into the fake fur of her coat collar. A few yards from the pub and she was at the edge of the wood. The moon had joined forces with the stars to make the night magical. The path ahead was scattered in silver light that showed the way home.

Albania surprised herself by making up her mind so definitely. It was unthinkable that she would leave the house where she had lived for almost fifty years to move in with her brother. She didn't like the unfriendliness of London or the airless grandeur of Braithwaite Mansions, and wasn't sure that she liked Hector, certainly not enough to give her life over to his. That would be the way of it. Within a few weeks she would be no more than unpaid housekeeper. It was an unkind thought. Age had treated her more kindly than it had treated her brother. He forgot, he muddled, he dozed and went in and out of dreams filled with long-redecorated courtrooms, forgotten trials, mis-remembered verdicts. She would tell him at once. As soon as the work was completed on his apartments, he must return home. Alone.

It was an unpleasant duty, but she owed it to herself as much as to her brother. He was sitting in the garden, his legs splayed in a deckchair that had never looked more rigid and unyielding. To her surprise, he seemed disinterested in what she had to say, as if the dilemma had never been mentioned, and smiled gently at her, as if he'd not understood what she was saying. Gazing down at him, his face drawn close in the afternoon sun, she felt a pang of something that surprised her. It was, possibly, affection, and more than a little sorrow at how their lives had come to this pass. In her bedroom, she buried her head in the ice-cream chill of the satin eiderdown.

Hector Postgate dreamed on, of childhood, of Albania calling to him across the sands at Worthing, her words crashed across the waves that were working up a storm. He couldn't make out what she was saying, only aware how eager she was to have him by her side, a brother and protector. A steamroller driven by a fork-tongued beast was hurtling towards where Albania waited, crying for help, at the edge of the sea, when he awoke, steadying himself with his hands at the edges of the deckchair for fear of falling under the steamroller. The sharpness of the sun blinded him for a moment, until he looked around at his sister's garden and the woman standing across the patio.

Jen lifted her face, making a sunshield of her hands. It must have been a trick of the light, but for a moment Hector Postgate was transformed into a younger man. How handsome he must once have been.

'I thought,' he said, letting the mumble go. 'A lovely morning.'

'Yes,' said Jen. 'Perfect.'

He saw what she must mean: she was on her knees at a flower bed, forking the soil and tenderly setting aside young plants ready for putting out.

'I do not think my sister could manage so well without you. There is a difference between a house and a home. She tells me you have a way with plants. It is a knack, that way with nature. Green fingers. Such a strange expression, but apt, as if in being so much in contact with plant life, our very bodies turn to the green. My fingers are not, never have been, green. They are white. My hands are very white. I sometimes wish they were otherwise, that I had been closer to things that naturally belong to the earth.'

'It's not too late to start,' said Jen. 'Such things are a solace to the most unexpected of people. People say they lose themselves in a garden.'

'Hampton Court maze.'

'I think they mean that they forget the other things, the things they most need to forget. Plants have been a solace to me,' said Jen. 'I was much alone once.'

'Beyond a window-box, there is not much evidence of nature at work at Braithwaite Mansions. I return there as soon as is convenient. It is for the best. I have been uncertain where I belong.'

'I understand.'

'Yes,' he said, looking at her, her face half shadowed where the straw hat lapped her hair. 'I believe you do.'

The pause fell between them like a wall, beyond which each waited expectantly for something that would change everything. Jen thought she heard the old man's heart beating, a gentle pulse and occasionally a soft thud as it coursed its way through his body. Hector heard himself sucking air into tired lungs, but all the time listening for the breath of the woman stooped to the ground before him, her eyes fixed on him as if imploring him to be the first to speak.

'Your name is not that of a flower. Not a flower,' he said at last, and stood.

'No, not a flower,' said Jen.

'I was telling my sister that many such came before me when I was sitting. Roses, Myrtles, ladies of the night. Mayfair

Lily. I wonder where she is now. She always winked at me, you know, after I had fined her or sent her to cool her heels for a few weeks in Holloway. Perhaps I would have liked Mayfair Lily had we met in a different world. She had a kind face. She must have retired long ago.' He lifted his chin higher, as if to get a better look at the sky. 'You are not one of those.'

'No. I was much traduced, but never that.'

'What then?'

'Can you have forgotten me? I have never forgotten you. If I were a delicate soul, your not remembering me would have robbed me of my last dignity. How unfair, that you should have been the cause of so much of my unhappiness, but have probably never given me another thought. I believe you *have* forgotten me. It's almost funny.'

His shoulders snapped his head up and his body seemed to crumple deeper where he sat.

'I knew there was something,' he said. 'I knew from the first, but I couldn't remember where or when.'

'At least in your book of reminiscences you mentioned the case. Not my name, of course. It was the only case of hederin poisoning you encountered. It hasn't featured much in chronicles of murder. You made quite a thing of it. I always suspected that the facts meant much more to you than did the lives of the people involved.'

He looked down at Jen, his eyes full of the last shreds of doubt, and said 'Of course! Ivy Betts.'

'Yes. Ivy Betts. I don't wonder that you didn't recognise me. Naturally, I have had to change myself. Sixteen years ago you sentenced me to death for the murder of my husband. Charlie died from hederin poisoning. How you all scratched your heads over that. There was no doubt that he had digested the dust from ivy, in sufficient quantities for it to cause his death. We had been working in the garden of our employer all day, pulling the ivy from the walls, wrenching it away from the carpet it created wherever it clung. The air was turgid with ivy dust. The prosecution argued that I had administered the poisoned ivy to Charlie either in the form of a drink or mixed into the food I prepared for his lunch. My defence argued that he had simply ingested the dust throughout the day. The cumulative effect killed him.'

'But the evidence … don't I recall that there was a clear motive? Letters read in court … The jury looking disapprovingly towards you as the words were read out … Words of such passion … a young groom that took you as his lover …'

'No. You have that the wrong way round, judge. It was I that took him. Bobby. Dear, darling Bobby. They heard what they wanted to hear. Charlie was a cruel husband. Bobby was younger than me, and I thought, "That's wrong, that's not how it should be." They wanted to believe the worst of me, that I was an immoral woman who should hang her head in shame, but I knew that wasn't the truth. I adored Bobby. I worshipped him. And he adored and worshipped me. My soul, my body. I've had rapture that you couldn't begin to conceive of, enough to flood my senses for ever.'

'Have you no shame? Still, all the years after, no shame?'

'I shuffled shame off because I knew it to be false.'

'But the evidence,' said Postgate, almost murmuring. 'The jury … the judge can only act in accordance …'

'The court was so still. I think in the middle of the most vast desert there could have been no more stillness. You wore the black cap and passed sentence on me, and the air stopped.'

'But I remember,' he pleaded, as if in distress. 'You were reprieved.'

'Was I? In a way, yes. I escaped the hangman's noose, but not the prison cell. The shadows of it were there for me to hide myself in. You didn't mention them, in your book.'

'It was an interesting case, an unusual case, and of course I knew that you had been reprieved. The Home Secretary …'

'Reprieved, yes, but not spared. It was the very last moment, you know. They took me from the cell that morning, the parson ready with his book, expecting me to believe in a god whose existence I had long ago denied. The walls of my cell fell away … they only pulled the wardrobe concealing the door to the execution shed to one side. Of course, by then, the hangman was standing with me. I looked into his eyes. Very briefly, oh so briefly … the merest seconds, and I could hear life already choking in my head.'

'Dear God. Dear God.'

Jen stood, brushing earth back to where it belonged, and faced him.

'You have forgotten me, judge, but I have never forgotten your face, just as I never forgot the face of my executioner. Strange, but I've seen him, too. Seen both of you, stood before each of you as if nothing mattered, as if we might mean nothing out of the ordinary to one another. In a way, it's made me wonder if there might, after all, be a god, one god. God. God, bringing the three of us to this place.'

'But you were saved. Thank God for that.'

'It was very last minute, and no thanks to you. A few seconds more, and it would have been of no use to me.'

Jen smiled at him. The hawk-like twist of his face had gone, perhaps lost years before. She saw an old man, almost unaware of what was happening, uninterested in the fact that her young lover had himself died from natural causes a few weeks after the birth of their only son.

'I am happy here,' she said. 'Happier than I've ever been. My lovely son ... Jimmy has the eyes of Bobby, and the smile that Bobby kept for Sundays. And your sister needs me here. The garden is chalk, you see. It must be respected, and tamed. With care, it will prosper. The prison governor at Holloway looked kindly on me. I don't suppose you ever came across her, although you must have sent many people her way. We liked to speak together of plants, of what might grow in the prison yard, heavily chalked as it was. Understandably, not many plants were enthusiastic about being there, but I found, with persistence and time, and goodness knows I had enough of that ... She brought me a book she had been given as a prize at school. *The Garden of Ignorance* by Mrs George Cran became my constant companion, and Mrs Cran knew exactly what would grow in chalk. Wallflowers and snapdragons ...'

'Oh, dear God.'

'.... phlox and Canterbury bells.'

'Oh, merciful God.'

'.. geraniums ...'

He had taken her wrist in his hand, his grip firm but not frightening.

'Forgive me, he whispered.

'Forgiveness,' said Francis. 'That's the key to it. When Jen went into the Wedded Stoat she recognised John Scott at once. How could she not? He had stood before her at the moment she faced death. He was the executioner about to end her life on earth. Isn't it inevitable that his face would stay with her for ever?'

'It's horrible,' said Gordon.

'It's the law,' replied Francis, 'and will continue to be so until humanity prevails.'

'More to the point, how do you know all this? It's not as if we were personally involved in any of it.'

'Jen's son is in my class at school. He often needed a shoulder, if not to cry on, to spill on. I happened to be walking behind Miss Simms on the day she saw John Scott and Jen kissing in the Wedded Stoat. When she hid behind that tree, I simply hid behind the one behind her. The view was quite good. I was walking through the village that night when Bess and Jen came out of the Wedded Stoat and John Scott stood at the door. They didn't see me, it was a dark sky. It taught me to look carefully at faces, especially when they're not talking. Then, there was the man in the camel coat ... I knew there was something, but I didn't know what. There was a sense that a moment had been reached, when the past would meet up with the present, when the elements of Jen's life came together in the most extraordinary way.'

'But how did John Scott become a hangman? Why would anyone *want* to be a hangman?'

'It's an ancient office, and a repulsive one. You must ask the question of John Scott himself, but I'm not sure you'll get a satisfactory answer. His grandfather and father were hangmen before him. It is not unusual for the trade to pass down from generation to generation.'

'What a ghastly inheritance!'

'I think John Scott was essentially an unhappy man, a man saddled with a secret that no one would want exposed. For a time, it seemed as if his marriage would break the links, bring him the contentment he longed for, but it didn't work out. He was disappointed with life. And disillusion can lead into dangerous waters. Knowing his parentage and the family's history, the Home Office approached him, enticing him back into the family business. With his family's past at his coat tails, the poor chap was easy prey. It was only when his marriage to Pat finally collapsed that he realised he had had enough of the execution shed. He wanted a new life. And needed to forget the old.'

'Of course. As the landlord of a pub in a remote Norfolk village where nobody would know who he was or what he'd been.'

'Yes, but he hadn't reckoned on the man in the camel coat.'

'What was all that about?' asked Gordon.

'I think he may have been an old associate of Mr Scott's. He knew what his life had been before he became a publican, so he tried one of the nastiest tricks imaginable.'

'Blackmail!' exclaimed Gordon.

'Yes. If John Scott wouldn't pay up, he'd expose him.'

'But how did you work that out?'

'The piece of paper that Bess found after Camel Coat had left the pub one night. She'd seen him and John Scott playing some sort of game on paper. On one side there was what looked like an upside-down insect. When she brought the paper to me, I simply turned the paper the other way round and immediately saw how sinister this affair might be … She might easily have seen it herself; she just hadn't turned the paper round! I saw that it was a body hanging from a gallows. They had been playing Hangman! It was another example of Camel Coat's callousness. On the reverse side of the paper was a list of cities and dates, with one line that had been crossed out.'

'So?'

'That's where I have to thank Uncle Peter's collection. He's wonderfully liberal. He's done all he can to influence an abolition of the death penalty. Two years ago his interest reached a fever pitch with the case of Ruth Ellis. The public recoiled at the idea of a woman being hanged in Britain in the middle of the twentieth century. And I recognised the date of her execution on Camel Coat's piece of paper. He'd crossed out that date because he'd realised that it was one occasion when John Scott hadn't been involved.'

'Have you confronted Camel Coat about all this?'

'I have. He decided that it might be more sensible to fade from the picture rather than have his activities reported to Inspector Slaughter or Sergeant Cudd.'

'… and the other dates?'

'I checked Uncle Peter's notebooks. He'd kept a list of executions and notes of the prisons where they were carried out. That alerted me to what Camel Coat might be doing, and the fact that John Scott had told Bess that one of the reasons his marriage had broken up was that he sometimes went away for a couple of days. His wife was convinced he was having an affair.'

'Anything else?'

'Bess told me the remarks Camel Coat came out with. "Tell John I'll be dropping in again" or "I just came in for a drop" or "No point hanging about if John isn't here."'

'Of course! Amazing how the evidence mounts up!' exclaimed Gordon.

'And he used to call John Scott "Jack".'

'Nothing so unusual about that, surely?'

'Except that Jack is a generic name for a hangman. Jack Ketch worked as executioner to Charles II.'

'It all sort of adds up in a horrible way. What will happen now?'

'Nothing much,' said Francis. He fell into the sofa and took up the Penguin paperback of Raymond Postgate's *Verdict of Twelve*. 'The usual, I expect. Some people's lives will go on a little better, and some a little worse. I expect that Bess's name will join John Scott's above the door of The Wedded Stoat. Jen will probably decide to take up Mrs Timson's offer and move in with her, especially now that her brother has gone back to London. He told one of the porters at the railway station that he was saying his goodbye to Norfolk. His sister was there to see him off, apparently. They were hugging one another on the platform, and the old boy almost missed the train. And now, if you don't mind, I'd like to get on with a *real* mystery.'

'Just one thing more,' said Gordon. '*Did she do it?*'

'Did who do what?'

'Ivy Betts, of course. Did she murder her husband?'

Francis wearily closed his Penguin.

'I tell you why I ask, Francis. *Ivy* Betts. It's weird, I know, but it's the name that worries me. The case was about hederin poisoning, wasn't it? Hederin poisoning, caused by the digestion of ivy.'

'So?'

'So, did those facts about hederin poisoning – a very rare thing – come to her because she was called Ivy, or is it just coincidence that someone called Ivy should be accused of ivy poisoning?'

'Please to remember that the someone called Ivy Betts is now Jen. Jen Bagnold.'

Francis gave a deep sigh, closed his eyes and gave Gordon one last look of exasperation.

'Be content that we've answers enough, Gordon. Perhaps we've learned something about forgiveness, too. Just as Jen forgave John Scott for what he might have done and forgiven Judge Postgate, others have forgiven what some might think unforgivable. Remember, Anne Boleyn forgave her executioner on the scaffold. And if nothing else, we've learned that coincidence may play its part in any mystery. Has it occurred to you that the judge in this case is *Judge* Postgate, and that the book I have been attempting to read is by *Raymond* Postgate? That is what you call a coincidence. And now, if you wouldn't mind shutting up, I will discover whether coincidence plays any part in Mr Postgate's latest detective novel.'

Happy Bunny

Ferruick does itself no favours by not adding by-the-Sea to its title. Motorists passing through Cornwall from one beauty spot to another avoid the little coastal settlement only by half a mile when they might have been tempted by a more alluring signpost. Those adventurous enough to turn off the main thoroughfare are surprised when the by-road takes an upward curve and the sea, a rolling blue brilliance on a good summer day, comes into view. There is no betwixt or between about the sea at Ferruick; it is either in or out. The harbour wall lets it know how far it can go.

The once grand promenade is nothing to write home about now. Sculpture-like, a few time-spattered cars reside permanently in the rutted cliff-top car-park, seagulls circling above like watchful traffic wardens. There's a flyblown teashop with grimy windows along 'Olde English' lines, a wool shop with faded bundles of pastel colours on display and patterns that went out of fashion before the war, interspersed with shoelaces and prices for key-cutting, a Bingo Hall with associated amusements, and a public information kiosk (closed). There's a red-bricked shelter declared open by a local alderman in Edwardian days, and a church intended as Perpendicular but now United Reformed. There's the Peter Pan

Kiddy Arcade, incongruously close to the three or four fine old houses that remain from a more genteel age … and, the most recent addition, a milk bar.

On a chilly morning in April, casual visitors may peer into the Olde English Tea Rooms as hard as they may but there is no trace of life. The welcoming words in the window, '*FROTHY COFFEE now available*', strike an ingenuous note. There is no such reticence about the milk bar, even now, just gone ten o'clock. The shiny façade exudes light and confidence, and loud music from a jukebox, and just so there is no mistake about it, a neon sign confirming that this is a 'Milk Bar'.

Janice looks forward to the first customer of the day. Since Mr Baldry trained her, she's the one who starts the place up as Ferruick wakes. She unlocks the door, switches on the lights, wipes the scarlet plastic-topped stools, props the menus on the formica tables. It's a routine, just like the one she had when she'd worked at Morthingtons, but the difference here is the customers. All sorts, really, the only thing they have in common (obviously) being that they like milk.

Not that she hadn't liked working at Morthingtons. She'd been lucky to be taken on there. In the Home, they'd scratched their heads as to what she might do when it was time for her to leave. Janice had not worried half as much, just walked into the laundry yard and asked if there were any jobs going. The works manager, Mr Clerkson, took her on a month's appro, but after the four weeks was up no-one mentioned anything about her leaving, so she'd stayed. Young Mr Morthington (not the Mr Morthington who'd started the firm, because he was dead and buried long ago, nor the original Mr Morthington's son, also deceased), smiled at her if he caught her eye across the floor, but Janice could sometimes have done without the other girls. Break times were the hardest. The canteen made her uncomfortable in more senses than one. During working hours she was standing so it didn't matter, but in the canteen the tables and chairs were bolted to the floor, as if the management suspected someone might make off with them, and the gaps were so narrow she struggled getting in and out of them. She heard the giggles on her first morning, not that she wasn't used to them, on the bus, in the shops, in the hairdressing salon where the steel arms of the seats clamped around her and some of her spilled out beyond the padding. She saw the eyes swivel and heard the disguised whispering when people thought she wasn't aware. That was when she realised how safe she'd felt in the Home, where the outside world was something you looked at through windows.

Of course, even at the milk bar there were days she wondered why she bothered about the polishing and the sweeping into the corners. People came and went, but even when they didn't come she thought how lucky she was, sometimes the luckiest of all when the place went quiet as a tomb. At Morthingtons there was always the chatter above the machinery and the other people who might spoil her day. She still missed Danny, though. He'd spoken to her the day she started at the laundry, asked her name, said something about the weather and the cardigan she was wearing that her gran had knitted especially for her. She sometimes wished she'd kept in touch with her gran. Too late now. She felt bad when she remembered that. There were bound to be things you did that you knew you shouldn't have done. And things you didn't know how to put right.

*

'It's called mucking-in,' explained Gordon. 'Also known as youth hostelling.'

'Mucking in?'

Francis injected more scorn into his voice than Gordon thought possible.

'Slave labour, more like. The facilities in this, as you insist on calling it, "youth hostel", are positively antique. We've only been here an hour and we've already peeled endless root vegetables, made our own beds, apparently constructed from planks that Captain Hook intended the Darling family to walk, endured prolonged bouts of community singing – surely one of the most ridiculous activities known to mankind – and promised not to leave gates open in the country for fear of loosing mad bulls.'

'Quite correct!' agreed Gordon cheerfully. 'And you really should wear your Youth Hostel badge, and at all times carry your Youth Hostel membership card, whose number you must memorize, and which you must produce on demand.'

'What's more, they expect you to wear shorts at every available opportunity. I mean, have you seen some of those *knees*? The whole thing's a nightmare. I've never experienced so many thistles and mosquitoes. It makes Dotheboys Hall look like the Ritz. And I absolutely refuse to join in another chorus of "Ging Gang Goolie"'.

'I do wish you'd stop moaning,' said Gordon. 'We're in the middle of the most beautiful countryside. Endless things to explore.'

'But everything's so organised,' replied Francis, fearful for his free spirit.

'We can escape whenever we like. Mr Tethers won't mind.'

Roland Tethers was one of the most sympathetic English

masters at St Basil's, at least to someone as vivid as Francis. Why on earth had Tethers been chosen to superintend this expedition? His head was full of Chaucer and Tennyson. He was the last person equipped to cope with thirty parent-free grammar school boys going native in Cornwall.

'I told him we might skip tomorrow's hike and do our own thing,' said Gordon. 'They're going down a tin mine and walking ten miles.'

'Presumably not in that order?'

'I thought we might go to Ferruick. It's a beauty spot on the coast, so there'll be birds and caves and things. There's Trethennick Wood, with a deep lake at its centre. We can cycle there in the morning. It's only half an hour away.'

Francis didn't respond. At such times it would be a sign of weakness to have him fall in so easily with his cousin's plans. But as the coach approached the hostel he had seen a placard outside a newsagent's shop that read '*Girl Missing at Ferruick*'. A morning spent there might not be a complete waste of time.

1 … 2 … 3 …

He watches. Waits and watches. How many years on the sidelines of other people's lives, alive but, unlike Molly Malone's cockles and mussels, not alive-o? Forever clinging to the shadows, on the margin of light, at a bus stop, turning into nobody of importance in a crowd, counting up to one hundred with a metronomic beat, telling himself that when he gets to one hundred he'll move on. Yes, he'll move when he's counted to one hundred.

Of course, there's always the temptation to drag the counting out. All you do is make the gaps between the numbers last longer, slow down the metronome. Change the beat, drawl out the minutes into hours. Hope that you won't have to get to one hundred before the thing you want to happen happens. Not that he minds, really.

There's always another time.

And another one hundred.

It had been the same at school, finding that solitary place behind the kitchens where nobody went, that hidden corner of the playground while the other boys kicked a football, or each other, rather than him. Sunday school was no better, despite the pious faces and simple hymns. He knew why he was there, his mother tugging at him to get a move on, away from the house and off to his grandmother. The Sunday school had nothing to do with Jesus, even if they kept on about Him wanting him for a sunbeam. His mother wanted him out of the way. On Sundays he was a parcel whose label was mislaid. He had no intention of becoming a sunbeam.

Morthingtons had been the constant in his life, listening for the hooter fog-horning through the neighbouring streets four times a day: the cockcrow ten-minute warning that workers should be setting off for the laundry, the hooter that told them it was time for lunch and, an hour later, that lunch was over, and at the end of the day came the finale of the leaving-off hooter. That meant he had to leave, and in many ways he preferred the laundry. Sometimes he felt he was in paradise with all those girls, their warm bodies close by, always smiling, cracking a joke. Sometimes they made him blush. His mother would have smacked the back of his legs if he'd repeated the stuff they came out with, so he kept it to himself.

He remembered the first girl, *that* girl, as if through clouds of steam. She'd called out to him at leaving-off time. He was late going through the gates that day. Most of the others had long gone. She was bending over her bike as if she didn't know what was best. The chain had come off. He'd always been good at fixing things. She crouched beside him as he put it right, so close that her breath, sweet and peppery, brushed his face. She was going to her auntie's for the evening. She said as how they'd have tea and listen to the radio like they always did on a Friday until she prepared the old lady a hot drink and said goodnight. The last bus left so early, so she needed the bike more on a Friday than any other day of the week. She was very grateful when he mended it. She said 'Thanks ever so'.

Thing was, he knew where her auntie lived, because he'd seen the girl the week before, wheeling her bike into the hallway. He was across the road by the time the last bus went by, so he knew she must still be there, and he'd wrapped up warm because the nights were still cold, and they'd said a frost was likely although it was April. She wouldn't be long. He knew she would appear, so he didn't mind the wait.

28 … 29 … 30 … He dragged out the counting, breathing in and out slowly, and breathing in again and breathing out, before he went on. 31 … 32 …

He didn't know what he'd say when they met. It would be too late to suggest they go for a drink together. That was all to the good. He hated the smell of pubs, the stink of the unwashed. Some vague recollection of Sunday School-administered warnings of the evils of alcohol kicked in, and anyway the pictures (not that the sort they showed nowadays were the sort his mother would have approved of) would be over.

She wouldn't be expecting to see him. He started up the engine when at last she came out of the house. She waved to her aunt and wheeled the bike into the street. It was five minutes past eleven. It was a scandal that the buses stopped running so early when young women needed to get home safely.

No one was about.

He let her get as far as the corner, saw her turn into the narrow street that ran parallel to Trethennick Wood. He let in the clutch and put on a little speed. The moon obligingly slid behind a cloud.

98 … 99 …

Then, he began to count another hundred …

Janice knows about it. Even if she didn't, people coming into the milk bar mention it, look over their shoulders, start whispering. She can't think what's happened to that girl, the one who'd gone missing. Only the other day a pineapple shake had started on about how careful a girl should be. Was Janice always in the shop on her own? Did she have far to go home? She should make sure to have a torch with her. Did she go back and forwards on the bus? She should keep a whistle in her handbag.

Janice hadn't said much, and nothing about catching a bus because she didn't have to. Along with the job, Mr Baldry had offered her the room above the milk bar, and since she'd come out of the Home, and after being at Morthingtons, she knew a little more about men. Some of the girls there were mucky-minded, but they didn't mean anything by it. They said Mr Baldry was up to something, imagining him climbing the stairs to her room and interfering with her.

As it happened, he'd told her he wasn't interested in women and had a policeman friend called Harry in a nearby town. Mr Baldry showed her a photograph of a man in constabulary uniform, and Janice said 'Oh, Harry does looks nice' but Mr

Baldry said 'No, that's me. Harry likes me to wear it sometimes.' So she only had the milk bar to worry about, and if the police ever asked if Mr Baldry knew anything about that missing girl – the papers said her name was Mary Shepstone – she could always tell them about Mr Baldry's friend.

'*Only* just a Victorian,' she tells people who ask, not that anyone does.

There can be no mistake when people see her in the street, standing at a bus stop, that she belongs to another age. When Harriet Braddle came into the world, plans were already laid for the imminent passing of the empire's old Queen. Sailors manning the royal yacht *Alberta* (no need to ask how it got that name) rehearsed their sovereign's final journey across the water from Osborne to Portsmouth. That mad cove, the copiously weeping Kaiser, would probably follow on in his own yacht, where the on-deck chairs probably had towels draped across them.

'You're only *just* a Victorian,' Harriet's mother would tell her years later, reviving the memory of England's squat little monarch and her bad teeth. The information was not especially useful to Harriet; it told her only what she was not, and gave no clue as to what she might become. The word 'ordinary' was often spoken, and linked with 'respectable'. Such labels were offered by her parents as the surest protection against the disappointments of the world. It was one from which Harriet would surely depart, not like the Empress of India on a gun carriage, but with ten minutes use of a Church of England vicar in a sparsely occupied crematorium where the heating was stingy.

Her parents had attained ordinariness and respectability by keeping a tobacconist and newsagent shop in a Bishopsgate backstreet. In the way of being an only daughter, Harriet left school when a child and worked behind the counter. So called, she supposed, because it was the place where money was counted and people encountered and she counted the dreary hours from morning to late night closing. The shop was seedy and smelled of thick newsprint and the foggy breath of the smokers who kept her parents in business.

When the last of them died, she shut it up, turned the key in the lock of London, and her face to the south coast. An employment agency approved her submissively ladylike demeanour by sending her for interviews with prospective employers who sought companionship. The positions she held saw her satisfactorily through many years until her latest employer, a French widow, died. Relatives, by whom this agreeable old lady had never previously been bothered, arrived as if from nowhere, without delay turning Harriet Braddle into the street. Homeless again – but had she ever really been otherwise? – she packed her suitcase and, enabled by her modest savings, treated herself to a holiday in Cornwall. Something about the name Ferruick appealed to her.

"Roselea" was a pleasant enough place to stay. More used to being the server than the served, Harriet's uneasiness came naturally, but she recognised kindness when it touched her. She relished the confinement of the third floor back, with its view over the rooftops towards the sea. Sometimes the tang of salt-air found its way inside. The smell of breakfast winding up the stairs each morning, the devilled kidneys and sunny eggs, the decorum of the dining room, exchanges about the weather with fellow guests: these refreshed her, made her slightly more of a person. She was taken aback when the landlady asked where she was planning on going at the end of her two weeks in Ferruick. Before Harriet could reply, the woman said 'You seem to like it here. It's a nice place, Ferruick. Unspoilt, even though it's changing. Can't stop change, can we?'

The next day Harriet saw the card in the post office window: 'Female Live-In Companion Wanted by Elderly Ferruick Resident. Details available at post office counter within.' It seemed the most natural thing in the world, the world, in fact, falling into Harriet's lap, a place the world had never before fallen into. The post office assistant had no doubt that here was the perfect applicant.

'Mrs Rampton-Cornett will be delighted,' she said.

A frisson of fear went through Harriet; it sounded such an uncompromising name. She instinctively felt her parents would never have considered her being associated with a hyphenated person.

'I'll telephone if you wish,' said the assistant. 'Shall I make an appointment? Fancy you just happening to be staying at "Roselea"! It's very select.'

Only then did Harriet realise that she had passed Mrs Rampton-Cornett's house each day on her way from the lodgings into town. Like Harriet, it was probably only just Victorian, a finely proportioned house, for some reason almost islanded on the promenade, flanked by the Peter Pan Kiddy Arcade. Three stories, windows gleaming, sills seagull-white, walls fresh as if a child's paintbox had just been closed up. It did, however, give nothing of itself away, like a box of chocolates with no printed guide to its contents.

The appointment was for the next day. That morning at "Roselea", Harriet helped herself to an extra devilled kidney.

*

It was 9.50 and moonlight by the time the boys wheeled their bicycles into the grounds of the hostel. Their excursion had not been entirely successful. While in the area, Francis had set himself the challenge of searching out some of Cornwall's rare species of flora.

'Cornish heather, Cornish butcher's broom, Cornish yellow wallpepper, Cornish lizard clover …'

'Cornish pasty,' said Gordon.

'At least we found the pasty. A more disgusting parcel of edibles would be difficult to imagine.'

'We should have come back hours ago. Ten minutes later and we'd be sleeping in the hedge,' said Gordon, who had studied the Youth Hostel Handbook assiduously. 'Then we'd be in hot water with Mr Tethers.'

'It looks as if someone's in hot water already,' said Francis. The Wolseley police car had spread itself ominously across the front entrance. 'Someone's probably made an official complaint about the community singing.'

'Well, what time do you call this?'

Mr Tethers wasn't quite in his pyjamas but looked as if the responsibility of keeping track of thirty boys on the loose in Cornwall had left its mark.

'You two'll be the death of me. I was about to set up a search party. Get your bikes put away and come in. You're wanted by the police.'

Once inside, Mr Tethers looked them up and down, straightened Gordon's collar and took them into the warden's office where a tall, well-dressed man in a blue serge suit was sitting, his fingers steepled as if in deep thought.

'This is Francis and Gordon, sir,' said Mr Tethers. 'Despite appearances to the contrary, they're relatively harmless. Shall I fix us some cocoa?' He gave the boys what Francis described as 'a look' and hissed 'Chief Superintendent Scott, C.I.D.' at them as he left the room. The man in the serge suit beamed.

'Nothing to worry about, lads, but I am here on official business. I've been in contact with the Norfolk constabulary who put me on to Inspector Slaughter. He told me you were on this school trip, and recommended that I have a word with you.'

Gordon's eyes almost popped out of his head.

'Inspector Slaughter *recommended* us?'

'Well, perhaps that's not quite the right word. When I mentioned your names he had a severe choking fit.'

'And turned a nasty colour too, I should think,' added Gordon.

'Constabularies are trying to cooperate with one another much more nowadays. There's a girl gone missing. Of course there's dozens who disappear every year. Most turn up safe and sound within a few hours, but this one hasn't. There's a feeling abroad that not enough's being done to find her. Her name's Mary Shepstone, aged seventeen. Last seen two weeks ago. She lived with her aunt and uncle.'

'How dreadful,' said Francis. 'Surely someone must have an idea where she is? Had she a boyfriend?'

'Apparently not. A quiet girl, by all accounts.'

Francis sighed deeply if unconvincingly. 'I don't see how this concerns us, sir.'

'I read about you two likely lads in the *Daily Sketch*.'

'Yes,' said Francis, 'I'm afraid we are occasionally mentioned in the popular press.'

'It was the Mallingering Affair, if I remember correctly. It stayed in my mind as a classic example of detective work.'

'The Mallingering Affair? I don't recall it,' said Francis with a faraway look. 'Do you recall it, Gordon?'

'Of course I do!' said Gordon, knowing that Francis remembered it perfectly well too. How irritating Francis was when he came over all Sherlock Holmes and treated Gordon as if he were Dr Watson.

'I believe the case involved the Crown Prince of Narpithiia?' said Scott.

'That's right, sir. He was abducted and kept prisoner, and attempts were made to smuggle another boy, Toby Mallingering, out of the country disguised as His Highness.'

'Of course,' said Francis. 'Now it comes back to me. My suspicions were aroused when I discovered that the Crown Prince's equerry had purchased a tin of Dark Tan Cherry Blossom Boot Polish. His Highness only ever wore black shoes, you see, patent, and the entire court always wore black shoes. For what reason would the equerry need a tin of Dark Tan? Obviously, to change the appearance of the severely anaemic Toby Mallingering so that he would pass for the dusky-skinned Crown Prince.'

'Thus solving a most puzzling case!' cried the Superintendent.

'Not to mention at the same time averting civil war in Narpithiia,' said Francis, who had no intention of not mentioning it.

'The long and short of it is that we want you boys to give us any assistance you can to discover what has happened to Mary Shepstone.'

'We're only here for two days,' said Gordon. 'Youth hostel regulations forbid any extension.'

'You needn't worry about that. Your school has been informed, and the Youth Hostel HQ has given you special dispensation to stay here as long as you wish. Naturally, we don't want to spoil your holiday. If you would rather devote yourself to your Youth Hostel expedition, and move on with the rest of your school to the next hostel as arranged, we shall perfectly understand.'

Mr Tethers returned with the cocoa. It was lukewarm, and a thick skin had formed on its surface. The lugubrious voice of the warden called 'Lights Out!' from some crevice of the building. From even deeper within came yet another mournful chorus of 'Ging Gang Goolie'.

'We shall need a few more details,' said Francis. 'And Gordon and I have absolutely no experience of missing persons cases.'

'They can be among the most distressing,' said Scott. 'It's the element of uncertainty as much as anything. There's no doubt that the first forty-eight hours are crucial. If in that time the person isn't found ... the likelihood of finding them alive and well diminishes. There will always be people who want to vanish, who simply don't want to be found. Even if we find them they can't be forced to go back to their old lives.'

'Forty eight hours,' mumbled Francis. 'And Mary Shepstone has been missing how long?'

'Two weeks,' said Scott. 'And we're no nearer finding her than we were two weeks ago.'

'Presumably you've interviewed everyone who knew her? Traced her last known movements?'

'All of that, of course. The last person known to have seen her was one of her two aunts, Mrs Roseberry. It was only after Mary was reported missing by her parents ... well, not exactly parents ... she was taken out of the Childrens' Home by another aunt and her husband ... that her bicycle was found abandoned beside the lake in Trethennick Wood.'

'And … the lake?'

'Dredged. Nothing found, thank goodness. And we've spoken to everyone that might have a clue as to what's happened, the people at the Childrens' Home, the people at the laundry where she worked, her relatives – but nothing concrete has come of any of it.'

'In fact, Mary Shepstone has vanished into thin air,' said Francis.

'Precisely.'

To her surprise, Harriet Braddle's acceptance of her plight gave way to making the best of a bad job, then to realising that others were worse off than she, and then to an unexpected contentment. Seeing her future employer's house for the first time, it had appeared grim, granite, Gothic-unwelcoming. Only later did she see how proudly it stood on Ferruick's promenade.

The days of Harriet's holiday had been cloudless, so it was unfortunate that on the morning of her interview gulls banged about in a grey sky crossed with coal-black cloud. A squall pushed in over the sea just as she left the boarding-house. The rain whipped at her woollen-stockinged legs. She arrived for the appointment feeling like Dorothy blown in from Kansas, before Technicolor began.

'It's raining' she said, dripping on the doormat. The tiny woman who looked enquiringly back at her had not answered the door since 1939, this having been one of the onerous duties of her previous companion, now called to the side of a needy relative in Broadstairs.

'Miss Braddle?' the woman asked, looking even further up at her visitor. 'Come in, do. Mind the Colonel. He juts out under the stairs.'

Harriet edged her way through the hall, looking out for an elderly be-medalled soldier. The Colonel was Mrs Rampton-Cornett's bath-chair.

'My last companion was of foreign extraction,' said Mrs Rampton-Cornett, lifting an apostle spoon as if it were a feather. 'French. You do not subscribe to the Can-Can, Miss Braddle?'

'I've never seen the Can-Can, although I have heard it disparaged. I've always imagined it might be quite fun, if a little exhausting. My tastes are quite conservative.'

'Politics need not concern us. They drive a wedge that is seldom necessary. Would you care to look at your room? It's at the top of the house. Quite comfortable, I think, although extravagance has not been encouraged. The room was exorcised in 1902, having been occupied by the mischievous spirit of an Indian mystic. I have retained his turban. I won't come up with you, Miss Braddle. My legs, you know. Do mind the Colonel. He does jut out so. I think you'll suit. That is, of course, if I suit. I find it might be so, but we must guard against life's disappointments as well as we are able. Your eyes tell me you have had many, and have survived them to reach my door.'

The room at the top of the house had all but spoken to Harriet Braddle when she walked into it. 'You must take me as I am,' it said. It was a day or two before she looked with growing pleasure at the view from the window. There, within reach, was the sea, so close that within a stretch or two of her arms it seemed she might touch it. With a turn of her head, she grew to know its mood, quiescent, disturbed, the light crusting its waves, toppling, dozy under moonlight. And the room itself, just as Mrs Rampton-Cornett had hoped, was comfortable, the sort of room that, when she walked into it, felt as if it had been waiting for her all day.

Routine kept the house and Mrs Rampton-Cornett going. It was one of Harriet's tasks to wheel her employer out each day in the Colonel, whatever the weather, along the length of the sea wall, perhaps bumping into an acquaintance of Mrs Rampton-Cornett, pausing to comment on the weather or absorb a titbit of gossip.

Harriet had time for letter-writing, mostly to a far-away niece of whom she was especially fond. There was food to be organised. To her surprise, she found that she enjoyed housekeeping duties. A daily woman came to cook and lay out the meals. After lunch, Mrs Rampton-Cornett dozed in her bedroom below Harriet's room. Above, Harriet dozed in synchronization with Mrs Rampton-Cornett below. There was no television or radio. In the evenings, Harriet read to her employer from the works of Dickens or Thackeray. It was on that first evening, after Harriet had unpacked her battered attaché case, that Mrs Rampton-Cornett said 'Your voice is surprisingly pleasant, Miss Braddle. Woody notes. You might have flourished on the stage. Your features suggest it, too.'

Few people came to the house. Old Mr Morthington was the most regular visitor. There was the doctor, with whom her employer was registered as a private patient. Henry Porter had served all the Morthingtons in his time, cradle to grave, inspecting their bodies before passing years and propriety forbad it. Another visitor was a school-friend of Mrs Rampton-Cornett's from childhood days spent in Switzerland. An elderly man came from London once a month, and stayed to lunch (fish and salad, fruit and wine). These were the only meetings during which Mrs Rampton-Cornett must not be interrupted. It was two or three years before Harriet discovered the identity of this distinguished visitor. He was collecting his hat and coat when he said 'I really believe, Miss Braddle, that you have had a great effect on Mrs Rampton-Cornett.'

Harriet looked blankly back at him.

'Since you arrived, her work has taken a new turn. Yes, quite changed course. A turn for the better, distinctly.'

She must have looked puzzled, because he paused on the threshold and said 'Her most recent work has rejuvenated her reputation.'

His eyes almost twinkled as he set his trilby on his head.

'I fancy that one of the most notable novelists of the twentieth century owes more than a little debt to *you*, Miss Braddle. Good-day.'

On the train back to London, he wondered at the fact that Mrs Rampton-Cornett's companion seemed to know nothing of her employer's place in the literary world. During his visits, he had only the faintest impression of the companion's character. Harriet could barely take in his words. Perhaps, after all, her employer's afternoons had not been spent dozing, but writing. All the time, beneath this roof, words were being pulled together, stories told, characters invented. Being a person of limited imagination, Harriet could not imagine how this might be. She somehow knew she should not mention this to her employer, that there was no need to do so, that this secret had developed naturally, and it would do no good to either to expose it.

The years passed, with routine in place as it had always been at Ferruick. Older now, Harriet liked to rest after wheeling the Colonel along the promenade. The Colonel took it out of her. Managing the house took it out of her. Reading Dickens and Thackeray took it out of her. Mrs Rampton-Cornett's school-friend from the Alps no longer visited; Harriet wondered if she had been eliminated by avalanche.

Of course, the most regular caller to the house in the early days had been old Mr Morthington, regal but alarmingly dandruffed in his nineties. He arrived for his weekly visit in a chauffeur-driven Bentley, and was Mrs Rampton-Cornett's elder brother, the man who had taken over Morthingtons from his founding father. Under his guidance, the laundry had grown to be the main source of employment for miles around.

When the second Mr Morthington died in 1953, his son Mark, the latest 'young' Mr Morthington, inherited not only the laundry but his father's weekly visit to Ferruick. Harriet thought he must be the youngest person ever to have set foot in the house, and almost certainly the handsomest. She came to welcome his arrival, putting out flowers in the rooms, and taking extra trouble with food and fresh coffee. It was a coincidence that he enjoyed the same menu (fish and salad, fresh fruit and wine) as that she always arranged for the elderly gentleman from London.

Doctor Porter came too, of course, out of necessity and the need to earn his fees, for he was now years older than most of his patients, and kept the most effective drugs for himself. He remarked on Mrs Rampton-Cornett's much improved health, her increased mobility, and there she was, proving the doctor's words by stepping out into the garden and walking out on to the promenade to take a breath of fresh sea air, as Harriet watched from her window. The Colonel spent the rest of his days under the stairs, jutting out as never before. One spring day Mrs Rampton-Cornett strode into the garden wielding secateurs, a measuring tape and seed catalogues. Harriet knew that things would never again be the same, and in this she was right: within a month Mrs Rampton-Cornett was dead. The better-class newspapers lamented the passing of the celebrated novelist Selina Rampton-Cornett.

Anna Morthington turned her perfectly made-up face to her husband, the hint of a sad smile on her lips, but one eyebrow raised as if questioning his sanity.

'Oh, Mark! Not the 28th! I'm in London for lunch at Claridges with Jasper and Delia. Can't you rearrange?'

'Rearrange? It's a funeral, for heaven's sake, not an appointment at the dentist. It won't hurt you to put yourself out just this once. It would look very odd if you weren't there.'

'What time is it? If it's morning, I suppose I might catch a later train. Funerals often over-run and then there'll be some sort of gathering, won't there? All those relatives you only see at such moments. How would it look odd?'

'I know you weren't on the closest terms with Aunt Selina, but she was my only surviving relative.'

'*Will* there be a do? It would be very difficult to get away.'

'What?'

'Afterwards. Little cocktaily things and a glass of sherry for the poor devils who've withstood the arctic temperature of St Crispin's. Perhaps you're expecting me to organise it? Much more sensible to get Losey's to do the catering, or the works' canteen. So much cheaper and I don't suppose there'll be coach-parties of mourners.'

Anna turned the pages of her diary with perfectly ivory fingers. Her husband may not have been listening; certainly, he was gazing distractedly out of the window.

'There's an express leaves at mid-day that would get me into London in time for afternoon tea.'

'Whatever you wish.'

'Or at a pinch I could cancel luncheon, leave mid-afternoon, go straight to the hotel and change for the Festival Hall concert. Where will it be?'

'On the South Bank, where it's always been.'

'No, darling. The wake!'

'At Aunt Selina's, or here, I suppose.'

'*Here?*'

She rested the diary in her lap, the afternoon sun casting the glint of a diamond solitaire. He watched the curve of her eyes as she looked around the room, still showing that smile freckled with disdain. His legs seemed not to belong to him, as if he were expecting a tidal wave. Ordinarily, he coped with the problems of the works, his loveless marriage, the absence of children, what it meant to be the last standing Morthington now that his aunt had died.

'Perhaps that would be best,' said Anna. 'No one's going to want to go to that dreary house. Triangulated sandwiches, don't you think, and individual trifles? A seed cake might be suitably Victorian. A Dickensian atmosphere would sit well with Aunt Selina. Those unreadable books she wrote were stuffed with it.'

He wasn't listening, only hearing words that didn't matter to him, but said 'Miss Braddle will miss her.'

He looked into the street again, imagining the emptiness in the old house at Ferruick, the house that had once been the family home, from where the Morthingtons had set out on life.

'I really think you'd be wiser to book a room at the Ferruick Arms, darling. It will save you so much trouble.'

Anna closed the diary, pressing its dainty pencil into its pouch.

'Do you think Robinsons could arrange an earlier slot at the crematorium? After all, it's not as if auntie's being disposed of by the Co-Op. Such a worry for you, darling. I'm sure Robinsons would co-operate. Of course, if I caught the 11.15 …'

At the window, she catches a glimpse of Clerkson, driving along the road towards the promenade. It takes him past the Baptist church, past the little wool shop that has every type of knitting needle known to woman, past the Milk Bar. As he passes, there's a plump girl lingering at its door. She goes in before he can see her face plainly, but he guesses she's still a schoolgirl. If he saw her photograph in the newspaper a week later, he couldn't be expected to recognise her.

He hadn't meant to hurt her. Of course he hadn't. Anyone at Morthingtons could have told you that. How many of *them* had been to Sunday School, regularly every week, half past two till four? He'd learned a lot there, how to behave, sit quietly on a wooden bench, wait. 'The Lord Will Provide' – that at least had sunk in. And he was still waiting.

He'd followed her, trailed her as she wheeled her bicycle round the back of her auntie's house. She'd looked left and right then, wondering which way to go, which way would be quickest because a steady rain was starting. The moon was out again, and it would cut the journey by ten minutes if she went through Trethennick Wood. He sensed her hesitate for a moment, before she strode off into the thick of the trees. He followed her along the track that led to the lake.

What was it about the lake that fascinated him? Warm as the night might be, or however hot the day, its stillness unnerved him. It wouldn't do to get too close to a lake. It showed your reflection, for a start. It just *was*. Water in a stream was one thing – it trickled, gurgled, tickled over stones and kept within its banks – it had the measure of time, and the sound of it, too; liquid and unhurried. The father of all water, the sea, was the most unpredictable: surly, spectacularly upset, dead, welcoming, however the mood took it. You never knew with the sea, changeable as English weather. But a lake? The plop of a bird, perhaps, a fish thirsty for air breaking cover in a mad leap, but otherwise nothing stirred, only willing to throw back shadow at those who peered into it, or support the lilies that alone clung to the lake, endlessly placid.

She'd propped the bicycle up against a tree, its handlebars arched across a supporting branch, the back wheel twisted. At the water's edge, she sat. The moonlit night flooded the lake with silver, accentuating the darkness at its edges.

He would watch for a bit.

When he'd counted to one hundred, he'd walk away, as quietly as he'd come.

The main road through Ferruick was surprisingly close to where the wood dipped into a bowl, so that safety never seemed far away. At the frightening splutter of a night-bird crashing through the trees, you were only ever a hair's breadth away from the reassuring thrum of traffic. The ground must have been mossy, only pine needles strewn across it, for his walking couldn't be heard, only the sound of what he took to be an animal turning over for the night.

It wasn't. It was the girl, humming to herself. She wasn't close enough to the lake to be able to see herself in it, until she leaned across its edge.

By the time he walked back up to the road, there was barely a ripple on its surface. He'd only counted up to 73.

*

'*Not* brilliant.'

Mark Morthington didn't move. The works manager had poured out such a catalogue of woe that Mark would have been forgiven for falling to his knees and burying his head in the sand, but he was still standing at the third-floor window of the laundry, looking down on the little industrial empire he had inherited.

'I never wanted any of this, Steve,' he said. 'It was never really part of me, not like it was with grandfather. He was so ambitious. When he met my grandmother they were both poor as church mice. For years, they lived on practically nothing, bread and dripping for tea. She darned the saucepans when they wore out. She'd done a night course in soldering. She'd go off on a potato lorry after she'd done a long day at the shoe factory, to work for another three hours in the fields. One day she complained there was nowhere nearby where they could get their clothes cleaned. That's how all this started.'

Even as he said it, he wasn't thinking of his grandparents but of Anna. No sooner had the first clod of earth clumped onto Aunt Selina's coffin than Anna made off for the London train. He'd seen the lifted eyebrows, the whispered carping, among the mourners. And who wore such flashy clothes to a funeral?

'So,' said Clerkson, 'what do we do about Despatch?'

His sallow face crumpled at the edges. Anyone looking at him might imagine a weak man, but Mark knew differently. Clerkson had taken much of the responsibility for running the laundry from his shoulders.

'Despatch?' It was as if Mark hadn't heard him.

'Things as they are, we can't afford to keep two drivers. I've done the figures. We could manage the collections and deliveries without Danny Drake.'

'Pity. He's a good worker. Good lad. Can't we use him elsewhere in the works?'

'What would be the point? We'd still have to pay him. There'd be no advantage in it. I know he comes over nice as pie, but he's already had a run in with the police. He's a load of trouble waiting to happen, that lad.'

'Maybe we'll have to let him go eventually, but I'd rather give him a chance. Surely we can afford to keep him on for a bit.'

'Business is down 40 per cent on last year. If you want to run Morthingtons as a charity …'

'It's those damned automatic washing machines.' Mark smiled as he said it, as if none of it mattered. 'Once housewives took the washing down to the stream.'

Clerkson gave a sympathetic sigh. 'The new machines haven't helped, obviously. And people don't want the trouble of getting their laundry ready for collection or collecting it … or paying for the privilege, for that matter.'

'My wife,' said Mark, and he paused so slightly that only someone of Clerkson's finely tuned perception could make anything of it, 'my wife told me they've opened a launderette in Ferruick.'

'They're popping up all over the place. Cicely Courtneidge and Jack Hulbert opened one the other day. Thousands turned up to see them. It was on Pathé News. Jack said that watching the machines go round was better than watching TV.'

'How the mighty are fallen! It's not going to get better than this, is it? That's the thing about progress. Too much is lost and forgotten in too short a time. Where will it end, Steve? Where are we headed?'

'Well, there's no need to despair, not yet. With careful management' (and something in the way he said it left Mark in no doubt that Clerkson was referring to himself) 'there's no reason why the company shouldn't be here into the unforeseeable future.'

'Empires fall,' said Mark, as if he hadn't heard a word. 'They go on until one day …'

When Clerkson left the office, Mark shuddered as he realised what he had never quite appreciated before: the works were where he belonged. It wasn't the fact that his family had built it up, it wasn't the comfortable lifestyle the works brought him. He liked the smell of the place, the people, the women with Morthingtons running through their veins like Blackpool through a stick of rock, the banter on the shop floor, their excitement at the prospect of the works' outing, the Christmas parties Mark had instigated for their children. Declining business threatened to put an end to it all. Of course, Steve was right. Eventually, Danny would probably have to go. Meanwhile, there was Aunt Selina's will to consider. He had never expected her to leave him the house. In a way, he supposed he'd inherited Harriet Braddle as well.

Those boys have arrived,' said Steve Clerkson. 'One's a bit toffee-nosed, the other one's ginger with freckles. What do you want me to do with them?'

'I think it's more a question of what they want to do with us. According to Superintendent Scott, they may be of real use in finding out what happened to Mary Shepstone.'

'They're schoolboys, for heaven's sake. They don't know the area. They don't know the people. It's a joke! The police are treating this as if it's something out of the *Beano*.'

'Oh, come on, Steve. I suppose they think they might as well give it a go. They don't seem any closer to finding the girl than they were two weeks ago. A tight-knit community like this, it's making people uneasy.'

Francis hadn't expected anyone as young as Mark Morthington. Directors of companies were supposed to be staid, mature men, possibly (especially in a laundry) starchy. Francis' first thought was that when he grew up he wouldn't mind becoming the sort of man that Mark Morthington seemed to be. After all, Francis was never going to have the tight, muscular body of Morthington's works manager, with that granite face and cleft chin. Aware as he was of all this going through Francis' head, Gordon lapsed into Prince Philip mode, setting himself aside so that his cousin could lead the field, as business-like as usual.

'We certainly don't want to formally interview anyone,' said Francis. Pompous little runt, thought Clerkson.

'Without sounding too pompous,' Francis continued, casting a look at the works manager, 'I think Gordon and I would just like to look around the laundry, as informally as possible. No need for anyone to know we're here at the invitation of the police.'

'That's exactly how I imagined you would wish to behave,' said Mark. 'We've already made it known that you'd be visiting.'

'Yes, we do a lot of factory visiting with our school in Norfolk, so we're used to the drill,' said Gordon.

'We've told everyone that you've come to see how a laundry works. I'll leave you free to roam. How does that sound?'

'Perfect,' replied Francis. 'What sort of girl was ... I mean, *is* ... Mary Shepstone?'

Mark leaned back in his chair, lifting his fingers to his lips in contemplation.

'A dependable, polite girl. Wouldn't you say, Steve?'

The works manager shrugged his shoulders. 'Nothing out of the ordinary. She did her work well enough.'

'Shy, I think. Quite a gentle soul. Hardly said a word at her interview. Blushed when I spoke to her. Not the brightest card in the pack, but she's sensible.'

'How long had she worked here?' asked Francis.

'How long, Steve? A couple of years?'

'Bit less.' Clerkson gave the impression that so far as Mary Shepstone was concerned, details didn't matter.

'It didn't come as a surprise that she seemed uncomfortable,' said Mark. 'She'd scarcely been out in the world before we saw her. She came to us from one of the local Childrens' Homes. Her parents had died, and at the time it seems it wasn't possible for her to live with any other members of her family. Then, shortly after she started here, I think she moved in with an aunt and her husband. These sort of situations are nothing unusual when it comes to children put into care. Some are effectively abandoned when they reach the maximum age for qualifying to stay in the Home. When it comes time for them to leave the protection of those places, the kids have to start fending for themselves.'

'Was it unusual to employ someone straight out of a Childrens' Home?'

Standing behind his boss's chair, Clerkson smiled wryly, his lip slightly curled. It seemed to Francis that Mark Morthington had sensed that look of amused frustration.

'No. The Childrens' Homes around here have been in existence as long as the laundry – longer, I think. My grandfather started the company by hiring from them. It's always been Morthington's policy to recruit from such places if we can, although I think Mr Clerkson doesn't altogether agree with it.'

'Well, look at what's just happened,' said Clerkson. 'And all this publicity doesn't do the laundry any good. I thought Mary Shepstone was a problem from the first moment I set eyes on her. She'd only been here a week or more when she started wearing skirts that were too short.' His lip re-set into the curl. 'Knees. I had to speak to her about her dress.'

'Given time, she'd have been fine,' said Mark. 'Sometimes they need a lot of space. It's a new environment, and the one they've known has already done so much to them. They have to find themselves.'

'Despite appearances, Morthingtons isn't a registered charity,' said Clerkson.

'We're a family. I'm not sure she mixed especially well with the other girls, but altogether they're a good lot. And if we couldn't take some of them on, where else would they find employment?'

Clerkson sighed. 'They think we're an easy touch.'

Gordon felt certain he heard Clerkson stifle a derisory snort, but his boss leaned forward.

'I've tried to keep the spirit of this place going. It's not getting any easier, what with pressure on the business and rising costs. Of course, some of the people we employ have problems – don't we all? – but is that a reason to turn them away?'

'It sounds a great place to work,' said Gordon. 'Soviet Russia would be envious.'

Francis bristled at so tactless a remark, and managed a quick thunderous look at his cousin, but Gordon was relieved to see that Mark Morthington was smiling widely.

'Do you know if Mary formed a close relationship with anyone here?'

Mark looked enquiringly towards Clerkson.

'Not specially. Not that one of them wouldn't have minded.'

It seemed to both of the boys that Clerkson had dropped the remark to invite further interest. It seemed natural to wait for more information.

'Danny Drake. Works in Despatch.'

'Did he know Mary well?' asked Gordon.

'No better than he knew any of the others,' said Clerkson. 'Probably not as well as he'd have liked.'

'Danny Drake's a lad we got from one of the local Homes. Sadly, it looks as if we may have to let him go.'

'Let him go where?' asked Francis.

'Sack him. The business isn't doing as well as it was. Cutting costs can be a brutal business. We may have to manage the Despatch department with one less staff member.'

'Perhaps it's for the best,' said Clerkson. 'He'd been nothing but trouble when he was in the Home, and recently we had the police wanting to speak to him.'

'Nothing came of it,' said Mark. 'The boy only needs a chance to prove himself.'

'Will I be able to have a word with him?'

Mark referred to Clerkson.

'The police said he'd been following some girl or other,' said Clerkson. 'Like I say, you don't bring in these waifs and strays without taking on a load of trouble. He's out on a delivery today. Won't be back till late this afternoon.'

The shrug of Clerkson's shoulders didn't offer much hope of further assistance.

*

Much to Gordon's surprise, Francis was reasonably relaxed as they made their apparently haphazard tour of the works. Gordon was in his element, chatting to anyone and everyone that came within his orbit, while Francis seemed always never quite at the centre of things. How Gordon wished his cousin would let people get closer to him. It came naturally to Gordon, and people weren't put off by his mop of unruly hair that owed more than a little to Burne-Jones, the wire-rimmed spectacles, and the more than occasional freckle.

It helped that much of the laundry was so noisy – shouting to be heard above the machinery gave the place a friendlier, informal feel. Never mind the giggling that Gordon's appearance started off; when the laughter ended, the girls treated him as if they'd known him for ever.

'You're a great bunch,' he said. As he was surrounded by several of them, it seemed a politically sensible comment. 'This feels like a good place to work.'

Oh yes, they agreed, but there was a sigh in the agreement.

'S'alright. But it isn't what it was,' said one.

'Why's that?'

'You must have heard about Mary?' asked another. 'Mary's gone, and no one knows where she is.'

'Oh yes. I saw something about that in the newspaper. She worked here, with you?'

'Yes. Everyone here knows everyone else. You can't keep no secrets!'

'I can imagine. Did Mary have any? Secrets, I mean.'

The girls agreed that despite the fact she had worked at the laundry long enough for everything to be known about her, she had pretty well kept herself to herself.

'Had she any special friends here?' asked Francis. 'One friend above all others?'

It seemed No, not really. Trying to get her to say anything was difficult enough, apparently. She would have made an awkward sort of friend. Not much to say about anything. The girls didn't ostracise her, though. They saw she was the quiet type, respected something about her that kept her always at arm's length. Several of them had come from Childrens' Homes, so they understood the sort of stuff she might be dealing with.

'Of course, she may have been a dark horse,' Francis suggested. 'Didn't any of you ever see her outside of work?'

They looked at one another. Oh, no. No one had ever seen her anywhere. No boyfriends, then, asked Gordon, as nonchalantly as he could.

A couple of the girls looked gingerly one to the other.

'Danny Drake, given half the chance!'

'Was Danny her boyfriend?'

'Was he?' They laughed at the suggestion. 'No, 'course not. He wouldn't know where to begin!'

'So, no idea if she had any special ... male friend?'

'Well ...' The voices lowered. 'We were thinking ... she did mention ... just once or twice ...'

'More than that,' added one of the girls. 'I've heard her more than once.'

'What?'

'Joe.'

'Who?'

'Joe. No idea who he was. But she said she couldn't wait to see him. Her eyes'd light up when she said it.'

'Yes,' agreed one of the others. 'That's the one time I

ever saw her, you know, looking happy. As if she was looking forward to something.'

'And did anyone here know who Joe might be? Someone in the laundry, do you think?'

'No, shouldn't think so for a minute. Not much selection here!'

They managed to laugh again, but now it was muted.

'It might not have been his name,' suggested one of the girls. 'I mean, she could have just made it up, made up the thing about having a boyfriend, to make us think she had one. Anyway, there's no one here called Joe.' She looked around as if for confirmation. 'Does anyone here know a Joe? Thought not.'

The girls agreed that between them they didn't know a single Joe.

After half an hour it was obvious the boys were unlikely to learn any more about Mary's life from her colleagues.

'At least we've learned that there might have been a boyfriend called Joe,' said Francis. 'That's something, isn't it?'

'Is it?' replied Gordon. 'There may or may not be a boyfriend called Joe. But if you take away the 'e' …. *you've got a girl called Jo.*'

'*You* might as well,' said Janice. 'As you're here.'

Danny Drake didn't need persuading. He was ahead of schedule as it was, only one more delivery to make before he made his way back to Morthingtons depot. He moved awkwardly but gently, reminding Janice of a giraffe that had unexpectedly got lost in a model village. Funny, him being like a giraffe, long and lean, his stretching neck somehow removing him even further from Janice, as if he breathed a different air.

'What flavour?'

'What?'

'Milk shake ... What flavour?' She felt empowered in saying 'On the house. Sit yourself down. You've got a couple of minutes, haven't you? Raspberry's good, or banana.'

It had been a good day. Mr Baldry had called in around lunchtime and looked at the takings and said things were looking up. He'd said with any luck she'd be getting a rise in a couple of weeks. He laughed and nudged her when he mentioned his policeman friend. Some nice customers had been into the milk bar. Two people on holiday from France. They'd pigeon-Englished their way through the menu and shaken her hand when they left. A party of hikers who'd broken into song. An elderly married couple who'd met on Ferruick promenade years ago when they were young and hadn't been back since, so Janice listened to how the place had changed, and then they put money in the jukebox and did a dance that made them all laugh because it reminded them of days gone by. Then the two boys who'd arrived shortly before Danny rolled up in Morthingtons' van.

The boys asked her about the missing girl, and said she should be careful because you never knew. Of course, Janice told them she hadn't known the girl at all well when she worked at the laundry, only to say hello to, because she'd worked in a different department to Mary Shepstone. Funny really, but all the talk about Mary made Janice wish she had known her better.

Danny chose banana. He watched as Janice did complicated operations that magically ended in her placing the foaming chalice in front of him. Looking on, Francis thought it had the dignity of a votive offering. There was something faintly ecclesiastical in the girl's gesture, the lightness of her dimpled hands as she brought the glass to him, the striped straw leaned against its side in a lop-sided sophistication.

Danny spoiled the moment by downing the milk shake with astonishing speed and not stopping when the straw began making embarrassing sounds. It made the whole business less sacred, like the unfrocking of a naughty vicar. The yellow liquid lined his lips when he'd drained the glass, turning him for a few seconds into an unfunny clown. It was an inappropriate moment for Janice to ask if he'd known the girl at the laundry who'd gone missing.

'No,' said Danny. He waited a moment before smearing his hand across his mouth. 'I mean, I said hello to her if I bumped into her. Never knew her.'

If Danny looked anything like a giraffe, he suddenly looked like a *frightened* giraffe.

'They asked me about her,' he said. 'The police. Like I told them, I never knew her, only to say hello.'

He'd better be going, he said. That hunted look had stayed in his eyes. Francis and Gordon wondered what he would be going back to. What would happen to Danny Drake, who'd done so well to get a job at Morthingtons after being in a childrens' Home? If Clerkson had his way, this might be the last time Danny dropped off the milk bar's laundry.

'I heard as how policemen were getting younger, but this is ridiculous.'

Gordon had been consigned to visit Mary's Aunt Ada, officially titled Mrs Roseberry. She answered the door in a flurry of polka-dots, her pink and white skirt puffed out by starched petticoats, her hair as exquisitely manicured as professional topiary, her feet snow-white and surprisingly tiny when compared with the bulk they carried. The white open-toed sandals completed the suspicion that here was a woman who remembered her youth and didn't mean to let it go. Gordon relished her gloriously Cornish burr with words. They curdled in the air. Somehow, she belonged to every one of them, just as she was perfectly matched with her little white-walled cottage that might have been something out of Hansel and Gretel. The word snug might have been invented for her, sitting like a contented forest animal by her smouldering fire, her chapped housekeeping hands spreading to catch its warmth, as her skirts rustled before settling.

'That nice inspector did say as how a Master Jones'd be calling. "Well," I said, "it mayn't do no good but it can't do no harm. Anything to bring our Mary back."'

'I believe Mary was your niece?'

'That's right. The one and only. My sister Florrie's child. *Her* one and only, and all.'

'Tell me about Mary, Mrs Roseberry. I get the feeling you were fond of her.'

'Fond of her?' The woman gaped at Gordon as if he'd asked the most preposterously unnecessary question of all time. 'I should say I was. A lovely girl, Master Jones.'

'Are you a close family?'

'Well, we was and we aren't, if you see what I mean. I was the eldest of three sisters, Beryl and Florrie besides me, and we were brought up good, you know. Not spoilt, oh goodness no, but never wanted for nowt. The three of us were more than sisters when we was young, soul-mates you might as well say, never happy to be apart for more than a few minutes if we could help it. I don't think between us we had a care in the world. When I think of how it turned out …' Her head drooped.

'How do you mean?'

'The three of us married, you see. Florrie married Reg. I was matron of honour. That were one of the happiest days of my life.'

'Really?'

'Of course, on account of Florrie being so blissful. She loved Reg, oh she adored him she did. He was a good man. He was thrilled to bits when Mary was born. The proudest father you could imagine. Trouble is, the good ones don't last long as the bad ones. Reg died, and Florrie not long after. The worst thing for her was leaving little Mary behind. She was twelve when we lost Florrie. Oh, a terrible time it was.'

'Yes, to lose your parents …' Gordon faltered. He wasn't going to upset this kind-hearted woman by explaining that he'd lost his. 'It's something you don't get over.'

'Of course that meant Mary was motherless *and* fatherless. Oh, I don't like to think of it, even after all these years.' Her voice broke as she turned her head away, hiding her emotion as well as she could.

'When her mother died, Mary had to be taken into that Childrens' Home. I don't know how it got to that, but get to that it did. Awful, it was. At the time my hubby was very unwell. Whenever Wilfred was ill, he always did it seriously. Know what I mean? It looked as if he might die. What with one thing and another, I couldn't see as how I could take Mary in. What a mistake that was. To tell you the truth, I couldn't have done anything about it. I had as what the doctor said was a breakdown. That's what it is, Mrs Roseberry, he said, you've broken down as sure as if you was an old car that's got too many miles on the clock. So poor Mary had to go into that Home. It wasn't more than a year later that Wilfred passed over. I never forgiven myself. Never should have said I couldn't take her in.'

'I can understand why you couldn't. You shouldn't blame yourself. What happened?'

'What happened?' Ada Roseberry's face turned sour. 'When the time came for the Home to get rid of her, up stepped my sister Beryl and her husband, that's what happened. I suppose at the time I was grateful they did. I tell myself that if push'd come to shove and there'd been that threat of her having nowhere else to go, I'd have taken her in anyway, never mind what a problem I had with Wilfred being so poorly. Trouble is, you see, when Beryl got married she … sort of changed.'

'In what way?'

'How can I put it? … She stopped being Beryl. She became Mrs Shepstone, and that's something you wouldn't wish on your worst enemy. I never took to that husband of hers. From the first day he showed up at our house, I seemed to take against him, him and his bible what he kept bringing into every conversation. Made you feel unclean, he did, as if you'd done something you was going to regret.'

Gordon was already wondering what Francis was making of his visit to the Shepstones. Would Francis' opinion chime with that of Mrs Roseberry? He decided to change tack.

'I believe Mary visited you on the night she disappeared?'

'That's right. Oh, I can't bear to think of it. Such a nice cosy evening we'd had, just like we always do … *did*. Every Friday night, she never missed. We'd have our tea and sit round like I'm sitting with you now, nice and comfy as everything, and talk about what she'd been up to at her work.'

'At Morthingtons?'

'Thass right. She loved it there. And we'd listen to a play on the wireless likely as not. Not this Friday, though. There was a concert from Scarborough. We both enjoyed it. *The Chocolate Soldier*.'

'There was nothing different about her that night?'

'Different? I don't know, really. If anything, she seemed a bit brighter than usual, sort of as if she was looking forward to something. I don't think she had much fun at home. That Shepstone don't know the meaning of the word.'

'Did she mention anyone?'

'Mention who?'

'Anything about where she'd been recently, or if she'd met anyone?'

Ada Roseberry looked into the fire for inspiration, but there was nothing there.

'Did she ever speak about having a boyfriend? A boy called Joe?'

'Oh, no. No boyfriend. Not as far as I know, anyway. Funny, that. I wonder now if she'd have told me about it if there had been. I mean, she would have known I'd never have said anything. Might have been better for her if she had a boyfriend. It's what she needed, someone to love her.'

The words seemed to bring the woman back to a realisation of what might have happened to her niece. She stared at Gordon through frightened eyes.

'What makes you think you'll find her? You're no more than a chit of a boy. If the police can't make out what's happened, how can you hope to? They must be desperate, getting schoolboys to do their work for them.'

There was anger in her voice. Her face clouded, but she turned to Gordon and smiled again.

'Still, it's good of you to call round. It gets lonely nowadays, Wilfred gone and Florrie gone and now Mary.'

'I'm sure everyone's doing their best to find her.'

'Oh yes. I'm sure they'll find her,' said Ada Roseberry. 'But will she be *alive*?'

'I don't know what to say,' said Harriet.

'Say yes,' said Mark. 'It's the obvious solution.'

'Not quite. I mean, your aunt left the house to you.'

'Only out of family duty. It's what she would have wanted.'

'These last years, I've felt responsible for putting an end to her career.'

'You should,' said Mark. 'You *are* responsible. She knew you were the reason it ended.'

'But once she had told me about what she did, I did all I could to encourage her to go on writing, I really did. The first I knew of it was when her elderly gentleman visitor let it slip. All I knew of him was his name, Mr Quennell. He blamed me when she stopped writing. But I never had any influence over her. I had no idea of what she did, or who she was to the outside world. But when she stopped writing, he was quite put out about it.'

'I'm sure he was. Quennell was making a lot of money out of Aunt Selina. Don't let it worry you. Secretly, I think he has a great respect for you.'

'I used to say to her, "Write something new. It'll come back to you if you'll only start again." I bought her those sixpenny red exercise books that she'd always written her stories in. She'd smile and stack them in a neat pile, but she never wrote again.'

'She didn't need to,' said Mark. 'What would have been the point?'

'But if it had been you or I,' said Harriet, 'we would have wanted to go on while we could. It was a crime, really, the way she turned her back on her writing.'

'She didn't need it any more,' replied Mark. 'Has it ever occurred to you that most people have life to live? Just getting through it is a full time occupation, for which there's no training and as often as not little reward. I'm not sure that authors, writers and observers like Aunt Selina, ever really feel part of what the rest of us feel. They stand to one side, trying to make head or tail of how we are, what we are, what we do. Oh, and there's one proviso in our arrangement that I insist on. You will allow me to come and go in the house and support you in any way you may need in the future. And it's about time I called you Harriet, and you called me Mark.'

How had it come to this, she wondered? She had no words to thank him for this supreme act of generosity. She wanted to kiss him, as if she had been his aunt, but she had never before kissed a man, and didn't think this the moment to begin. Thirty, forty years ago, she might have chanced it, stood on tiptoe, a chaste kiss of gratitude.

'As soon as the arrangements can be finalised,' said Mark, taking her hand, 'the house is yours.'

The Shepstones lived in a prim pre-war bungalow on the edge of Ferruick. The living room was neat, uncluttered, bare magnolia walls, cheap patterned curtains at the windows. Not a photograph or ornament in sight, and a gas fire that violently hissed at Francis as he entered. The atmosphere was thickened by a smell, indefinable but oppressive. A faintly antiseptic aura hovered around the diminutive and skinny form of Beryl Shepstone. Although it was stiflingly hot, a frowsy blouse buttoned to the neck, over which stiffly hung a long-sleeved cardigan of an indeterminate mud-brown, left her bird-like hands on show. Her fingers twisted the cuffs.

'You're not the police, are you?' she asked. 'They are so young nowadays.'

'Don't be ridiculous, Beryl.'

Mr Shepstone indicated the sofa. It made a sherry trifle squelch as Francis descended. Having to look up at Mary Shepstone's father made him wish he'd remained standing. From his perspective, Shepstone's crocodile smile looked even less convincing. He turned a look of withering pity on his wife, before switching back to the tooth-filled face.

'Do you know where Mary is?' asked Mrs Shepstone. 'What do you think can have happened to her?'

'Sadly, nobody seems to have any idea at present, Mrs Shepstone,' said Francis. 'You have no suggestions as to where she may have gone? Could she have gone to stay with friends?'

'Friends?'

Her voice suggested this was unlikely.

'My daughter had no friends,' said Mr Shepstone. 'She had no need of them. We were her friends. The bosom of the family. She was a good girl who preferred to live quietly here.'

Francis didn't like to point out that Mary wasn't Shepstone's daughter, and never had been. Perhaps believing he was her father made him feel as if she belonged to him.

'She worked at Morthingtons. How long had she been there?'

'A year or so.'

'She must have known a lot of the girls there.'

'The police' – Mr Shepstone's teeth moved strangely as he squeezed the word out – 'the police have been unable to provide us with any information. And nobody at Morthingtons has been able to offer assistance.'

'Sadly, no. They don't seem to know very much about Mary at all. They're a friendly lot, but Mary wasn't one to mix easily, was she? They'd wanted her to join the works' social club, but she didn't.'

'Mary wouldn't touch alcohol,' said Shepstone, as if this would be the terrible outcome of any such association.

Hoping to irritate Shepstone further, Francis said, 'In such cases as these, sudden unexplained disappearances, there has to be a reason. Did she seem unhappy at home?'

'What right have you got to ask such questions? You're surely not suggesting that we are in any way responsible for what has happened? We've done our duty by the girl. When she came out of the Home – when we *rescued* her – she knew very little of decent family life. How could she have been expected to know, cooped up in that place? Do you suppose it was an easy thing for us to deal with? She could be difficult at times. A stubborn girl, and not always appreciative of the sacrifices we willingly made. I think, too, we should have mentioned to the police …'

Shepstone hesitated, shutting his eyes tight closed, as if unable to focus on this omission.

'Mentioned what, Mr Shepstone?'

'Oh dear. I'm sorry to have to say it, dear …' and at this he patted his wife on the shoulder as if she too was a difficult minor, 'but Mary was – how shall I say? – a trifle unstable.'

'Oh no,' interrupted Mrs Shepstone. Given the chance, she would have embellished her denial, but her husband patted her again on the shoulder, now with a faintly restraining air about it.

'No, no, Beryl. We should have mentioned it to the police. That would have only been law-abiding. Who knows, it may have some bearing on the events that have come to pass. Fortunately, I am a patient man, and could cope with her moods, even when she flew into one of her rages. Such shocking tantrums as she had, after all we did for her.' His face switched to a religious mode, eyes turned heavenward. 'Be slow unto wrath with all they that are young.'

From the gravity of Shepstone's manner Francis assumed this must be a biblical quotation. Mrs Shepstone snivelled into a handkerchief. Was it shame? Embarrassment? He wasn't sure.

'In the circumstances, there seems little we can do to add to what we have already told the authorities. Much as we appreciate your personal efforts,' and here Shepstone's teeth came into play again, 'my wife and I are quite unable to suggest any reason why Mary should have gone missing.'

Mrs Shepstone seemed to have shrunk even further into a corner of the room.

'A boyfriend?' asked Francis. Shepstone flinched. His wife fiddled with the buttons of her cardigan, making sure all were in place and that she was well protected.

'Mary had no time for anything of that sort,' said Shepstone. 'She worked all week. Sundays are our church days, and she taught at Sunday School. She was an important member of our congregation, serving the Lord. There is no reason she should have vanished as she has. The world was, we might say, at her feet. She was about to begin attendance at tambourine practice.'

'And there was nobody at your church that she befriended, or who took a particular interest in her?'

'No doubt if you were a churchgoer you would better appreciate the absurdity of such a suggestion,' said Shepstone. 'At church one is not interested in the individual. Bodies do not assume the importance they assume in more fleshly spheres. One's relationship is with the celestial being.' He made a vague attempt at another smile that went badly wrong. 'And now, if you have nothing more to ask …'

'I wonder if I might take a look at Mary's room?' asked Francis.

'Her *room?*'

'Superintendent Scott thought it might be a good idea.'

'But the police have already spent hours in there, dusting for fingerprints and riffling through the cupboards and drawers.'

'Naturally. I suppose the superintendent's idea was that as a younger person I might look at the room in a slightly different way from an adult – if that makes sense. Might see things that someone else didn't see.'

'It makes about as much sense as anything else in this business,' snapped Shepstone. 'I speak on behalf of my wife and myself when I say that this disturbing affair is becoming most wearisome, and more will be spoken of it to the police and in courtrooms. However … Very well. This way.'

The door to Mary's room opened. For one disconcerting moment it seemed to Francis that he was back at the youth hostel. His next thought was of his own bedroom at Red Cherry House, with its gaily decorated curtains – roses on a never-ending trellis – the quilted coverlet that his mother had patched into a work of naïve art, the welcoming dip of the old armchair as he sank into its arms at the end of the day – its variety of chintzy roses ever a comfort – the old armchair that had been retrieved from downstairs when the monstrosity of the new leatherette sofa arrived, the bulky valve wireless that Uncle Billy had bought for him at a second-hand shop in Norwich with its lattice-worked speakers in a rococo setting, the Indian cane-work table beside the bed, and the tilting heap of books topped, like icing on a cake, with his current reading. On Mr Tethers' recommendation, Francis was working his way through J B Priestley's 'time' plays, currently *They Came to a City*. This, after all, was surely what a room was supposed to do: to protect you from the outer world but make you ready for it, a room in which Time with a capital 'T' played with truth and possibilities, as well as offering reassurance, peace, pleasure.

There was no hint of it here. Mary's room was little more than a cell. He wouldn't have been surprised if the murky window had been barred. Had it ever been opened? He suspected that nothing as controversial as fresh air had blown into that desolate space. The dark brown dado of the walls suggested a waiting room where you awaited desolation. The walls themselves were bare, where Francis might have expected to see some magazine cut-outs of Elvis Presley or Johnnie Ray or a pinned-up James Dean, the unreachable desires of a growing girl. There was nothing to suggest that Mary Shepstone had ever lived in the room, nothing that caught or diverted the eye or senses, no hint of ornament except for a canister of fly repellent.

The air was sickly, as if the darkly wall-papered walls themselves had digested it. Catching at his throat, it unsteadied Francis for an instant, his head reeling as if the floor was lifting beneath, giddiness running through him. He held on to the windowsill, leaning in to press his forehead against the clammy glass, fearful of collapsing in this mean, confined space. There was a moment when he knew he was about to fall. The threat appalled him, the thought that he was losing control colliding with the bile rising at the back of his throat. He must have blacked out for a while – only a spasm of time – closing his eyes in an attempt to regain equilibrium, his stomach rocking to a ghastly rhythm over which he seemed to have no control.

When he came to, he was standing at the window, his aching head, ice-cold, pressed against it, as if he had hoped the glass might let him through. The waves of nausea had gone as quickly as they'd arrived. A cold sweat sent trickles past his collar, but he knew the worst was over. He heard himself breathe again, hugely relieved that neither Gordon or the Shepstones had witnessed what had happened. He opened his eyes. The patch of earth beyond the window was another prison. Nothing grew or stirred except tangles of weed divided by a concrete path. A washing line hung limp between rusted poles, pegs dangling as if they too had lost interest in being there. A battered dog kennel, its slats broken, as if they might have been kicked in, and a drinking bowl, half-upended, old rainwater slanting.

Turning, Francis saw a shape in the doorway.

It was Gordon.

McGillivrays was at the very point where Ferruick's promenade gave up to the sea. Because the nearby towns were considered too refined to have a fair of their own, and never allowed a travelling fair to put down for a Bank Holiday, McGillivray had no competition for miles around. The big dipper wasn't as big as the one at Blackpool or as frightening as Clacton, but people said the ghost train elicited more screams than any other in England. Mr McGillivray sat picking his teeth with a knife in the booth outside, oblivious to the terrified cries because his hearing aid had stopped working in 1953 and he had never exploited the National Health.

Janice loved the idea of the fair, its far-off sounds, the mechanical glockenspiely chimes of the carousel, the coloured lights, the glass reflected every which way. The very thought of it, seeing it from afar, was so magical and alluring that the thought of being part of it was enough. Here at least was an enchantment of childhood from which she couldn't be barred. To be fair, when she was in the Home they'd organised an outing to McGillivrays every summer.

'People are so very generous', she heard the woman who ran the Home say, so Janice knew that it was charity, that they'd raised money so that she and the others could go on the rides and enjoy the stickiness of the candy floss. Last time she'd been, they had to stop the coach on the way back because two of the children were sick, but Janice wasn't.

It was when they said she'd have to leave the Home that they took her on at Morthingtons. Mr Morthington said he had high hopes of her, those were his exact words. He'd made a point of coming to see how she was getting on after a day or so, and the other girls had giggled behind their hands and said things and giggled again, because he'd singled her out. The laundry gave her hay fever but she didn't mind the work, and the girls were mostly friendly considering how big she was.

She'd been at Morthingtons a few months that Christmas when the girls said they were having a night out at McGillivrays. 'You might meet your handsome prince,' one of them said, probably thinking of Snow White, giggling like they always did because they didn't mean it, not for a moment. When the girls got off the bus that Saturday evening the sun was already going down and a chill wind was blowing in from the sea. The banners proclaiming McGillivrays and the brightly coloured bunting decorating the arch at its entrance flapped excitedly, like the promise of a special evening when anything might happen to change your life. The Morthington girls linked arms, a wall of laughter and expectation . People had to step aside to let them by, but not before seeing how they'd made up their faces with make-up from Woolies.

Janice smiled back at them. She had no idea how it had happened, but tonight she was the most exotic of all the girls. Her outfit was topped by a green beret she'd crocheted from a pattern in *Woman's Weekly*, and tailed it with a pair of high heels she supposed had once belonged to her mother. When they reached the entrance to McGillivray's, her mouth dried. She hung back for a moment, wriggled her toes because she was starting a blister, until one of the girls from the laundry said something rude and they all began laughing again. She touched her charm bracelet and strode on. She wished they hadn't said that about finding her prince.

'Have you taken leave of your senses? You're giving away the house?'

'Of course I'm not giving it away,' said Mark. 'What's it to you if I did? You've always said you hated the place, that it smelled of old people and pee. You never liked going there.'

'For God's sake, it's nothing to do with my liking it or not liking it. That house must be worth a fortune. I know it needs doing-up, but … Selina never spent money on it; it's an ice-house in winter. Ferruick is on the up and up, and it's the biggest house on the promenade. There can't be many properties as grand for miles around, and you're handing it on a plate to that Braddle woman. How could you be so selfish?'

'I didn't know I was.'

'You're not thinking of us in all this, are you? What's going to happen to us? The business isn't doing well, is it? If you lost the laundry, where would we be? How's she going to afford living there, anyway? Unless you've decided to pay for her upkeep as well?'

'That won't be necessary. Miss Braddle isn't destitute. There was the money she got from selling her parents' shop.'

'It all sounds pretty sordid.'

'And Aunt Selina left her a little money.'

'It sounds like a conspiracy.'

'It seemed the right thing to do. Of course I haven't given the house away. I've told her she can go on living there as long as she wishes. For all I know, she may not want to stay.'

'You're joking of course! Why on earth should she consider leaving? At a time when the cost of living is rising …'

'*Your* cost of living is certainly rising. You already have everything you could want, Anna. The sports car, your smart friends in London, the clothes, the diamonds. I can't think of anything you *don't* want. Nothing seems to make you happy. Nothing's ever enough.'

'No. No, Mark, it isn't. I hate this place. I hate the sea, always there, always doing something when all you want is to forget it's there. No theatres, no smart restaurants, no decent shops, the tedious parochialness of it all. And I hate the laundry. I hate the idea that we're dependent on trade. I have nothing in common with you, Mark, and I hate being Mrs Morthington.'

She sank exhausted into a chair, twisting her head away from him to look towards the sea that she had so recently cursed.

'Well, it's good to hear you saying what you really think at last.'

'What do you mean?'

'You don't belong here, Anna. I'm not sure you'll ever belong anywhere, because you're always looking for something else, more, different.' .

He heard the silk rustle of her dress as she walked to the window of their bedroom. It might have been the passing of a ghost. She brushed aside a little of the curtain and peered into the street below.

'Is it there?' asked Mark from somewhere behind and beyond her. 'Can you see it from the window? Your life, the life you really want, is it outside there? I'm sorry, Anna. I wonder sometimes why I ever fell in love with you. I don't think you ever fell in love with me.'

She couldn't turn back into the room, because then he'd see the start of tears, and that couldn't happen. He would be away soon, back at the laundry. She would be alone in the house by the time the delivery man arrived. Mark wouldn't approve of it at first, but he had always come round to everything she had ever done in the past, and there was no doubt that she needed a washing machine. Steve Clerkson had laughed when she told him that Mark wouldn't have one in the house. Laughed, before he took her throat in his hand, crushed her lips to his and began what had happened so many, many times before.

He was standing in the middle. Not so much standing, really, as swaying, this way and that with the music, his body seen again in the glass panels at the core of the carousel, his fingers encircling a horse's head or his brawny arms switching from pole to pole to steady himself as he spun ever faster. Janice knew that nothing anyone had ever said, whatever warning a kindly milk shake had handed her, meant nothing. She had never seen anyone so fanciable, didn't know what the word meant until that moment, and there, as she'd heard someone somewhere once say, was the man that proved that handsome is as handsome does. The girls had moved off, some shrieking at themselves in the distorted mirrors, some acting horror as their dresses flew high above their knickers on the wibbly-wobbly cakewalk. To Janice it was as if no one else had come out tonight, that she alone was here at McGillivray's, she and that gorgeous man on the carousel. She felt ridiculous. Tore off the beret, which she'd crocheted wrongly anyway. It wasn't long before the horses slowed down, and stopped. People got off and new people got on, as she stood watching him.

'Hello.'

She hadn't taken her eyes off him, waiting for that fraction of a moment when the carousel turned and brought him back, a flash of heaven, until he was gone again, but she hadn't even seen his lips move.

'Hello again.'

The voice was behind her. Danny from the laundry, holding up candy floss, obscuring part of his (much less good-looking than the man on the carousel) face. It sort of went in where it might more sensibly have gone out, and then turned back on itself somewhere around his nose. He stood there, a great ball of pink fluff like cotton-wool teased beyond repair hiding his eyes.

'I got you one,' he said, and passed the stick to her.

He'd come to the fair with some mates from the laundry and a couple he'd been in the Home with, on a convoy of motorbikes. She'd never have guessed from his hair polished with Brylcreem, with a quiff that set off his unlined brow and set a crown over his mathematically equal eyebrows. Green eyes, she thought, like a cat she'd once stroked. Eyes she'd never noticed at the laundry.

She liked watching him trying to eat the candy floss, his head darting about around it. The companionable silence seemed natural, even in that swirl of noise and illusion. When they'd finished he took out a handkerchief ('Freshly laundered by Morthingtons' he laughed) and wiped the stickiness from her fingers.

Most of Janice's girls and most of Danny's mates had paired up and scattered around the fair's stalls. She wasn't sure if this was a good or bad thing. It was growing colder, and her teeth chattered in the night air. He took off his jacket and slipped it over her shoulders. They laughed because her arms were too short and the ends of the sleeves dangled like ghosts at the panto were supposed to. The jacket and the laughing warmed her up. Danny looked better without it on anyway. He was slim and dark, but he'd been in some bother with the law, one of the girls had told her. As they made for the heart of the fairground, Janice looked back to the carousel. Something stirred in her that Danny might never incite, but she instinctively knew that if the man on the carousel offered her his jacket he would have wanted something from her in return.

Gordon wanted to find Mary, but the mystery of her disappearance had never fired him in the way it had Francis. He couldn't see what they could do. How foolish of Francis to take on such a problem, with negligible chances of finding a solution. As the days went on, and the calendar struck off the days until they had no option but to return home, it seemed to Gordon that Francis was only intent on not being seen to have failed. What if he did? There would be disappointments ahead of them; they couldn't be expected to clear up every mystery. Let Francis make a fool of himself; it would teach him a lesson, if nothing else. The possibility that something appalling had happened to Mary Shepstone was too much to bear, and he didn't want Francis feeling he had let everyone down.

There seemed nothing amiss at the laundry. Mark Morthington had been helpful, concerned, but unable to cast any light. Clerkson had seemed genuinely upset by the business. 'It's like they're your responsibility,' he told Francis. 'The kids become one of us, you know, like a family. You feel it strongly when something like this happens, know what I mean?' The family that perhaps Mary had never had, thought Francis, remembering the sterile little bungalow, and Mary's buttoned-up aunt, the plain walls, the overbearing heat firing from radiators, the broken garden.

Francis had been back to Trethennick Wood several times since he and Gordon had first visited it.

'I don't like it,' said Gordon, shivering. 'I don't like the stillness of it. It's creepy.'

'They think this is the last place Mary was known to have come. Her bicycle was found here.'

'It's horrible, but that's where the scent grows cold, isn't it? Superintendent Scott told us they'd already dragged the lake. Look at it, just sitting there looking back at us in that unperturbed way! – and thank goodness they found nothing.'

'Yes, that's the one spark of hope there is about this whole affair. There's still the chance that she could be alive.'

So, what reason was there for his cousin to keep going back to that desolate place where the water waited? The wood itself was small. Was there a word for a small wood? There could scarcely be one smaller, and a thorough search of it had revealed nothing of interest. For Francis, though, there was something about the place that made him wonder why a girl like Mary would ever have come to such a place. Was this the first time she had come here? Had she arranged to meet someone? In the dark of night, the wood was big enough and thick enough to be convincingly uninviting, but perhaps Mary felt safe here. Francis looked up and around, took in the breath of the trees, the faint, almost imperceptible living sounds that happened every now and again around the lake. However she had left that spot, it wasn't on her bicycle. A car? Mary didn't drive. Something had spirited her away, Francis simply didn't know what it was.

For some reason, in the darkest moments when no answer suggested itself, he remembered a line from the Priestley play he'd been reading, *They Came to a City*. How perceptive it was of Mr Tethers to suggest it! Francis had decided there and then that it was worth putting up with the pipe-sucking Yorkshireman's political prosletizing. It had been a thrill to discover the film version, too. It touched him as much, probably more deeply, than reading the play, this story of characters who turn a corner in their everyday lives to find themselves inexplicably lost, arriving at the gate to a golden city of friends. Francis was hypnotized by one scene, when Googie Withers discovered a great door embossed with a radiant star. The door had no handle, but the old charlady Mrs Batley knew her onions. 'That door'll open when it wants to open, and not before', she told them. It's silly cockney philosophy, Francis told himself, but the line resounded in his head. He never wanted to lose that thought. He wondered if, rather than some terrible door closing on Mary, another sort of door had opened. Of course the wood, and the lake, were frightening; Gordon had made no mistake. But what if the wood, with the lake at its dark centre, had been the perfect place for Mary to be on that particular night?

Of course, Janice knew that most of the girls at the laundry liked Danny. One had said he was better looking than Tommy Steele, and Janice said that wouldn't be difficult and Danny had much nicer teeth and the girl hadn't spoken to her for a week. There'd been that hoo-hah with the police, about some girl or other, but it had come to nothing. Some said he was half way to being a Teddy Boy, until someone else said that they were going out of fashion. Danny had the sort of face and manner that wouldn't have made it matter very much anyway. She couldn't make up her mind about that face. It altered sometimes when you looked at it and then went back again to how it had looked the day before.

'Let's get you a goldfish.'

They swam in glass bowls at the side of the shooting gallery. The rifle (was it a real one, she wondered?) was surprisingly light, as if she had hold of a feather. Danny stood behind her, wrapped his arms around hers, steadied the gun, so close she could hear his breath, young, warmly whispering in her ears. She missed at the first pop, and the ducks, bobbing about as nimble as the goldfish, moved about too fast, but at the second attempt, and of course it was Danny who pulled the trigger, one of the ducks went down. And then another. Two hits got a woolly stuffed animal, not that there was much choice. A wormy rabbit, one ear more lopsided than intentional, every colour of the rainbow. Danny said the goldfish were better looking, and laughed, but Janice blushed and stuck to her guns. The stallholder made the presentation. Close to, the smell of the woolly rabbit was musty damp, because it had spent too much time out in the evening air, for too many years, just another relic of McGillivrays' fair.

'At least you won't have to feed him,' said Danny, stroking its ears.

'What?'

'Not like the goldfish. What'll you call him? You'll have to call him something.'

Janice hadn't thought of it as a him, but she didn't see why not.

'He reminds me of you,' Danny said, and laughed again, a safe sound she would cherish in her memory. 'How about Happy Bunny?'

'It's not like us to leave a case unsolved,' said Gordon. He had completed packing his case for his return to what passed for civilisation, aka Norfolk.

He'd had quite enough of quaint Cornish cottages, fishermen wearing smocks and sou'westers that looked as if they'd come from a theatrical costumier, old Cornish legends of smuggling and coves (the rocky, not human, sort), and had fallen out of love with the Cornish pasty, on the composition of which nobody seemed to agree. What he wouldn't give for a solid British dumpling, except that he'd heard Fanny Cradock, wearing a ball-gown and colouring potato caterpillar green, insisting that dumplings were as French as Yorkshire pudding! That one woman could do so much damage to national cuisine seemed little less than treason.

'Who says we haven't solved it?' asked Francis, who had been remarkably subdued since returning from a visit to Superintendent Scott.

'Well, I don't like letting anyone down,' said Gordon, shuffling his feet. He couldn't understand why Francis was so sanguine about their failure. His cousin would usually have moved heaven and earth to solve any problem.

'Oh, I don't think you'd ever do that,' said Francis. 'As a matter of fact, Superintendent Scott was telling me what a very bright lad you are.'

'Superintendent Scott?'

'Do stop repeating everything I say. Very bright lads don't do that. Yes, he was here. He telephoned earlier and asked to meet us here, but as you'd selfishly decided to go off brass-rubbing …'

'A particularly interesting knight, twelfth century, dormant.'

'Well, he would be after all this time, wouldn't he?'

'Superintendent Scott must have been disappointed we've been unable to come up with anything.'

'As it happens, he didn't seem too concerned.'

'What do you mean? Have the police found her?'

'Not exactly.'

'Not exactly? Francis … what's that supposed to mean?'

'She's safe.'

'She's safe?' exclaimed Gordon.

'Perfectly. Half an hour ago Mary Shepstone knocked on the door of her Aunt Ada's house. I imagine there were tears shed by both Mary and Aunt Ada Roseberry. Tears of relief as well as happiness.'

'I don't believe it. It's wonderful!' Gordon could barely stop himself from dancing, but paused to give his cousin a piercing stare. 'You *knew* it would end this way, didn't you, Francis? You've known all along it would end like this!'

'Of course not. I *hoped* it would.'

'So, what had happened to Mary?'

'Through a sequence of circumstances she wound up with the wrong relatives. You must have felt it too, the day you arrived just in the nick of time to gather me up at the Shepstones. You're not telling me you liked the man?'

'He gave me the willies. I thought he was a quite unpleasant character. That room was so hot he might as well have come up from Hell. You couldn't breathe in there.'

'Exactly, Gordon. You've hit on something at once. It was airless, claustrophobic. How could a young life prosper in a place like that? And then the way he described Mary's existence. Looking around, there seemed not a shred of evidence that she had ever lived there.'

'No photographs. No ornaments. Bare walls and those heavy net curtains at the window. It was like a prison.'

'It was a stifling atmosphere that would make anybody want to escape, long to feel the breeze blow through their hair.'

'Except David Nixon,' suggested Gordon.

'You couldn't imagine contentment taking root there. Mrs Shepstone was no more than a desiccated husk of a woman beaten down by her marriage. Remember how nervous she was, unable to settle to anything, her eyes never resting.'

'She seemed very buttoned-up. Even her clothes pressed in on her, as if the only reason they were there was to suppress whatever personality she might once have had.'

'That's psychologically very observant of you, Gordon, although I suspect the truth is somewhat more sinister.'

'In what way?'

'The sweltering heat of that place. It made you want to rip your clothes off, but there she was, sweating in a long-sleeved blouse and cardigan, as if they were protective armour. She couldn't take them off, you see.'

'No. I don't see.'

'She was hiding the bruises.'

'Bruises?' Gordon gasped as a penny dropped. 'How awful.'

'Yes. It's only one aspect of this sorry case that the police will want to discuss with Mr Shepstone. There was something else at the house that set me wondering, too, apart from that scary look that came into his eyes whenever he got round to reminding us of the Old Testament. I looked into the garden.'

'Crikey! What a mess that was. Percy Thrower would have had a fit.'

'But amongst the broken bric-a-brac and decrepit debris there was a dog kennel.'

'So? Perhaps they'd once had a dog. Something else he could mistreat.'

'Yes. The kennel might have been out there for years. It was in a rotten state. But outside its entrance was a bowl of water. It was then I realised what made the heat of that room even more insufferable. The missing ingredient. A warm, foggy smell.'

'Canine!' announced Gordon.

'Precisely.'

'So, where was the dog?'

'If there was a dog on the premises, it was the dog that didn't bark in the afternoon. I'd asked the Shepstones if they knew the Joe that Mary was always talking about at work. Mrs Shepstone sort of folded up, until I couldn't tell her from that ghastly sofa, and Mr Shepstone's face folded into one of those artificial smiles he was so good at putting on and said that Mary had never mentioned a Joe. It seemed odd, when she would often tell the girls at Morthingtons that she couldn't wait to see this "Joe" again. Of course, girls being girls, they all thought Mary was talking about some boy she'd met. The Shepstones knew very well who Joe was. Mrs Shepstone was too frightened as to what might happen to her if she admitted it.'

'Joe was the name of the *dog*? But why didn't Ada Roseberry tell me that when I asked her?'

'I think perhaps you asked the wrong question.'

'The wrong question? … Oh, no! I think you're right. We'd assumed that Joe must be someone, a boy, that Mary knew. I asked Mrs Roseberry if Mary had ever mentioned a *boy* called Joe, and of course she said she hadn't. It didn't even occur to her that we might be talking about her *dog*. What a fool I was. But that doesn't tell me what happened.'

'Well, despite that rather appalling slip-up, basically you're an intelligent boy. You should be able to work it out for yourself. Essentially, Mary Shepstone was desperately unhappy. On the night of her disappearance, she went to pay her weekly visit to Mrs Roseberry. It was probably her happiest moment of the week, her aunt being the only relative who cared about her. Another girl in that situation might have unburdened herself to her aunt, but Mary was so brow-beaten, so emotionally squashed, that she couldn't contemplate it. She waved goodbye to her aunt, wheeled her bicycle into the street and started for home.'

'Home? The poor girl didn't know the meaning of the word. And that very word … Home. The place she'd been put because nobody wanted her.'

'Quite. Her way took her to the edge of Trethennick Wood. It was dark. She was alone. The world around her was still. And it was then that the Priestley thing happened …'

Gordon waited for an explanation, but Francis was staring ahead as if in some sort of trance. There looked little hope of him ever coming out of it …

'The Priestley thing? I'm lost, and you're in danger of becoming pretentious.'

'Mary was lost, too. But – perhaps it was a change of look in the moon, a clearing of cloud in the sky, some inexplicable electricity in the air – something happened. *The door opened.*'

Francis turned piercing eyes onto his cousin, as if this was explanation enough.

'You're talking in riddles, Francis. Pass that to me again.'

'Priestley's door. It opened … "That door'll open when it wants to open, and not before. That's the sort of door it is."'

'What on earth are you talking about?' asked Gordon. 'Animal, vegetable or mineral? Is this door you're talking about an *allegorical* door?'

Francis ignored this, so Gordon thought it must be.

'I think Mary knew that somehow or other her life would never be the same again. She walked into the wood. A sort of renewed baptism, if you like. She wheeled her bicycle to the edge of the lake. I don't know how long she sat there. I don't know if she was alone in the wood. It's not a safe place to be at dead of night.'

'Might someone have been watching her? Lurking in the shadows. It makes you shudder to think of it.'

'I don't suppose we will ever know. But luck, Fate, whatever you like to call it, was with her that night. When she was ready, she simply walked out of the wood.'

'Abandoning the bicycle?'

'It was a symbolic gesture, I think. Leaving something of the old life behind.'

'Where did she go then?'

'I think she carried on walking into Ferruick, until she reached the promenade. She looked to the sea, looked to it for answers. People have gone down to the sea through the ages, scanning the horizon, waiting for answers. None came, of course. The sea doesn't do answers. She might have sat there forever, still be sitting there for all we know, but someone saw her.'

Gordon edged forward. There was something irritating and mesmeric about Francis at such crucial moments.

'Being Mary, she still had the natural need to shy away from the world. If she looked out to sea, it had to be from a secluded spot where she was least likely to be seen. The curve at the furthest part of the sea wall was the most discreet point.'

'That would be across the promenade from where Miss Braddle lives. Almost opposite, isn't it?'

'Yes. From one of the upstairs windows Harriet Braddle had a perfect view. At first glance, she thought nothing of it, a young girl sitting on a sea wall late at night. Two hours later, it was a different matter.'

'I think I see where this is going. She went down to the promenade and …'

'I never doubted that Harriet Braddle was a good woman. A Good Samaritan, in fact. In her way, she had already been one to Mrs Rampton-Cornett, just as Mrs Rampton-Cornett had been a Good Samaritan in taking in Harriet Braddle.'

'She took Mary in? Mary has been with Miss Braddle all the time!'

'Yes and no. She had no idea who the girl sitting on the wall was. When she saw the photograph in the newspapers that the police issued of the missing person, she simply didn't recognise her.'

'Didn't want to, you mean?

'Perhaps. I suspect Shepstone thought so little of Mary that he gave the police the least flattering likeness of her he could find. He didn't particularly want her back, you see. And it was only three days after Mary vanished that he told the police she was missing. When Morthingtons rang her home to ask where she was, Shepstone said she was poorly and couldn't come to work. By that time, Miss Braddle was frightened of what would happen if she went to the police. Furthermore, Mary pleaded with her not to do so. The thought of her having to go home was horror to her. Miss Braddle was trapped. Mary didn't want to be Mary Shepstone any more.'

'So, you went to see Miss Braddle?'

'We had a chat, yes. You see, the other day – You were off in search of one of your knights dormant – I went for a stroll along Ferruick promenade. It was a soft day, hardly a murmur of breeze, and I heard a dog. Crisp, happy little barks. The sound came from Miss Braddle's. She must have seen me from the window, because I saw her hurriedly close it. I don't suppose I'd have thought much more of it, but just then the owner of the Milk Bar came out onto the prom for a cigarette, and nodded a how do you do. "My goodness" I said, "Miss Braddle's dog has been letting rip." He said, "She hasn't got a dog." And that's when I decided that Miss Braddle and I should have a chat.'

'You're not telling me …?'

'It was Joe. He'd run away from home. An intelligent creature. Like Mary, he'd had quite enough of the Shepstones's hospitality, and went looking for the one person in the world that he knew loved him.'

'If you could avoid sentimentality, I'd be grateful,' said

Gordon. 'All this will be dreadful for Miss Braddle, won't it? Abduction? Kidnapping? Wasting police time?'

'None of the above,' announced Francis. 'I don't think you should worry your head about it.'

'Please don't patronise me.'

'The Superintendent and I came to an understanding. What Miss Braddle did may have been unwise, but it was done out of kindness.'

'Naïvety, more like.'

'Naïvety may be a virtue rather than a vice. As I told the inspector, it's a matter of Priestley's door, accepting the fact that things only happen at a certain moment, and when the moment has gone, your chances go with it.'

Gordon lifted the eyebrow he usually lifted on such occasions.

'Really! And what was the inspector's reaction?'

'He said "*What?*" and I told him, "That door will only open when it wants to. It's that sort of door." And then he gave me a long look, and his eyes glazed over.'

'Now, why doesn't that surprise me?' sighed Gordon.

A new day, he thinks, a fresh beginning, opening windows and letting air in. The Morthington empire belongs to him again, and he begins to relish the challenge. This is what he is heir to, and he turns his face to it once more. He hears the laughter and the silly chatter and absorbs some of the worries of the girls in the laundry, suspecting their little despairs, and will do his damnedest to keep the laundry going for as long as he can. Let launderettes, washing machines, Cicely Courtneidge and Jack Hulbert do what they may.

Janice is no less content than she was before. Mr Baldry

sleeps contentedly and occasionally alongside his policeman, knowing the Milk Bar is in good hands. It may be mere coincidence that he has let the third floor flat above the Milk Bar to Danny, so naturally he and Janice pass on the stairs, and he comes into the shop, looking through the menu and deciding what flavour to have. On his way out, Janice waves to him, and Danny waves back. Neither knows what the other is thinking. When she opens the door of her flat, the first thing Janice sees is Happy Bunny, lop-sided as ever.

Francis had barely left the police station before Superintendent Scott sent a car to the Shepstones. In the antiseptic utility kitchen, a young WPC made Mrs Shepstone a cup of tea as her husband was questioned in the living room. The officers asked him to turn off the radiators, and opened windows. The WPC gently persuaded Mrs Shepstone to take off her cardigan. She hugged Mrs Shepstone, poured another cup of tea, and left the room to whisper into the ear of her fellow officers. Mr Shepstone, as if he had turned to rock, was clutching a bible.

If Priestley's door hasn't opened fully for Mark Morthington, a chink of light shows beneath the lintel. He sleeps alone now. Anna has gone, presumably with Steve Clerkson, for she and Clerkson vanished the same day. Mark feels relief rather than despair, and regret can be reconciled. He wonders what will become of Anna. He isn't to know that Clerkson, infatuated with her as he may be at the moment, will tire of her, and consider how he might be freed. Clerkson needn't hurry. He's used to waiting. 93 … 94 … 95 …

Miss Braddle, Ada Roseberry and Mary get on like a house on fire, wondering as they sit, legs akimbo, Joe staring at one then another, how they ever managed before. Late at night,

Harriet Braddle, almost a Victorian, sits in the window of the house that Mrs Rampton-Cornett and Mark Morthington bequeathed her, and looks to the sea wall, in case another girl is waiting there.

She never is.

AFTERWORD

Francis and Gordon Jones owe their existence to Anthony Wilson's creations Norman and Henry Bones, whose solving of mysteries was a highlight of the BBC's Childrens' Hour. I hope he would have appreciated these accounts of Francis and Gordon as much as I have enjoyed writing them. Anthony's stories were, of course, intended for children; mine are not.

Margaret Jones has been an encouraging influence almost from the moment the boy heroes were first thought of, and has cast her eye over their second outing, now and again preventing me from making too much of a fool of myself. Any idiocies that remain are my sole responsibility.

This may be the opportunity to mention some of those whose influences, either intentionally or subliminally, for good or ill, may have crept into the present volume. The clues are there for those who may care to recognise them. A list of the writers I most admired from my teens onwards and who may look over my shoulder would have to include Patrick Hamilton (unmatchable for British gloom, and surely the last sentences of *The Slaves of Solitude* are among the greatest in English literature), and early William Trevor; I remember the thrill of buying his first, gloriously cruel novel about ageing, *The Old*

Boys. My Aunt Gertrude bought me a complete set of the novels of Jean Rhys for my twenty-first birthday, and I like to think that, somewhere along the mysterious way, some of Rhys' elliptical style has brushed by. If you wish to be thoroughly depressed, Rhys is your woman. There is certainly a dash of L P Hartley, whose biographer I happened to become, in one of the stories, 'First and Last' in *The Voice of Doom*.

Another great writer, the now somewhat neglected Ivy Compton-Burnett, makes a personal appearance in 'Happy Bunny', concealed behind another hyphenation. After consuming all of Miss C-B's novels at too early an age, I was left friendless for much of my teens, having taken on her mode of speaking, shreds of which here and there inhabit the adventures of Francis and Gordon.

The occasional tipping of the hat to Conan Doyle is so obvious that it needs no pointing out, and the headmistress of detective fiction writers Agatha Christie is credited with helping out with 'The Coming Day' via her remarkable recounting of *The ABC Murders*. Elsewhere, (and Shakespeare stole many ideas from others, so why not us lesser mortals?) I have plundered the works of Enid Bagnold (regarding chalk) and Raymond Postgate (regarding something that an old song once sung by the music-hall artist Marie Kendall reminded us clung to the old garden wall). I have also given that grand old man of middle-class intellectualism J B Priestley the chance to get a word in about the best moment to open doors.

As for comedy, Richard Haydn was probably an enduring influence. Mr Haydn, who originally achieved notoriety through his fish impersonations at the Players Theatre, appearing in Hollywood's *The Sound of Music*, and as the dourest of butlers in Hollywood's 1945 version of an Agatha

Christie much-renamed novel, also deserves to be remembered for his quirkily hilarious *The Journal of Edwin Carp*.

Those reaching for a map of Norfolk should know that Branlingham and many other locations in these pages do not exist, although their inhabitants seem real to the author: the Revd. Challis; the post-office-bound and tambourine-trained Miss Simms; the pastry-maker and corsetry specialist par excellence Doris Jones; the aristocratic gorgon Lady Darting (one of my own favourites, a sort of amalgam of some of the wonderful old ladies I have been privileged to know); her irresistibly handsome nephew Rufus; the appalling and blithely incompetent Inspector 'Tod' Slaughter (named for a British film star whose existence should brighten everyone's life); his long-suffering sidekick Sergeant Cudd, and – of course – Francis and Gordon themselves.